smithy goes across
to Bryn's. Stacey
excited to be home.

7. Eating - Nessa
talking -

Stacey + Pam
making dinner - invitation
- Gavin + Mick come
home.
Mick goes to
Get Nessa

mention
in ep 3
re vegetarianism.

EP
N.T.
Hows Jase -
Stace cafe
ACE.

How do you
knees 43
Red car 64
Danny La Rue
52.
Brighton Line
59

① Gout of

Office

Essex
smithy putting up
tellite dish for & Mrs
ny, talk about boys

ant to
r + Mick
car
oing
shee
yn Apple

Ho
convo what
will Nessa do
Gwen suggests
she moves in
with them. five

4. CAR.
Convo as driving -
end up in
drive Home.
19 + Stepmother

5. Drive Home
hatch.
Looking to
Smithy -
Smithy's
sister.
ORDERING
FOOD
7
Intro to Bryn.

6. House.
Run out of
convo -
Stacey is
doodling he
sh: Na.
7. Driving
Smithy alone
1
Boys -
advice -
Mick.

8. House.
Stacey in he
room alone
Gwen - alright
she's deep
though
They'

Nessa +

Gavin's done
toast +
apologises +
A stocking
don't knickers
crisps

Mick preparing
food in + out of
kitchen/ lounge
Stacey arranging
presents & Bryn
Pam wrapping
Gwen makes
㉖

SMITHY ARRIVES
DAVE HAS TAKEN
NIEL FOR A WALK
㉗

LUNCH.
Jokes + CRACKERS
PAM TURKEY
MOMENT NICK
IS BIG DAVE
㉘

PRESENTS
㉙
-

PROPOSAL ㉚
㉝
MICK TINKLES
GAV COMES IN.
...LGS

HAVE A ㉜
MERRY LITTL
XMAS

DON'T MARRY
HIM

④
P + M, PRESE
TURKEY

⑤
ext Nessa
GROTTO

GAV GETS IN

⑥
N + G. NEED
THE ROOM

⑦
SMITHY in car
TALK TO GAVIN

⑧
B + h + Dolls
on Doorstep.

⑨
SMITHY + STACE
@ N + S. Under
for Lucy

⑩ P + M
Jason + Pete
call by to
collect turkey
St. MIKE

①
Burny -
G + B get
picked up -

Gavin
Stacey
wn

When
Gavin
met
Stacey

and everything in between

www.penguin.co.uk

When Gavin met Stacey

and everything in between

a story of love and friendship

Ruth Jones
and James Corden

bantam

TRANSWORLD PUBLISHERS

UK | USA | Canada | Ireland | Australia
India | New Zealand | South Africa

Transworld is part of the Penguin Random House group of companies whose
addresses can be found at global.penguinrandomhouse.com.

Penguin Random House UK, One Embassy Gardens,
8 Viaduct Gardens, London SW11 7BW

penguin.co.uk

Penguin
Random House
UK

First published in Great Britain in 2025 by Bantam
an imprint of Transworld Publishers

001

Typeset in 13/18pt Imprint MT Pro by Six Red Marbles UK, Thetford, Norfolk
Printed and bound in Great Britain by Clays Ltd, Elcograf S.p.A.

The authorized representative in the EEA is Penguin Random House Ireland,
Morrison Chambers, 32 Nassau Street, Dublin D02 YH68.

A CIP catalogue record for this book is available from the British Library.

ISBNs: 9780857507440 (hb)
9780857507457 (tpb)

Penguin Random House is committed to a sustainable future
for our business, our readers and our planet. This book is made
from Forest Stewardship Council® certified paper.

MIX
Paper | Supporting
responsible forestry
FSC® C018179

GAVIN & STACEY

by

James Corden and Ruth Jones

EPISODE 1

Shooting Script

28th October 2006

Baby Cow Manchester Ltd
C/0 77 Oxford Street
London W1D 2ES
Tel: 020 7399 1267
Fax: 020 7399 1262

Dedicated to our dear friend and
brilliant director, Christine Gernon

CONTENTS

INTRODUCTION

We may never see its like again. A romantic comedy that started out as a modest, little-heralded series about a love-at-first-sight romance between an Essex boy and a Welsh girl and the thornier relationship between their seemingly incompatible best friends Vanessa and Smithy, airing on the BBC's 'youth' channel, watched by barely half a million viewers. Seventeen years later, having made stars of its creators, built an ever-increasing, loyal audience and moved to its spiritual home on mainstream BBC One, from the 2008 Christmas Special onwards *Gavin & Stacey* has become the most-watched scripted TV show since records began, a symbol of the national public service broadcaster's power – even in these days of streaming blockbusters – to bring millions of people together, still, to watch a TV show.

Across its twenty-two episodes, all directed by Christine Gernon, *Gavin & Stacey* has given us many indelible moments, from having a heated debate over the best motorway service station to finding the eroticism in a KFC corn on the cob, the poetry in an Indian takeaway order, and the joy in a new pair of fully functioning oven gloves. Not forgetting the mysterious fishing trip, whose secrets still remain tantalizingly out of reach. Probably for the best.

Now, with the benefit of hindsight, the show feels like a sure thing, with that core ensemble of perfectly cast actors – Mathew Horne, Joanna Page, Rob Brydon, Alison Steadman, Larry Lamb, Julia Davis, Adrian Scarborough, Melanie Walters, Robert Wilfort and Steffan Rhodri – playing an extended family of funny, fundamentally decent people with peculiar foibles living relatively modest lives; the kind of people who are rarely seen on television, characters for whom drama means pretending to go vegetarian or making an omelette.

There are no superheroes or aliens here, no major crimes, no dead bodies (apart from the one Mick discovers on his way to work, leading to his blink-and-you'll-miss-it appearance on BBC News). Instead, there's a Wales/Essex culture clash, a love that dare not speak its name, and one that just needs a bit of hard work and a dominatrix every now and then. It's about the life events that affect us all: the births and marriages, the unexpected romances, the moments when friendships crystallize over a 'Do They Know It's Christmas?' singalong or a 'World In Motion' dance routine, the little things and the big, life-changing moments.

More than anything, this is a show in touch with its emotions. So when the 2019 Christmas Special arrived, it built up to a cliffhanger for the ages as Vanessa Shanessa 'Nessa' Jenkins went down on one knee and proposed to Neil Noel Edmund 'Smithy'

Smith. A breathtaking moment – and then the world had to wait five years to find out what the hell happened next. And what happened next was that the finale on Christmas Day 2024 broke all ratings records and has now been watched by upwards of 21 million people. Of course, Ruth and James have gone on to huge success with myriad other projects, but *Gavin & Stacey* is where their unique partnership as friends and creative colleagues began. That's the legacy of *Gavin & Stacey*, the little show that could. And most certainly did.

Boyd Hilton

PROLOGUE

May 2000. A church hall in Headingley, Leeds. It's the read-through of Kay Mellor's brand-new series *Fat Friends*, charting the lives of a group of Yorkshire slimmers, which will become Britain's highest-rated weight-loss-related comedy drama! Sitting with scripts in hand, a few chairs apart, are thirty-three-year-old Ruth Jones and twenty-one-year-old James Corden. There's a polite hello between them that day, nothing more. But twenty-five years later, James Corden and Ruth Jones have become the best of friends, who between them have created one of Britain's best-loved TV shows.

This is the story of that unexpected friendship and the even more unexpected success of a TV show called *Gavin & Stacey*.

CHAPTER 1

When Ruth met James:
the backstories

JAMES: What was odd about that first read-through was that it was just for episodes one, two and three, and my character, Jamie, only really popped up every now and then. I only had one or two lines in those episodes.

RUTH: **People ask me what my first impression of you was back then – I just thought you were very nice and sweet, and very young.**

Well, I remember that you were really, really good. I remember thinking, 'Oh, she's brilliant.'

Did you keep that opinion of me or did it change?

Well, we all change, Ruth!

So were you not in the scenes we did in the National Super Slimmers' Competition – with Richard Whiteley and Alison Steadman's character, Betty, having that fantasy sequence?

No, I wasn't there. I was literally only in the local slimmers' club scenes, where Janet Dibley's character . . .

Carol something . . . McGary!

. . . Yeah, she'd go, 'Oh, well done, Jamie – you're down two pounds.' And I'd go, 'Thanks.' Or she'd go, 'You've got to do better,' and I'd say, 'I'm trying.' And that was it.

I remember one bit of dialogue where Carol goes to you, 'Jamie, you've put on five pounds,' and you go, 'We've had visitors.' And Carol says, 'What did you do – EAT them?'

Oh yeah . . . classic Kay Mellor, that! Then when I did my episode, everyone pretty much disappeared because it was mainly about me on my own at school, getting bullied.

You were superb in that ep. Didn't you get an RTS [Royal Television Society] nomination for it?

Yeah, but I got beaten by Rob Brydon.

He *is* the better actor, to be fair.

I know.

That scene, though, where you got attacked by those school kids, when they smashed up your mother's birthday cake – it was horrible . . . D'you remember?

Yeah, I'm incredibly proud of what I had to do in that scene. What I didn't know, though, was that the rest of the cast had to stop themselves laughing because they all had to run down a hill in the park where I was getting beaten up!

We weren't laughing at your traumatic scene, though; it was just funny that we suddenly had to run down a hill to get to you. Cos I know this will surprise you, but I'm not actually a runner. And nor was Alison Steadman, and we just got a bit hysterical about it all.

There was quite a gap between series one and series two of *Fat Friends*, and I was in it a lot more in that second series, and that's when you and I would start to hang out and chat in the bar of the Crowne Plaza hotel.

Ah, the Crowne Plaza Leeds ... where we stayed during filming. And where *Gavin & Stacey* was eventually born.

That's right ... but not till we were filming series three of *Fat Friends* in 2003.

It had very orange decor, didn't it? The Crowne Plaza.

Yeah, and there was this sort of mezzanine, with a bar, and these sofas which looked inwards to the reception. And we all used to gravitate to that one area and sit there, and almost always, if you came down after a filming day, you'd find a couple of members of the *Fat Friends* cast there. You'd just join them, and then more people would join. Some nights after filming there'd be fifteen people there. Some nights there'd be three. Some nights people would drink till eleven p.m., twelve midnight, or on other nights everyone would head to bed at nine thirty p.m.

You didn't really drink much back then, did you?

No, but when I first met you, you were a teetotal vegetarian!

Oh yes. That didn't last long ...

Well, it lasted through series one, then it really fell off . . .

Anyway, one night in 2003, while we were filming series three of *Fat Friends*, we were sat in that bar and I told you about how I had been to a wedding with an ex-girlfriend of mine from Barry Island, which is a place I'd been to before because she had family there.

And I remember it was just the two of us talking, and you described it so vividly.

It was so weird that no one else was at the bar that night at the hotel, and actually, had anyone else at all been around, I don't think we would have had that conversation and we wouldn't be sitting here today. No question.

It's so odd thinking things like that . . . Can you imagine!

The wedding was at this place called St Mellons, which we ended up using in *Gavin & Stacey* – it's actually where Dawn and Pete renewed their vows, and it's also where Smithy and Nessa ended up having their register office ceremony in *The Finale*.

I'm so glad you said 'register office' then and not 'regis-try office'. It's one of my bugbears. Like when people say 'sicth' instead of 'sixth'.

Yeah, sicth.

No, it's SIXTH – it's the number SIX, not SIC.

Yeah, sicth. So I'd been at this wedding, and I didn't know many people there and it was a long day. It started at one p.m. with the actual wedding, then we waited around for the photos, then there was a sit-down meal. Then everyone left and went into this other area while all the tables were taken out, and the dance floor was put in, and they had a partition in the room. Then when they pulled the partition in the room back, suddenly it looked like a theatre. It struck me that it looked like a proscen-ium arch.

Anyway, I didn't know many people there, and my ex-girlfriend knew lots of people, so she was off chatting, and I was just sitting there looking at everything going on, taking it all in, and thinking, 'Fuck . . . all human life is here, in this room of people.' The bride was Welsh, from Barry, and he was English, but a lot of these people didn't know each other, and there were people flirting, and there were people speaking excitedly or drunkenly, and all kinds of stuff was happening. And you saw this ripple effect of this one event, this wedding, having this impact on all these people's lives just for one day, because two people were to stand up in front of all their friends and family and declare their love for each other.

So as you talked to me about that wedding day, I remember at some point we both said it could be a really good basis for a TV show, a one-hour comedy drama, about a wedding and the people that you meet when you go to one. The show would just be these little vignettes of people's conversations. It wouldn't even need to have a particular structure. And we were going to call it *It's My Day*, because the mother of the bride was going to be this really overpowering character who overshadowed her own daughter and felt that it was *her* day. (Actually, that character became the mother of the groom – aka Alison Steadman's Pam in *Gavin & Stacey*.) But it's interesting that some of the details you told me about from the wedding, little bits of overheard dialogue, did end up in the final script, like the discussion about the digital camera . . .

Which is a real thing that I heard when I was there at the wedding . . . We used it in the final episode of series one:

```
        BRYN (wielding his digital
            camera to show Budgie)
        Ever seen one of these?


                BUDGIE
        What?


                BRYN
        No film in there. Digital!
        I've got night mode, and
        black and white . . . I'll
        use that later probably, for
        effect. It's got 'seppiah', or
        sepia. I don't know how you
        say it. I've got a feeling
        it's faulty. It just makes
        everything go brown.
```

**We came up with this treatment for *It's My Day* and some
of the lines from *that* ended up in the script, like the motto
on Dave Coaches' bus – *'We'll get you there – if we possibly
can!'* – as well as Nessa's lines at the end of Stacey's hen
night, which became quite an iconic Nessa speech.**

Towards the end of the night everyone is worse for wear
and the philosophising is in full flow. Nessa is lighting three
fags at the same time and giving them out to the girls who
are all sat around her listening. She doesn't actually make
a point – but sounds as if she does:
**"I not bein' funny . . . , don't get me wrong . . . , but to
be honest, at the end of the day, . . . if truth be told, no
word of a lie, . . . d'you know what I mean?"**
And after a lot of thought the girls all say, **"Yeah."**

Another thing that I heard there, at the wedding, was my ex's uncle talking about his Citroën Picasso, saying, 'It's got a three-year warranty or 50,000 miles, whichever comes first. Well, let me tell you, if I do 50,000 miles, I'll be a walking miracle.' And we put that straight into the mouth of Bryn as well.

Oh yeah – in ep three, when the Barry lot go to Essex for the first time.

And so I was telling you about all these things I heard people say, and when we were sat there at the Crowne Plaza, there was an event happening in the hotel – a conference of some kind, with lots of people walking in and out – and we were observing them and deciding, 'Oh, they're from Barry,' or, 'They're from Essex.'

Yeah, we were already thinking of possible characters for the show: that's the drunken auntie, and that's the nerdy uncle . . .

We should also say that another key element in the birth of the show was that I actually had a mate called Gavin, who had met his wife through their work. She worked in sales, and he worked in purchasing or whatever, and they met over the phone and they would speak every week. I used to go to West Ham with him, and he would say to me, 'Oh man, I was only supposed to be on the phone for a few minutes to this girl, but we've just started talking.' And this was before the internet. She couldn't google him. He couldn't look her up on Facebook. None of those things. It was completely pure. They didn't know what each other looked like, and eventually they met up, had a brilliant weekend together, and then later they got married. It really happened . . . So the idea for *Gavin & Stacey* was a mix of that story and the wedding I'd been to.

Then a few days later you said to me, 'James, I keep thinking about that idea. Why don't we try and write it?' And I was like, 'Yeah, OK.' And actors say that all the time. You constantly meet actors who are writing something, and you never hear anything more of it, you never read it. It never gets finished. And truthfully, without your passion for it, I think I'd have just let this idea go by the wayside. But you were insistent, saying, 'No, come on. We think we've got a good idea for a show. We could both be in it, so let's do it.' And I was like, 'Great!'

But I'd never written anything ever in my life.

At that point I'd only written an episode of *Fat Friends* and a couple of screenplays, but nothing came of them ... One of the screenplays was called *Never*

Greener, which I ended up turning into a novel many years later . . . You love my books, don't you, James?

I've read every one.

(You haven't!)

And the episode of Fat Friends I wrote – it was in series four and it was Lynda Baron's story, d'you remember?

'The Baroness', we called her. She played Nurse Gladys in *Open All Hours*.

When you think about it, Kay Mellor played a massive part in the creation of Gavin & Stacey. We may have never met if it wasn't for Kay. God bless you, Kay Mellor!

The first time we wrote together was the day we went on *This Morning* in 2005. To promote *Fat Friends*. And you had been very, very adamant that we write this thing. You said, 'We're both going to London to be guests on *This Morning*. Why don't we meet and try to hammer it out and see if we can make something of it?' So we met before the show, at the Marriott hotel in London by the river.

The old GLC building . . .

And that was the first time we'd put anything down. I came to see you very early, we worked a bit on the treatment, then we went on *This Morning*, and afterwards we went back to the hotel and carried on working on it some more.

I remember we had a late check-out. Which was handy!

The important thing to say is, when we'd written this treatment, you said, 'I'll tidy it up, and then I'll show it to you to look over before we send it.' Then I called you and said, 'I think it looks great. I think it's good.' And you said – and this is so pivotal – 'Should we put the characters' backstories in?' And I said, 'I don't know. Does it not make it look too big?' Because we really just wrote the backstories for us, to know who the characters were. But you suggested it could be, like, a companion alongside the main thrust of the treatment; I remember you saying, 'I don't think it can do any harm. I'm going to put it in.' And I said, 'Sure, fine.' And had we just sent the standalone treatment, and not included all the backstory stuff, it wouldn't have got green-lit because all the backstory stuff is what the show is.

So, here are a couple of extracts from that first treatment and scene ideas for the wedding. It's funny re-reading it now, because actually a lot of the stuff in

there is NOT what we're about any more. And not very *Gavin & Stacey* at all. I think we just didn't know what it was at that stage, we were just finding our way . . .

'*It's My Day*' by James Corden and Ruth Jones (Feb 12, 2005)

A sixty minute drama about the coming together of two different worlds – Buckhurst Hill in Essex and Barry Island in South Wales. A hundred and four people who would never normally meet are spending the best part of fourteen hours together.

Because today is special.

Because today, as Stacey's mum will point out later on, "is my day."

Gavin West, 26 is from Buckhurst Hill in Essex. Stacey Shipman, his intended, is 30 – she's from Barry Island in South Wales. Stacey's been engaged before. Twice.

Gavin works for Bedmores Electronics, a Leytonstone company that makes circuit boards for CB radios. Stacey works in the offices of Wenvoe based company Shellfords. They sell CB radios.

For two years Gavin and Stacey talked and flirted regularly on the phone and in emails whenever Shellfords had orders to place. And yet they never actually met. Gavin listened to all the ins and outs, ups and downs of Stacey's colourful love life and will often be quoted as saying, *"there ain't nuffin' I don't know about that girl."*

Then a year ago, Stacey was off on a trip to London with the girls to see Marti Pellow in "Chicago" (they'd all loved the film but they loved Wet Wet Wet even more). The idea was that they get the coach up, see a matinee, get wrecked in the night and crash at the Thistle hotel in Piccadilly. All booked through Cresswells of Barry – a local travel agent whose motto is *"We'll get you there! – if we possibly can!"* Gavin seized the opportunity of Stacey's

trip to the Big Smoke and arranged to meet her, impressing
both Stacey and the girls by getting them half price tickets
for the Hippodrome.

The night was a huge success – Stacey and Gavin got
it together – so much so that they had sex down the
side alley of Mr Woo's all-you-can-eat Cantonese buffet.
As Stacey says in hindsight, *"What was the point of
waiting? We'd known each other 2 years all told. And
at the end of the day, I knew straight away he was my
soul mate."*

She took him back to the Thistle where she was sharing
a twin room with Nessa (aka Vanessa) who'd managed to
cop off with Gavin's best mate Kyle. Out of politeness Kyle
and Nessa offered to do it in the ensuite, but Gav pointed
out that they were all friends together and as long as the
lights were off no-one need be any the wiser.

The next morning the girls were at Victoria Station waiting
for the National Express to Cardiff. Stacey and Gavin
couldn't let each other alone. They snogged relentlessly –
eating each other's faces despite the other passengers.
When it came to the sweet sorrow of parting, Stacey
became almost hysterical with grief. As her mother often
says, *"She's fond of a bit of drama is Stace."* Looking
back on the event Gavin says *"There was no getting away
from it. I'd found my soul mate."*

Kyle said goodbye to Nessa a little less lovingly, *"See you
round. Like a rissole."* To which Nessa replied, *"Don't be
a twat Kyle. Come on girls – down the back so we can
smoke."*

Kyle and Gavin waved them off and headed for the tube.
Kyle told Gavin that Nessa nearly let him go up her arse –
and wondered how far he got with Stacey. But Gavin was in
love and refused to be drawn. *"I knew straight away she
was a lady and an angel."*

By the time the coach pulled into Cardiff station, Gavin
had been home, picked up his car, driven down the M4 and

was there to meet Stacey off the bus clutching a bunch of wilting Spar carnations. She of course was delighted. And they spent two hours together before Gavin set off for home. Kyle told him he was off his head.

And so began the love story that is Gavin West and Stacey Shipman. They could only see each other on weekends – she'd go up, he'd come down. And of course – they'd continue to talk all the time on the phone.

After six months Gavin took Stacey to Madame Tussauds for a Christmas treat and whilst marvelling at the workmanship that'd gone into the waxen Robbie Williams, Gavin got down on one knee, told her he wanted to grow old with her and together watch their grandchildren play. (He'd heard this line in 1991 on an episode of *Home And Away* and always knew that's how he would propose when he met the right girl).

Then he told her to look in Robbie's hand – **"*I know you'd probably rather marry Robbie, but will I do instead?*"** In her apoplectic excitement Stacey snapped off Robbie's thumb trying to get the ring. This set off the alarm and the happy couple got thrown out. Gavin didn't mind though, and was heard later to say – **"It was crap in there anyway. Kylie had a squint."**

The wedding was arranged for the following summer. A Cardiff wedding – at St Mellons Country Club – **"*We got to 'ave it in St Mellons. I's always dreamt it would be in St Mellons.*"**

And only when they return from honeymoon will the happy couple move in together – **"*I don' believe in pre habiting before marriage*"** says Stacey.

The photos
We don't see the photos being taken. We just see various groups of guests standing around with their sherries, most of them smoking, waiting to be called to come and be in shot. One such group might be the Essex

boys – Gavin's mates. They might be discussing the
bride's plump figure:

- **Well all I'm saying is, <u>see</u> the mother – <u>see</u> the
  bride. In 30 years time. And I don't mean no
  disrespect and you know that.**

They are interrupted by the photographer's ineffectual
assistant. **"Right then. Friends of the groom. Can I have
friends of the groom please? Come on lads."** Some of
the lads leave for the photo. But some of them carry on
smoking:

- **You comin' Phil? Friends of the groom.**
- **Nah fuck it.**
- **Yeh . . . See, I tried to tell him on the stag – and
  I'm not telling you nothing I wouldn't tell Gav.
  It's like a car innit – you clean the car to sell
  it, you get it serviced – get it looking the best
  you can.**
- **What you fuckin on about Mickey? She's not a
  fuckin car.**

Uncle Trefor

Stacey's uncle Trefor from Barry is obsessed with his
new digital camera. And he doesn't miss an opportunity
to tell anyone who'll listen, all about it. Trefor's
late brother was Stacey's dad. And secretly Trefor
believes that <u>he</u> should have given his niece away and
not Neil the family friend. He has managed to trap a
fellow guest:

**"Sit down a minute now. Right. Look. The thing is
with this, you take NO bad pictures – see – look I
mean, I dunno, I take that – look see? Bop. I don't
want it – so I gets rid of it. Take one of your shoe?
See? Bop. There it is. Don't want it. I gets rid of
it! That's the beauty of it. See? Now look at these**

right. These are what I've kept so far, right? There's Stacey this morning – with Neil. He gave her away . . . Whatever . . . My brother in law would turn in his grave if he knew. . . . But I'm not going to talk about it. He's not family. What I'VE had to say has been said. Forget it. If I don't want that picture – bop - I gets rid of it. But I DO want it so – bop - I keeps it. You got a computer? Get one of these. Easy. Not cheap. But cheap in the long run. Cos you don't spend the money on films."

Barry Boy and Essex Man

. . . are talking in metaphors.

    – The thing with me is I know what I am . . . I'm Mondeo man. I'm not Porsche man – I mean, I'd love to be Porsche man but I'm not. I'd love to be Mercedes Man but I'll tell you this, at least I'm not a Fiat. I'm certainly not a Punto. And that's their best selling car. No. I'm Mondeo man.
    – And that's a good car. Yeah – you'd love to be a Beamer. I daresay you'd like to be a volkswagon . . .
    – I'm a better man than a volkswagon.
    – D'you think?
    – Yes! Well I'm better than a golf. I'm certainly better than a polo.
    – But not a Passat.
    – No. No. Not a Passat I grant you. But I'm top of the range polo and a mid range golf. Which to all intents and purposes IS a Mondeo. Which is what I'm saying. I am Mondeo man.

Pause. Essex Man walks off whilst Barry Boy is looking around. Barry Boy carries on talking, unaware no-one's listening.

> – **Now Gareth by there now. Salt of the earth.
> Modest as fuck. He'd tell you he's an Astra. But
> in truth – he's your full spec Lexus. And he's
> only 28.**

He notices Essex man has gone. Pretends not to be
embarrassed. Sees Russell. Calls to him.

Two Welsh Aunties

. . . are discussing the misfortune of the bride and groom's
surnames. She's a Shipman and he's a West.

> – **That is bad luck by anyone's standards. I mean
> it's not as if she's not had enough problems
> what with her weight and her father dying. But
> no. Living for the day she can change her name.
> And look what she inherits.**
> – **Coulda been worse, Jean. He coulda been a Laden.**

Nessa holds forth

Towards the end of the night everyone is worse for wear
and the philosophising is in full flow. Nessa is lighting three
fags at the same time and giving them out to the girls who
are all sat around her listening. She doesn't actually make
a point – but sounds as if she does:

**"I not bein' funny . . . , don't get me wrong . . . , but to
be honest, at the end of the day, . . . if truth be told, no
word of a lie, . . . d'you know what I mean?"**

And after a lot of thought the girls all say, **"Yeah."**

So we sent that treatment to Sioned Wiliam, then
head of comedy at ITV, because we thought to begin
with that our show would work on ITV.

We also thought she'd understand it because she's
Welsh! And from Barry, in fact. And she did understand

it, to be fair, and she liked it. A lot. But she didn't think ITV would go for it. She said the 'offers people' just felt that it was a BBC Two show and not really commercial enough for ITV. They were very interested in the tone of the piece and the emphasis on realism. But in the end they were looking for something more mainstream. That was in May 2005 . . .

What's funny about that ITV response was that they were looking for something with a greater commercial appeal, and they wanted something for all the family, and I do see that this first version of the show doesn't read as one for all the family straight away.

There's a lot of swearing in that treatment, and it's very crude in places . . . I don't think we had more than a couple of 'fucks' in the final on-screen episodes . . .

Yeah, it wasn't exactly family viewing when we started writing and making it, but that did sort of organically happen to the show in the end. It ended up being watched by people of all ages, which we probably never intended.

So after we were rejected by ITV, we sent the treatment to Stuart Murphy, who was the controller of BBC Three. Then we had this email from Stuart:

22 June 2005

Email from Stuart Murphy to Ruth Jones

I was blown away by your script ideas - love them. I am just about to go to Level 1's (initial commissioning meeting) in about 15 mins to talk about this and other comedies, but just to fill you in now what I was going to say

Is there an indie or production unit (eg BBC Comedy in Manchester?) which this project is attached to?

I know you pitched it as a one hour special but I would much much rather have 6 x 30 mins, and call it Stacey & Gavin. I loved the notes on how they met in London for instance, and how he raced down the M4 to arrive at the National Express Coach Station with flowers - that is at least one ep I think. So what I am saying I guess Ruth is that I would only really go for this if you feel you could do it as 6 x 30 mins

Are there any scripts written? I know you said it would be pretty improvised, but would you have script outlines done?

If we did 6 x 30 mins, how soon would we be able to get it? Are you flat out with work at the moment?

Thanks so much for sending it to us. Really really appreciate it. I think it could be one of the best things we've done

Stuart

We read and re-read that email so many times. What he wrote at the end – 'it could be one of the best things we've done' – we just couldn't believe it. And we don't know what he saw in it, or what could have given him that thought. But we did what he asked us to do, and that was it, really.

Yeah, we couldn't believe it. So we have to thank Stuart, because he said there wasn't a slot for an hour-long comedy drama but suggested we could serialize the backstory.

And he said, 'Call it *Stacey & Gavin*!'

I can't remember when it became *Gavin & Stacey* – can you?

No, I can't, actually. It was also Stuart who suggested it should be a half-hour comedy show, and then he commissioned us to write one episode, which was so exciting. And suddenly it was like, 'Wow! Fuck! This is really happening.'

We had a good relationship with Stuart; partly, I guess, because I'd been in *Nighty Night* and *Little Britain*, which were both BBC Three shows . . .

Well, you knew Stuart much better than me. I didn't know him very well at all. But at that time it felt like you were carving a name for yourself as a really important figure in British comedy . . .

I didn't know you thought that about me! I get nervous when you say things like that, cos you sound all serious and grown-up.

I'm forty-eight now.

Yeah. Jeez. But of course, round that time, you were in Alan Bennett's *The History Boys* at the National Theatre, which became this massive hit. I remember meeting you in the early days of rehearsals – like, in week one – and you weren't sure about it cos there was a lot of French in it!

Yeah. Takes a while to get into something, I suppose.

It was a brilliant play, though. And he really encouraged you on the writing front, didn't he – Alan Bennett?

Yes, because I was, if I'm honest, a bit doubtful that I could write or co-write anything, let alone star in it as well.

That surprises me, you saying that . . . cos so many people had said to you that you had this special talent.

I remember when we were doing *Fat Friends*, Alison Steadman said that you should do stand-up comedy. You're such a great raconteur. Rob Brydon and I always say this about you: that you've just got this ability to hold people's attention. And sometimes there are silences in your storytelling. And whereas if I had a silence in one of my stories, people would just go, 'Yeah, anyway, should we get some coffee?', with you, you manage to keep people interested even through the silences. And I think it's a really huge skill. So I think a lot of us knew that you were going to be really good at all that.

I did learn a lot from being in rehearsals for *The History Boys*. It was a life-changing thing for me. I'd never been in a play before, and when I auditioned for it, there were defined parts for some of the school pupils. There was Dakin, Posner, Rudge, Scripps. Then there were these other characters who were referred to as 'Boy 1', 'Boy 2', 'Boy 3', 'Boy 4', and they weren't defined. And there was a chance that I wouldn't have been able to be in series four of *Fat Friends* if I was going to sign up to do this play and get one of those roles, so it was a bit of a dilemma.

I didn't know that!

Yeah . . . and it all happened on the same day. I auditioned for *The History Boys* in the morning, got offered it in the afternoon, and I was in my agent's office, and she was saying, 'I think you've got to do this play. You really, really should.' And I was like, 'But I don't know what the part is. What if I've just got four lines? At the moment there is no specific character there.' It was just one of the deliberately vague, undefined roles. So then Alan Bennett, who was in the National Theatre at the time, came and spoke to me and said, 'Look, the part isn't going to be as big as those other parts. The core four roles are very, very defined. But I promise you, if you commit, I'll give you some interesting, fun things to do.' Which he really, really did.

So how did you get into talking about *Gavin & Stacey*?

Well, when we got in the rehearsal room, I was messing about and joking and telling him ideas I had, and he would tell me quite often that some of the stuff I was saying was funny, and that I should write some of it down. 'You need to know I'm serious,' he said. And I remember we were in the National Theatre canteen once, and he asked, 'Have you started doing any writing yet?' And I said, 'No. Well, my friend Ruth and I have got this thing that we're working on, but I feel a bit of a fraud, because loads of actors are writing stuff.' And he said, 'Well, if you can make a rehearsal room in the National Theatre laugh, you can make anybody laugh, because they don't *want* to laugh at anybody.'

And then he did an extraordinary thing.

He read the scripts of episodes one, two and three of *Gavin & Stacey*, which you and I had written, and he didn't give any notes. In fact, he was full of praise for the scripts.

That's so bizarre – the idea of Alan Bennett reading and enjoying lines like, 'A kiss, a cuddle, a cheeky finger . . . just don't go givin him the whole farm.' I mean, I suppose when you think about it, a lot of his writing is about the minutiae of life, isn't it? The quite pedestrian things people say that are actually really funny . . . And I guess *Gavin & Stacey* had a lot of that sort of day-to-day stuff. Just not said in a Yorkshire accent.

When the show came out on BBC Three in 2007 with the first two episodes, I was waiting to hear from him. And I didn't. And then episode three went out: heard nothing. Four went out: nothing. And he *is* the type of person to call. He's such a lovely man, I totally expected him to call. So I thought, 'He just doesn't like it.' I knew he would have seen it. So I assumed he was just going to let it be rather than have to tell me what he really thought. Finally, episode six went out. And he called ten minutes after the end of the episode . . .

I was like, 'Alan, I was waiting to hear from you. Honestly, I convinced myself that you didn't like the show.' And in one breath, he rendered every television critic pointless, because he said, 'Well, I was waiting till I'd watched it all. Why would I call you after one or two episodes? It's like somebody writing a review after seeing half an hour of one of my plays.' And I was like, 'You're absolutely right! TV critics should only be allowed to write reviews after they've watched the entire series.' And now we're in this situation where people decide what they think of a show after ten minutes . . .

That's so true.

Yeah, Alan Bennett liked it, and that meant the world.

But before all that, when Stuart Murphy asked for a script for the first episode, there couldn't have been anything more exciting, and I would argue that nothing I've done in my career since has been as exciting as the notion that me and you, Ruth, were going to write our own show for BBC Three. This was fucking nuts.

Gav and Stace – outline 1

1 Barry Island – Stacey on the phone to Gavin
2 Ilford Essex – Gavin on phone to Stacey – you know what I look like I sent you those photos. . I know but it's not the same
3 Barry, Stacey's house – night before – Nessa turns up ready for the trip – with just a bag – meet uncle Trefor
4 Essex, Gav's house – night before – intro Smithy – est his on/off relationship and the fact that it's a sort of double date tomorrow – meet Gav's parents – Smithy flirts with Gav's mother – father really dour – thinks the ideas mad – she could be a rapist.
5. Next day – Stace and Ness on a coach
6. Gav and Smithy on tube
7 The meeting Smithy pissed off cos Nessa's fat – Gav points out that "with respect, so are you!"
8 Nightclub – Gav and Stacey chatting, Ness and Smithy grinding – getting it on
9 Mr Woo's – Chinese meal – down the side alley, being sick – kissing?
10. Girls invite them back to the hotel.
11. In the cab – snogging each others' faces off
12 Hotel – Smithy offers to go in the ensuite – Nessa doesn't understand why. Agree to go in the ensuite for the first one – compromise
13 Gav and Stace – beautiful moment – play music on Stacey's ipod and speakers – "Shot to the Heart!" – am I how you imagined? No – you're better than I imagined Really gentle, loving, quiet Bring it right down And the background noise is Ness and Smithy having really aggressive sex.
14 Next morning – Smithy on the floor? Or maybe go straight to the coach station? Gav and Stace all coupley – Ness and Smithy not speaking – just smoking. See you round like a rissole – don't be a twat all your life Kyle The name's Smithy Whatever Stace in tears – they say good bye – watch the coach go
15 Smithy's got the guilt about his girlfriend – why didn't you stop me? Or talking about how far they both got. Ness let him up the arse Gav won't be drawn – she's a lady and an angel. Still Welsh tho
16. Gav suddenly disappears – cut to him driving down the M4.
17 Girls on coach? Ness bored with the love story – or setting the alarm off trying to have a fag in the WC?
18 See Gav go over the Severn Bridge – pull in at Magor services – buy flowers from garage

19 Gav at the station meeting Stacey off the coach. Nessa's reaction – this is the start of something beautiful. Christ give me strength.

SHELLEYS LINE TK MAX – CAN'T GO WRONG

NESSA AND THE AUSTRALIAN ON THE HEN NIGHT DISCUSSING THE THE BENEFITS OF ANOREXIA AND PURGING – YEAH I USED TO DO IT MYSELF – LOOK AT YOU – YOU GOT A CRACKING FIGURE – WHY NOT

STAG NIGHT – BRYN NOT INVITED SO GAV HAS TO ORGANISE ANOTHER ONE IN THE PARK HOTEL – BRYN THINKS GAV'S FRIENDS ARE A SHOWER OF SHIT

SANDWICHES – VICAR – MARRIAGE GUIDANCE

SMITHY'S OBSESSION WITH SELF HARMERS

GAV AND SMITHY IN FOOTBALL MATCH – NESSA AND SMITHY'S GIRLFRIEND BOTH TURN UP – SMITHY LETS IN A GOAL.

Nessa's expression "simple as"

"he's an Aaaarse!" as heard in tescos

Could the rhys ifans character be gay – maybe the gay brother's boyfriend – not related – so bryn hasn't forgiven him for "turning " his nephew queer – against gays because he is one. Rhys ifans character comes on to bryn in the wedding – come on – let out your true nature

Holiday when they were younger – something happened that we never find out about

Rhys ifans could be the gay boyfriend of stacey's brother

Bryn really disapproving of the gay thing because he is a gay himself

Series 2
Stacey goes to live in essex – lasts 10 days hates it – has nessa to stay? Ends up moving back to barry – gavin works 5 days a week goes to barry on weekends – so we get to see the rest of the families. Strain on the relationship Stacey finds out she's pregnant. Loses the baby this brings them back together at end of the series

Comments from both sets of parents on their infertility also how unnatural it is for a married couple to be living apart Pam into alternative therapies – also she treats the miscarriage as if it's happened to her Everything in her life is like a soap opera

Ep 2 series 1 when gavin comes to barry for the first time – bryn introduces him to the internet – see this? Sit down – have a look at this www – just remember www The way I do it, whisky with water Or weather won't worry Basically anything that begins with w gavin says – like world wide web? Yeah if you like What is it you do then gavin. I work in computers

He's a little shit Yes but he's MY little shit.

___

Notes
Luther Van Dross If Only For One Night poss song for G and S first time together.

Wedding music like Kylie and Jason in Neighbours – Stacey insists on it

Senile relative – daughter main carer – "I won't lie to you – every morning I go in there and I hope she's dead. I've even thought of smothering her,"

Diabetes – grumpy old relative – someone excuses it – it's his bloodsugar – had this in Nighty Night tho.

Rhys Ifans character is Stacey's brother – he left under a cloud and Bryn won't speak to him because when he came out as gay he got off with Bryn's best friend

Breaking the news of the engagement – the emotional scene in Wales with bryn etc then gavin arranges to get his family together in Billericay – Stacey comes up with nessa – pam knows there's something exciting "as long as it's not cancer. Tell me it's not cancer" – and she's in the kitchen mixing up the egg mayo, nessa on doorstep having a fag – nessa lets the cat out of the bag – ruins the moment for pam and everyone - but has no remorse"oh get over it, you were gonna tell them anyway! What's the big deal – I just saved you the hassle – Christ when I think of the number of times I've been engaged – If I had to make a big thing of it every time – I'd be there all year!" – mick weirdly fascinated by nessa – yeah well how come you're still single

Episode 2 is the engagement and telling the parents   gwen reacts quite negatively – "oh for love of Christ not again! I'm calling your uncle Bryn"

The welsh family go to essex to share the news of the engagement Nessa shares a bed with gwen. Gav and Stacey in a bed. Mick and pam talking about who's gonna pay for the wedding And there's bryn on his own on the sofa bed. Mick offers him the porn channels He declines Although initially put out at the prospect of driving to London but is ultimately excited to be able to use his sat nav

Nana Shipman – Bryn's mother, Stacey's Nan, Gwen's mother in law Bryn

Crab stall – bryn calling ness Vanessa – ey that#s out of order and you know it is there's only 2 people I let call me that ..Craig... and Sylvia at hyper value

The crab stall?

Nessa can never leave the kiosk – there's over 70 pounds in here
GAVIN
I don't need this Where is she?
NESSA
Oi All I'm sayin is you hurt her again You got me to deal with. I got her back And Bryn's For reasons you don't need to know about But if you hurt her again - I'll break your legs And one of your arms

have you woken up deaf?

Places in barry – Talk of the Town (the Savoy) where they do karaoke

Let's establish that it's Barry and not Barry island where our family lives   there are no houses on Barry Island.

2 amusement arcades – caesars palace and phoenix nights. Both really really grim Maybe Vanessa has worked in both. Rivalry.

A tanning shop called TANFASTIC

Is Stacey's dad really dead – or is this what the family pretend to hide some great shame?

You were really crap Great but crap

Cheese cloth – g spot

I'm not kiddin – they gave me the worst haemorroids I've ever known

Gavin they are frying eggs on the streets of London

Jimmy Choos – Jackie Chan

SMITHY I WO0ULD LOVE TO HAVE A GO ON JEANETTE CRANKY – NOT IN THE OUTFIT AND AS LONG AS SHE DIDN'T DO THE VOICE
I TRY TO THINK OF A WOMAN – ANY WOMAN – WHO I WOULDN'T LET BLOW ME. AND I CAN'T. GO ON – NAME ANY WOMAN – GO ON – ANNE WIDECOMBE, WHY NOT – WE'D BOTH STAND UP TO DO IT NADIA FROM BIG BROTHER. I STILL THINK – YEAH SHUT YOUR EYES. GREAT PAIR OF TITS – WHO AM I TO QUIBBLE

REMEMBER THAT PAM IS NOW A VEGETARIAN – CARRY THIS THROUGH TO THE WEDDING – THE OTHER DAY I HAD SOME LAMB AND I CRIED INTO IT – MICK THOUGHT IT WAS GRAVY SHE SAYS SHE HAS TO START EATING MEAT AGAIN FOR HEALTH REASONS BECAUSE SHE'S IRON DEFICIENT

MICK RECKONS THAT PAM WEARS THE TROUSERS IN THEIR HOUSE – UNTIL HE WANTS THEM BACK

On stag – how old is lucy now four? No 17 and three quarters.

The Proposal
Gavin comes down to Barry meets gwen and bryn Suggests taking ttime off and
going London – they meet pam and mick – Stacey wants to go to madame tussauds –
mick you're paying 20 quid to stare at candles – look here you are – picks up candle –
who's that? Pam says I'll pay – no you won't – smithy calls round to see why gavin
didn't go to football pracice – say what you've got to say in front of staqcey – one
sniff of that girls minge – you wanted her here! – you used to bang birds all the time –
actually stace maybe you should step out – they end up talking privately – gavin tells
smithy he's going to propose – smithy thinks he's mad – mention of lucy – I've been
with lucy for nine years – I'm not going to marry her – but that'#s not a relationship
– how dare you – just cos I'm not drifing up and down the m4 – get across the
relationship between him and lucy – they go – gavin proposes

1   the office – gav and stace on the phone but it's different from before – he's not
     as flirty now because they've had sex.
2.

Ep 3
Telling the parents
Football – everyone comes – smithy has brought his girlfriend to prove that he does
things with his girlfriend – nessa and Stacey in the changing rooms – nessa's staying
put

Chinese Alan is not Chinese but there's an Alan and Chinese Alan. "Gav! Chinese
Alan's here" – at the stag

INT.
Essex Kitchen - the oven is open and MICK is showing his friend
PETE, only 5'3, a fine leg of lamb MICK is wearing an apron
MICK
It's garlic, olive oil and rosemary and I've bashed it all together in
the pestle.
PETE
Now - is the pestle the bowl or is that the mortar?
MICK
D'you know what Pete, I don't know! I've just always called it the
pestle . but that's by the by..
PETE
I'm gonna look that up.
MICK
Yeah Let me know. . so what I've done is just massaged it, rubbed
it - all over the joint And then I've let it stand - marinade - for an
hour
PETE

An hour??
MICK
An hour.
PETE
That is brave And you don't find it too overpowering?
MICK
No. Because none of it actually gets through. It just stays on the outside. And you wait till you taste the gravy!!!
They laugh as if MICK has just told a filthy joke. MICK closes the oven door with aplomb - still wearing his oven gloves.
PETE
Can I ask you a personal question?
MICK
Fire away
PETE
Where d'you get those oven gloves? I tell you why I'm asking - Dawn got me a pair last Christmas. I loved the colour - it was like a charcoal grey
MICK
Nice
PETE
But I swear - I could have only picked up two, three baking trays four at tops and they melted straight through.
MICK
And you never replaced them?
PETE
No
MICK
So what you on - tea towels?
PETE
Yep
MICK
That's not good. Here - give these a try
He takes off his gloves and gives them to PETE who puts them on and opens the oven He lifts out the sizzling baking tin full of lamb
PETE
Yeah That is nice Can't feel a thing
MICK
Yeah
INT.
Essex Front room. PAM is sat with her friend DAWN, PETE's wife. They are having a gin and tonic and talking quietly.
DAWN

So he was flicking round the channels - bout half ten on a Sunday
night - and that film, wotsit, "Disclosure" comes on
PAM
With Demi Moore when she's the boss .
DAWN
And Michael Douglas So this is on - and there's quite a raunchy
scene - so I say to him, I say "Pete - I fancy a bit of role play - what
d'you think?"
PAM
Dawn! You are naughty!
DAWN
Yeah - I said "I'm gonna go upstairs and put on a blouse and skirt,
stockings and stillettoes and pretend to be your boss. Then I'm
going to sexually molest you in the workplace.
PAM IS ENJOYING BEING SHOCKED.
DAWN
And d'you know what he said?
PAM
Go on!
DAWN
He said that would never happen where I work. There's only me,
Andy and Russel and they'd never do anything like that
Pam laughs
DAWN
(so disgusted remembering it)
I mean - have you EVER heard
PAM
I feel for you Dawny I do And I know I'm a very lucky woman
Because I can honestly say, Mick has been open to ALL my
suggestions.
(the front door opens)
Even the Charles and Camilla stuff.
GAVIN walks in with a KFC bucket
PAM
(whispering to DAWN)
I bought him these ears. . I'll tell you later.
(to GAV)
Hello my little prince
DAWN starts singing the bridal march
GAVIN
Alright Dawn?
DAWN
Congratulations Gavin

(she kiss es him)
Who's that hiding in the hall?
SMITHY (O S)
Dawny!!!
HE COMES IN
DAWN
Come here and give me a kiss you big brute
They kiss and she grabs his arse PETE and MICK come in.

It's a bridal fayre. Maybe Mick talks to someone on a stall – oh
Stacey shipman – she's booked me five times now – opportunity
for everyone on different stalls – did you know you can get married
in deep space? Under water etc – bryn quite taken by this…dave's
coaches can be there – all aspects of the wedding…bridal dr3ess
woman who doesn't finish her sentences Sorry my love what was
that? Day trip mentality

In ep 2 – stace to ness – I will miss you what you gonna do – go
round Craig's – is that back on – no we'll probably just shag

Smithy doesn't know Jason is gay – even seen a gay porno film
men in black men

Nessa had advice from Jason about how to perform a certain
sexual act

Forgive me jesus – at the wedding

SMITHY
(to Gary'n'Simon and Gavin)
I'm gonna rip their heads off in a minute
ANDY
What you say?
SMITHY
What?
GAVIN
Calm down - I'm havin a great time
JESUS
Fingers! How d'you get on with that Dutch bird the other night?
FINGERS
It was a nightmare - we get back to her place, you saw what she
was like, all over me wasn't she dickhead?

DICKHEAD
Like a rash
FINGERS
So we're in the bedroom and she flicks the light on. I take one look
at the bed - she's got rubber bedsheets!
JESUS/GAVIN/SWEDE
Quality!/Shutup!/Oh My God!
FINGERS
She turns to me and she goes
(Dutch accent)
"You like the Shportsh?" I'm thinking - oh God - what she gonna
unload on me? I say "Sorry sweetheart . "

FINGERS
She says - "I need the Sports " So I shut my eyes thinking ...here it
comes, and she flicks the telly on. Sky Sports! She can only do it if
she's watching Sky Sports!

FINGERS
I said to her - you must be sent from heaven. I'd marry you if I
weren't already married.
They all laugh - they've come to the front of the queue but the
bouncer stops them coming in
BOUNCER
No stag parties - sorry

 LUCY'S HOUSE SMITHY is lying on the bed with LUCY, a 17
year old bleached blonde - attractive but plastic looking girl.
SMITHY is fiddling with her hair.
LUCY
So - you know Jurassic park. . is that real?
SMITHY
No! Lucy - baby . I told you this when we watched it... none of the
Jurassic parks are real, King Kong didn't actually happen but
Schindler's list did
LUCY
Oh . so they really did that to all those people?
SMITHY
Yes!
LUCY
That's awful
SMITHY's mobile rings

The music is really loud and the club is packed SMITHY is drunk and now surrounded by a group of girls with GAVIN next to him

SMITHY

No - look -

(pointing at his t-shirt)

"Best man" - and he's the groom So tonight is your last chance to get off with him

GAVIN

Yeah Last chance - come on who's first?

COLLETTE

I'll do it. Come here

Some of the other boys gather round GAVIN and COLLETTE start snogging People start cheering SMITHY starts whispering in COLLETTE's ear whilst she's snogging GAVIN.

SMITHY

You can get off with me too if you like, anytime .. tho tonight would be quite convenient   what with us both being in the area

SUZIE

Hurry up - I want a go

GAVIN

Hey - there's plenty go round. Come and join in.

GAVIN starts snogging both girls They are all giggling - all the stag boys start cheering

SMITHY

Room for another one??

And he sticks his tongue out and lurches towards the threesome trytng to join in They all pull away

SMITHY

What you doing? Come on - God Chill out! Free Love!

GAVIN

I'm not snogging you!

GAVIN'S phone rings - he takes it out and walks off.

SMITHY

Oh yeah - bothered I got a girlfriend anyway. She's fitter than both of you.

LUGGY

Yeah - and how old is she now Smithy, four? Five?

SMITHY

She's seventeen and three quarters actually. So it's not me that looks stupid

He smiles at the girls who are now bored and walk away.

Episode 6 – plan
Office – empty chairs
Stacey's house – Gwen, Stacey and Nessa – being sick – Stacey needs the bathroom – Nessa looks in the mirror at herself. Jason there

Hotel – Smithy practicing his speech

Emotional scene with pam mick and gav

Bryn arrives with cars – in the car on way to church he gives her letter from her dad.

At church – all the boys are at the church who were at the stag night – couple of them are ushers

Some people turn up – get to meet new characters – Dawn and Pete,

Guest list – who's there

Smithy has put ribbons on his van – he drives them

Church
Photos
Reception
Speeches
Evening do

Loch Ness monster

Farmer's market in Billericay – called Barley Lands Farm

Woman with the turn in her eye – don't know which way she's looking..

Bryn glyn glan gwyn glen and gwen – all from Glan Llyn

Contortionist – Nessa "when I was working as a contortionist in South Korea" with Cirque de Soleil – they keep asking me back but I said no.

CHAPTER 2

Battling for the green light: the development

JAMES: So we got commissioned to write one script, and we had to write it very quickly, which is why that first episode has a very natural beginning, middle and end. And it ends with the hope that the viewer will want to see more of them. For us, it had a really nice ending, with Gavin saying, 'If you say it, I'll say it back', Stacey saying, 'I love you', Gavin saying, 'I love you too', and then her rape alarm going off.

RUTH: I remember we wrote that first ep in the Century Club in Soho and then in that hotel in Shepherd's Bush – is it still there? It was called the K West. We wrote it in three sessions of eight hours. Because I was filming *Nighty Night* and you were rehearsing, I think, so our time was a bit precious.

I found out many months later – at The South Bank
Show Awards, in fact – that Guy Garvey from Elbow
was in the hotel room above us writing songs for *The
Seldom Seen Kid*. So weird.

**Yeah, I can remember writing there so clearly, and us
really laughing at the Bryn dialogue with the rape alarm
and thinking, 'Well, if no one else finds it funny, at least
it's made us laugh.'**

It was a bit of a game-changer . . .

Here's the scene:

> GWEN
> What do I owe you for that
> alarm, Bryn:

> BRYN
> Oh don't worry about it. This
> was on me.

> GWEN
> No, come on!

> BRYN
> Hey these things are
> important. My brother would
> turn in his grave if he
> thought I wasn't looking after
> his little girl. Truth is: I

don't want anyone in this room
being raped, myself included.

GWEN

That's very good of you, love.

NESSA

Aye, fair play.

STACEY

Thanks uncle Bryn. [she
hugs Bryn]

BRYN

Ahhh come on now don't get me
started. Right! Man in the
shop says I should give you
a little demonstration, so,
Stace, I want you to run at
me, as if to all intents
and purposes, you are my
attacker.

STACEY

Oh you don't have to show me I
can work it out myself.

BRYN

Stace, tomorrow morning you
are going to London, England,
to meet a boy you never met
before. I offered to come with
you. You said no. I offered
to drive you there and wait

```
       in the car. You said no. Now
       you've met me half way on the
       rape alarm, at least have the
       decency to let me give you a
       demonstration, because - and
       I tell you this for nothing -
       if you come back Sunday, raped,
       and I showed you how to use it,
       I'll rest easy in my bed. You
       come back Sunday, raped, the
       fault will lie solely at your
       door. So please, attack me!
```

To be clear, we're not laughing at the mention of rape here . . .

No! It was just the ludicrousness of Bryn not realizing the inappropriacy of his words.

And so we sent the episode off and waited for feedback from the BBC.

I actually found my original email to Stuart . . .

14 September 2005
Re: Gavin & Stacey episode 1 . . .

---

hi Stuart - here it is then . . . it is absolutely a first draft - with nothing whatsoever done to it . . .

i am crossing fingers, toes, legs . . . the lot!

speak soon

ruth x

And a week later, he replied:

21 September 2005

I liked your script a lot. The only notes I would give would be the same as Cheryl's in the comedy commissioning bit - that I would start the emotional journey earlier, to establish the characters as single people before we see them as a couple. I think it is a world which has so many opportunities for comic potential i wonder if you are selling it a bit short, starting the story the day they first meet . . . just a thought

[Cheryl was Cheryl Taylor, who was Controller, Comedy Commissioning at the BBC at the time.]

Then, on 2 October, I emailed Lisa Holdsworth, a TV writer who'd written for *Fat Friends*. I was getting impatient . . .

Me and James Corden have written the first episode of a six part comedy which it looks like BBC3 want to do . . . but the red tape and the waiting on tenterhooks for green lights is all a bit much. i think actors are made of weaker stuff than proper writers. we tend to give in at the first hurdle! i think it's our egos needing constant massaging. sad but true . . . it would be great if it all works out tho, as we've written ourselves a couple of cracking characters . . . fingers crossed.

It was quite unusual to send a script directly to the BBC. The usual route was to go to a production company first of all and let them develop it before going to a broadcaster. Thinking back, I wonder what would have happened if we'd gone to a production company first of all? It may have become a different show altogether.

It may never have been made.

We were so lucky to have that connection with Stuart Murphy and to have been able to send it to him direct. And to get his direct approval on the script before anyone else got to look at it. Or change it.

But we knew we'd have to go to a production company with it eventually.

Yes, and Baby Cow [Steve Coogan's production company] felt like the natural place for us, because I'd worked with them on *Nighty Night*, and you'd worked with them on *Cruise of the Gods* [a one-off comedy for the BBC which also starred Rob Brydon]. Although Stuart Murphy suggested we could start our own production company – d'you remember?

But we didn't know anything about anything back then. We wouldn't have known where to start.

Can you imagine!

I think Henry Normal was the biggest pull of Baby Cow, because *The Royle Family* was a really important show about a working-class family, and the fact that he had been so integral to the success of that show. And at that point, they really were the go-to company for comedy: they were making *The Mighty Boosh, Nighty Night, Marion and Geoff*, Alan Partridge, so it was very natural if you had a half-hour comedy show to go to them.

I remember very, very clearly the biggest impact that Henry made on the show at the time was during that meeting at the BBC, after Cheryl Taylor said that they really liked episode one, that it was great, and they'd like to commission two more scripts.

D'you remember Cheryl Taylor said when she read it she was on the tube to work and missed the tube stop for the first time ever, because she was so gripped!

Oh yeah . . . Henry didn't speak very much in the meeting, because it was mostly us explaining where we thought *Gavin & Stacey* could go, and then

Henry just said, 'Ruth and James are busy actors, and if you commission two scripts, they'll squeeze them in amongst other work. I think it would be in the BBC's interest to commission five more scripts. And I think you'll get those scripts earlier, because then they will have to commit to start writing them and James is going to go on this tour of *The History Boys*. And Ruth is in demand. She's got *Little Britain* and *Nighty Night*. And there is a very definite win here. So I think you'll get where you are hoping to get quicker.'

And they said, 'Well, we'll have to talk about that.' Then I remember the next day they said, 'We'd like to commission five more scripts,' which I don't think we realized was such a big deal, but it really was. It was such a commitment. And that meeting with Cheryl Taylor where Henry got the script commission – that sort of thing just didn't happen! I sent my agent an email titled 'Open the champagne!'

17 October 2005

just spoke to Henry - the BBC want to commission another 5 scripts - yippee!

Speak soon

Ruth

But then later that day, on 17 October, in an email from my agent, we got a bit of a shock because it was suddenly announced that Stuart Murphy, who was so key in getting the show commissioned, was leaving the BBC. And I replied:

just spoke to Henry he'd just heard himself - he said
not to worry - that there are enough people other than
Stuart behind it and that certain other projects might
be more of a cause for concern - but he has no worries
for G and S. also he said it could take him a while
to leave.

cheers

ruth

Then later that same day, I emailed Stuart:

I can't believe it! On the day of joy when we find out
we're getting a series commissioned, I find out you're
leaving!!!! No!!!!! Don't do it!!! I'll miss you too much. Feel
very sad.

Ruth x

It was such a relief that it got commissioned before Stuart actually left. And so then we set about working on the scripts for episodes two, three, four and

five of series one in the autumn of 2005, in the hope
that the BBC would give us the green light to actually make the show.

**I didn't really understand the terminology back then:
I thought if something was commissioned, then it
was definitely going to get made. But you explained
to me about the 'green light'. Getting green-lit was the
actual go-ahead to film it. At that stage, we'd only been
commissioned to write the scripts. We'd written five
and a half of the six scripts before you went abroad to
do *The History Boys* on tour . . .**

Yeah, I was heading to Hong Kong, then New
Zealand . . . and then the Broadway run.

**So we would have been writing the scripts for the rest
of the series that autumn [2005]. Then it was the week
before Christmas, and we were about halfway through
episode six and we were in London. And we just didn't
manage it. We gave up and went to the pub instead! We
called Julia [Davis] to come and join us. Wasn't it in the
John Snow in Soho?**

Yeah, that's right, and we got drunk on this
organic wine.

We thought because it was organic, it was good for us!

And you were meant to be at some function in Cardiff which started at seven p.m. But we were still in the pub at eight.

Oh yeah! So Christmas came and went and we still hadn't finished episode six. And off you went on tour. You were away when I went to a meeting with the BBC in February 2006 and finally found out that we'd been given the green light to make the series. I think I messaged you and left a voicemail saying, 'Can you call me?'

I'd just arrived in New Zealand with the cast from *The History Boys*, and on my phone it said I had two new messages. I turned on the voicemail, and it was you, as Nessa, saying, 'Oh, Smithy, we got a green light.' And I remember just bounding over to the boys who were at the baggage reclaim, practically yelling, 'My BBC show has been green-lit! We've been green-lit!' And they were like, 'Cool.' I was expecting more of a reaction, to be honest, but we had just flown in from Hong Kong.

And then they all ended up being in it! Andy Knott was Dirtbox, Samuel Anderson was Fingers and Russell Tovey was Budgie. Such lovely boys. I came out twice to New York, didn't I? First time to finish ep six and the second to do the rewrites. And it must've been around then that we decided Nessa was pregnant.

And Smithy was the father!

Oh yeah . . . And so between February and October 2006, when you were away, that's when we would have been doing a lot of the prep stuff, including some casting sessions, all building up to start filming in the October.

It wasn't always plain sailing, though, was it?

No. In August 2006, I remember writing an email to Henry Normal asking what was going on with the acting budget, because we felt it was so low. I really offended him . . .

You were pretty harsh in that email, I remember.

Well, I was honest. And I was just saying what we both felt: that we were so gutted about how low the main cast fees were. You were away on the tour, and probably I should have run it by you first. We're pretty good at balancing each other out, aren't we? Calming each other down, kinda thing . . . But Henry was really upset. I think he felt insulted that I didn't trust him. In retrospect I can understand why he felt like that, and I think now, having been on the production side myself, I'd feel the same if the writer was questioning me like that, and asking about the budget. Having said that, I do think his reaction was disproportionate – he seemed to

think I was making all sorts of accusations about him and the company, which was simply untrue. Do I regret sending it? Yes, probably, because it didn't really resolve anything. We fell out for no real reason. Though we did meet and make up, and it was fine in the end. I was SO nervous going to London to meet him and sort it all out. I really wished you'd been there. I think I met him in a sushi place.

I suppose it just felt like we were no longer in control of it and, of course, if it was now – well, that wouldn't happen, like you said, because we've both got so much more experience between us, and we've got our own production companies. So, no, it wouldn't happen now, but back then we were in the dark about how it all worked. Maybe we should have taken the advice of Stuart Murphy to set up a production company, but we didn't. We couldn't! Still, there's a lot to be grateful to Baby Cow for, because Henry was brilliant in terms of helping us and teaching us about the industry.

And let's face it, hindsight is a wonderful thing . . .

CHAPTER 8

Naps, rows and
chocolate: the writing

RUTH: I'm the typist.

JAMES: Of course you are! Stephen Fry said once that in all writing partnerships there's someone who types and someone who wanders around. And that's our relationship. You're the head girl, and I'm in detention, right? That's just our nature.

It's true, I really was head girl. I also handled the admin and the emails. And it was my laptop we used from the start. The first one wasn't an Apple one. I just remember that it was kind of dark blue and chunky and didn't even have a trackpad. I can't remember what make it was. Sony, maybe? But I only discovered when we were writing *The Finale* that if you use two fingers on an Apple Mac trackpad, you can scroll up pages.

I said, 'Why do you take so long to get to the end of the page? Just do that. Just scroll up and down . . .'

It was a revelation! I was like: 'What? Oh my god. This is life-changing. I can't believe this.'

In the writing process I always think of you as being a bit like Tom Cruise in *Minority Report*, where you've just got this unbelievable ability to go, 'No . . . Maybe . . . Absolutely not . . . Oh yes, that's it!' And then we're locked. Basically, the writing experience is me doing lots of this: 'OK, what if we do this . . . Hang on, wait!' And then you go, 'I don't think that's right. What if we actually put that thing here instead of there?' And then I'll go, 'Yes, and then we can do that there.' And then that's it! As soon as we're locked, that's it, really.

I think a lot of the way we work comes from the fact that before we started writing *Gavin & Stacey*, I had written those two other things, so I was used to writing scripts on the laptop, and also I'm a touch typist. I did a night class in 1987 in Leamington Spa. So I can sit, we can be talking, and I will be typing it all out at the same time. Your handwriting is all in capitals, James, so I can imagine it would slow us down if you had to type as well. Practically, we would never get anything done. But the fact is

we seemed to fit into that groove, and it just seemed to work, really.

I do like writing the Post-its.

Oh yeah, all in capital letters! The Post-its are the very first stage after the initial chat. And we try to make them as succinct as possible – like, with just a handful of words. So it might say something like: *Bryn, roof rack, angry, Gwen, mysterious.*

And then what happens is: when we get to the stage of writing a scene, we will sit together at the laptop and read it out, and then we kind of amend it together, as it were.

So in the initial stages, I'm just sort of making notes, so that we've got something to work from to actually write the scenes. Then it's the Post-its. Then it's what should be the enjoyable bit, like building to the climax of a tennis match, as we act out all the dialogue.

And we do all the voices in a very defined way, so I'm always Pam, Smithy and Gwen, and you are often Bryn, Stacey, Nessa and Gavin.

But sometimes you are Nessa.

I'll sometimes do Nessa, yes. I actually love doing Nessa. And there are a couple of floaters. So sometimes I'll do a Bryn and you'll be doing a Gwen. But I'm always Pam and you're always Mick!

I sometimes think you channel your mum a bit when you do Pam. And friends of mine have said Nessa reminds them of my impression of my dad!

Writing is sort of 'playing', really, isn't it? And messing about. I mean, it feels like messing about but actually a lot of good stuff comes out of it. I took a lot from the shows I'd been in before where I'd been able to just 'play' and try things out. So with Julia Davis's *Nighty Night*, for example, certainly for series one, we did over three years of improvisation, coming up with ideas and stuff. I can remember things like the 'roll on, roll off' massage idea, when my character, Linda, is a masseur and she literally rolls on to this guy, one of her clients. I remember doing that at Steve Coogan's house down in Brighton, and it really was just *playing*. I knew Julia from an improvised comedy group that Rob Brydon and I were also part of in Bristol in the early nineties, and a lot of what we did was just messing around and I loved it. And that's why I love writing with you so much, James. We do just play, don't we? The number of times you would go, 'Imagine if . . .' and then we'd go on a flight of fantasy.

There was one time we were writing in the Soho Hotel in London and you were holding a plate that I think had a club sandwich, some crisps and salad on it. And you said, 'What would you do if I just threw this sandwich at your head?' Then we played it out. So I said, 'What are you doing?' And you went, 'I'm sorry, I didn't mean to.' And we acted out a whole scene . . . It was just nonsense, really, but that was like a lot of what went on in our writing rooms.

When we were doing series two and three, we used to write in a place on Oxford Street. We used to go off to get lunch, and we'd sometimes go separately, to different places, and we'd arrange to meet back at a certain time. But we'd often bump into each other by accident somewhere in Soho anyway, and we'd start an improvisation just to amuse each other. Like, as if it was years later and you and I had lost touch. I would go, 'James? James! It's Ruth Jones . . .'

And I'd go, 'Oh my god. Oh. My. God.'

I'd pretend to be really bitter at seeing you, cos my life hadn't worked out as I'd hoped . . .

And I'd pretend I'd married Geri Halliwell or something, and was living in LA.

And there was the pot pourri . . .

Oh yeah. There used to be a bowl of pot pourri in this Oxford Street office, and I got in there before you one time, and you opened the door and I just threw it all over you. I mean – why?

And then we had to spend ages picking it all up. So on another day, I resolved to get in there earlier than you. I think we were due to start at ten a.m., and I was there at, like, nine fifteen, just holding this bowl of pot pourri, ready . . .

So childish!

But so much fun.

And we used to sleep, didn't we? We napped. You some-times slept on the table, or under the table, or I would sleep on the table and you'd be on the floor. And when we weren't in hotel rooms, often we were in these serviced offices, and sometimes they would show prospective clients round. I remember one time we were having one of our naps and there was a knock on the door. We didn't answer because we couldn't be bothered. We were napping!

Then this guy arrived, saying to his client, 'I think

this room would be ideal for you. You just want to come in?' And he was greeted by the two of us waking up.

Also, we would often do this thing where somebody came in, and we'd both pretend to be crying. One time this woman came in and I decided to start crying, and you said to her, 'She's OK, don't worry ... she'll be all right.'

There was a lot of that going on when we wrote together. That's what our writing sessions were like, right up to the end.

And we've written the show everywhere, haven't we? In series one, we'd do half a week down in your house in Cardiff, half a week in my flat that was above a Chinese takeaway in Beaconsfield: we'd just split our time. You would sleep on my sofa bed. I'd go in your spare room. That's where we wrote to start with.

Then there was New York (because of *The History Boys* being on Broadway), where we did the rewrites for series one – some of which we did in Central Park. Me and Russell Tovey, aka Budgie, lived next door to each other on 72nd Street and Central Park West. You came out there twice and you stayed in my flat, and we just wrote all day. Then I'd pop off and do the play and come back, and we'd write more afterwards. We did that for a solid week, and one day it was so hot – you know, July-in-Manhattan hot – that we just took the laptop into the park. It was so surreal, writing these scenes set in Barry Island while we were sitting in Central Park.

I was in New York quite recently, with a friend, and I said, 'Can you believe we wrote *Gavin & Stacey* here?' It was crazy.

I remember how we wrote the 2008 Christmas special in a hotel that was kind of around the corner from Selfridges. That was seventeen years ago.

Can I just say, when we were there in that hotel, we were trying to save money by not spending loads of cash on food, because when we had our lunch breaks there was the temptation to get something from Selfridges. So we decided to boil some eggs in a kettle.

Yes, it was either room service or Selfridges Food-hall, which were both quite expensive. And we both fancied boiled eggs. So we bought some eggs from around the corner and we tried to boil them.

Well, first we tried to boil them in the ice bucket.

We thought if we poured boiling water on them and left them in there long enough, it would be OK. We then opened the bucket and it was the single most horrific smell I'd ever experienced. So then we tried to boil them in the kettle, but it obviously didn't work, so we just gave up on the notion of boiled eggs.

No one sold boiled eggs back then. They're everywhere now.

Then, when we wrote *The Finale*, we decided to go back to that hotel where we wrote the 2008 Christmas special.

Because it felt like magic. A magical place.

Yeah, it was great there. But I have to say, it is tired now. Those sixteen years had not been kind. I think it's under new ownership. And so we got there . . . we lasted just about an hour. And then went to a different hotel.

It's really weird. I'm actually quite amazed that we ever get any writing done at all because we talk a lot about all kinds of stuff, don't we?

We chat.

We usually start off the session by talking about anything and everything, kind of like gossip or just about life stuff.

Just how we're feeling.

And sometimes that can go on for quite a long time. And then we'll get a little bit of work done, but the writing day needs a lot of ingredients. It needs naps and it needs food and it needs chocolate.

Chocolate is key.

Well, we've had a whole history with chocolate. I tried to give it up many years ago, and although I hate the phrase 'struggled with my weight', I can't ever remember being slim. Maybe when I was seventeen? And one of my attempts to lose weight was to go to a Paul McKenna workshop using hypnosis. Apparently, he was on the radio the other day saying he'd cured my love of chocolate, but no, he bloody didn't, because I still eat it now!

Anyway, back at this workshop, he asked what my aim was and I said if I could stop eating chocolate, I would be fine, or at least feel better about myself. So he said, 'OK, I'm going to show you a technique; if you want to stop eating chocolate, this is going to stop it for good.' There must have been sixty people there in this hotel conference room and we got paired up and taught how to do what was basically aversion therapy, where you think of something that you would hate eating at the same time as the chocolate. So I would imagine eating some carpet, and then eating chocolate, and go back and forth. And you had to imagine it becoming a big piece of chocolate, and then it got even bigger and even bigger. And then you had to imagine walking through it. It was a really strange technique, to be honest, and I was a little bit cynical about it and thought it would never work.

But it did. It completely worked. And I did not eat chocolate for five years.

During those five years, I couldn't stand the smell of chocolate. Couldn't stand it. And when you and I were writing in this period, some of the hotels that we'd stay in – having progressed to slightly better ones – would often put a little bit of complimentary chocolate in the room. What I used to do was I always used to test myself to see if I was still not wanting to eat the chocolate. I'd inhale the scent of it. And I'd find it repellent. And you would keep testing me, either with the chocolate in the hotel, or you would buy Maltesers and you'd go, 'Just put one in your mouth.' Like a child, an absolute child.

This one hotel had a little box with four chocolates in it – four little things. And you smell it and go, 'No, I don't want to go near it. It's gross.'

So anyway, one day I got a bit fed up with all the emails from the people who had put on that workshop, so I unsubscribed from the Paul McKenna company. And I swear to god, the next day we were writing, and there were chocolates on the bed in this hotel room. And I picked them up, went to inhale the smell, and instead of the usual repulsion, I just wolfed them all down in one!

I'd gone into the bathroom for a wee, came back, and you were eating them.

You were like, 'Oh my god.'

You literally had chocolate hanging out of your mouth. You were holding them near your mouth and I was like, 'What? This is insane.'

It wasn't always messing around, though, was it? There were also the rows . . .

Oh yeah, the Easter Egg Row. It was quite a big row, really.

It started when I was travelling up from Cardiff for a writing session for series two. I was meeting you at the Charlotte Street Hotel, and I think I was going to stay the night there after the writing session. It's all a little bit vague. But I'd had a message from James Thornton, Jo Page's husband, a few days earlier, because he had this script idea and he'd said, 'Oh, would you mind reading it?' So I texted back to say, 'Oh, yes, by all means, send me the script and I'll have a look. Don't know if I can help, but I'm happy to have a look.' But instead of sending the text to James Thornton, I sent it to you, James Corden.

So then I messaged you and said, 'Oh, sorry, that wasn't meant for you.' And you asked, 'Who was it meant for?' And I don't know what possessed me, but I just went, 'Oh, it doesn't matter. I can't tell you about it.' And for some bizarre reason, you went, 'Oh my god, are you doing *Doctor Who?*' And I replied, 'I'm sorry. I can't tell you because I've signed a confidentiality clause.' You were *furious* with me. And I was basically playing a joke on you, which I rarely do. Because I'm not really a wind-up merchant, honestly. I mean, you bloody are, but I don't do that sort of thing. But for some reason, I was really enjoying teasing you that one time by saying, 'No, I'm sorry, I can't tell you.' You took it really badly, and then you said to me, 'Oh, just forget it. I'm going to Benidorm.' I was like, 'What?' And then *I* got really cross and I said, 'Hang on, I'm coming all the way up from Cardiff to write with you. You can't just go to Benidorm.' We were really cross with each other. We met up in the bar in the Charlotte Street Hotel. And I said, 'Oh, for god's sake, I was just winding you up.'

So we had that pathetic little sibling row, made friends, and then we went across the road and bought some Easter eggs.

That's right – we decided to go for a walk and we bought two giant Cadbury Easter eggs. We lay on the bed in this hotel room, opened them, and just lay there with the chocolate eggs on our faces. Then it was shortly after that that we wrote Dawn and Pete's vows, when she changes the words to the lyrics from Michael Jackson's 'Ben'. That was an idea that arrived at 11.45 p.m. in the hotel, after a crap day. And I just went, 'What if Julia says, "Pete, the two of us need look no more . . ." and recites the whole song?'

Yes. We went up to the room. Ate the Easter eggs. Had a sugar rush. Had a sugar low. Fell asleep. Woke up. And wrote the Pete and Dawn vows scene.

I remember getting really hysterical writing it, because once we'd got the lyrics in place – you know, we changed it to, 'Pete, you're always running here and there' – it was just absolutely joyous. It was magic.

And also the bit that we never really mention, but that also came about from that day, was the ring that

Pete bought, which had a 'P' and 'D' on it, for Pete and Dawn. Or Puff Daddy! Or P-Diddy!

Anyway, that story does show how I have meltdowns with you sometimes, and get really annoyed and I overreact. I don't think I'm as bad now, but I used to really react to you, and you used to be able to wind me up so badly, which is why that story about accidentally sending the message to you was quite unusual; it was rare that it was reversed that way. And from my point of view, it was nothing compared to the NTAs argument.

Oh god, yeah, the National Television Awards in 2010! You and I were laughing about that recently. Maybe we should get to that later . . .

Yeah, we'll come to the NTAs. But in amongst all that arguing, being childish and eating and napping, I don't know quite how we get any writing done.

I think what we actually do is commit to the whole process. So we start at nine thirty or ten. We'll go till lunchtime. Then we'll leave and we'll always walk somewhere, like the other day we got some lunch and brought it back. Then maybe we'll do some work in the afternoon. Actually, when we were writing *The Finale*, we did quite a lot of late nights. Do you remember? We would do, like, ten a.m. till

ten or eleven p.m., just in these long processes of
getting all our ideas out. Because really, with *Gavin
& Stacey*, when people would come up to us and say,
'Oh god, we can't wait to see the next episode . . .
what's going to happen?' we'd often go, 'No, we're
excited to find out too! We don't know.' What it feels
like some days is we just open a sort of portal and
wait for the characters to arrive and tell us what's
going to happen.

**Yes, there have been times – not so much in recent
years, but back in the day – when I would get asked to
write something for somebody else. I don't know if I
could now, because I don't know if I'd be on the same
wavelength. I've got so used to how you and I work,
James.**

**It's interesting to think that in the original concep-
tion of the show, in that treatment we wrote, we said
that the cast would improvise, but when we wrote the
scripts that didn't happen at all. I think we realized
we really like writing funny but *real* dialogue. One of
the only times we included some improvisation was in
the wedding scene in series one with Julia [Davis] and
Adrian [Scarborough] as Dawn and Pete.**

Well, that was more of a vignette rather than part of
the script . . .

Yes, it was more like something that you'd overhear, a little bit of funny, natural dialogue, and Julia and Adrian were so good at all of that.

When you've got those two, and what you're going to need in a little scene is to show the passage of time within the day, if you put a camera on them, it *will* be great.

I think we also probably said in the treatment that it would be improvised maybe because we didn't fully think of ourselves as writers – writers of dialogue.

But then I come back to the feeling we had when the first show went out on BBC Three on a Sunday night. I remember we spoke on the Saturday, the day before, and I said to you, 'What percentage of the show would you change today if you could?' And you were like, 'Six per cent.' And I was like, 'I'm seven.' Therefore, success or failure, we wouldn't have changed anything, and it was really important to remember that.

We were happy with it. And we felt the same right up to *The Finale*. We are happy it's the show we wanted it to be.

What we've always done from the beginning is work out each series, so we decide how each series ends

first. Then we work out how the different episodes end. And then we have our Post-it notes and work it out on them. We're not very detailed in that regard, are we? We're very general to start with.

Well, we're not very slick. If you saw our room, it's literally eleven Post-its on a wall. And that's it.

We've always planned it so we know how each series starts and ends, like series one was: they meet in episode one, and they get married in episode six. But we had no idea that Nessa would be pregnant with Smithy's baby. Not a clue. Series two: Stacey's gonna move to London and not like it. Nessa will have the baby in episode seven. Series three . . .

. . . Gavin's moved to Wales.

And Gav and Stacey are going to be trying for a baby. They have a baby, and Smithy will stop Nessa marrying Dave. In the first Christmas special, we had the last scene out in the garden, and Smithy is just going, 'Don't marry him.' We had that before we had anything. I remember us running that dialogue, and acting what Nessa would be like. She was going to say something like, 'It's cold.' Then Smithy was going to say, 'Don't marry him? Don't worry. I'm not saying, marry me. That's not what I'm saying.

I'm just saying, don't marry him.' And then they go inside and they're singing 'Have Yourself A Merry Little Christmas' . . .

And Nessa and Smithy are having these little glances at each other while Larry Lamb is (not) playing the piano.

Then, in the 2019 special, we always knew that it would end like that, with Nessa's proposal. And with *The Finale*, we always knew it would end with Smithy and Nessa. So we've always started at the end, basically, and then worked back from that.

We do like having a destination.

Yeah.

A big element of writing the first series was figuring out the tone, and working out what it was about. I can remember being on a train going back to Cardiff after we'd filmed that series, and Ted Dowd, who was then the producer from Baby Cow, said we needed a synopsis or a strapline to describe the show. I was in one of those vestibules on the train, just going back and forth on the phone to you, both of us going, 'Well, what is it?' And then we came up with this idea that the show is all about the extraordinary in the ordinary, to show that seemingly 'ordinary' people are extraordinary.

I think that's it. Probably the biggest thing that we share, outside of our love of being silly and playing dress-up and all those things, is this idea that nobody is ordinary.

I know you feel like this, James, but if you just sit and listen to people – as I was listening to this woman at Pret this morning, for example, just talking about her life – then you realize that actually everybody is fascinating. If you said that to people on social media, they'd be very cynical about it, and assume that only famous people are exciting. But the truth is, everybody's got a story, everybody's got something going on in their life that's really quite intriguing . . .

And how rare it is to see some of these characters be front and centre. If you take people like Smithy and Nessa, whether it's down to society or the media, they would be defined in so many ways by how they look. If there's life on another planet and they come here, and they're looking for an example of human beings and how they operate, and they only look at film and TV, you're really going to think that anybody who looks like me and you doesn't fall in love. They have friends who fall in love, but *they* don't. They certainly wouldn't think they have great sex. But in our show, they do.

Smithy and Nessa definitely have great sex.

If there's something I'm most proud of in the show, it's that at the forefront is this really conventional boy-meets-girl love story, and that is it. They meet and they fall in love and they stay in love, and it's fucking beautiful. But that isn't always what love is, and not what love is for a lot of people like Nessa and Smithy, maybe. Love is complicated and it's messy and it's complex. And so to show both forms of love, and then familial love – that's something to celebrate.

When people ask why viewers love it so much, I think it's because it is about friendship and family and laughter and love, and those are all things that really keep us going. Actually, I think, no matter – even if you're not in a conventional family, your friends might be your family, for example. Like, say, how Pam and Mick are with Smithy. And I think that there's something reassuring about it as a show. Also, when you talk about the ordinariness of it – and you are really good at this, James – I think if you compare, say, my show *Stella* with *Gavin & Stacey*, if you drew a Venn diagram, the bit in the middle that those two shows share is family and warmth and the love that people have. But what I did in *Stella* was have an event per episode, when something quite big would happen, but I remember you

being conscious of the dangers of overly big stuff and saying, 'No, we can't make it that kind of show where big things happen.'

The classic example is I remember suggesting that one of our characters could be on the telly one week, maybe. My thinking was: one of the characters could be on *Stars in Their Eyes* or something. And you said, 'Yeah, they should go on telly, but it should be something so mundane and underplayed.' So in series two we came up with the whole idea of Mick being on the local TV news when a dismembered body is discovered in a Billericay car park. And everyone gets so excited, they all gather round their TV sets to watch him . . . but he's only on TV for a few fleeting moments. And everyone watching it is going, 'Is that it?!'

                        PAM
          Shh. It's on. It's on. Gavin!

                      MICK (on News)
          Well, it's the last thing you
          expect to find when you come
          into work in the morning.

                        PAM
          Is that it? (louder) IS
          THAT IT?

                      GWEN (In Barry)
          Was that it?

```
                    BRYN
          Well, I'm bitterly
          disappointed.


                    GAVIN
          Crikey dad, it was hardly
          worth mentioning.


                  . . . . .


                    SMITHY
          They've made you look a
          right tit.
```

Talking of the sex-positive element of the show, when it first started we were younger, and I think we were probably trying to cling to the kind of comedy that was popular at the time . . .

Yes, there was an element of 'let's be outrageous'. A little bit. Don't forget that the context we were writing in was shows like *Nighty Night* and *Little Britain*, but with the sort of 'James Corden with Ruth Jones' spin on it.

But in that first series, which probably was more edgy, I also think we didn't want to make something that was cynical. I think that's there in all our work, separately and together: that we both feel there's probably enough of that around.

I remember Steve Coogan, when I was doing his show *Saxondale* after the first series of *Gavin & Stacey* had gone out, came into my dressing room – well, it wasn't a dressing room, more an office where I was getting changed. More like a cupboard, in fact. Anyway, I remember Steve just sticking his head around the door and saying, 'I watched your series, by the way. Do you know what I liked about it? I found myself laughing *with* the people, not *at* them, and that was very good.'

But there is also an edge to it. I mean, you can't find anything edgier than calling the families the Wests and the Shipmans.

Remember we had a joke about Nessa needing some AA batteries so she could have some 'me time' in the second series? Well, I did this thing recently for the Welsh Rugby Union. They've made this really nice film about what rugby means to people in Wales, and it's lovely. It's very warm. And I remembered I did this thing back in 2008 after Wales had won the Grand Slam, where I went on as Nessa and I interviewed Ryan Jones, who was then the captain of the Wales team, and there was this big celebration of Wales's achievement and all that stuff. I did this interview, and then right at the end he said, 'Oh, and by the way, Ness, here's a present from all the boys.' And he took out a packet of AA batteries and said, 'Have a little bit of "me time" on

us' . . . Those tiny little cheeky things are there in the show. Now kids watch it and I do wonder what they think 'me time' is!

What's really interesting about the show, and something that's always been there quite subconsciously, is how it works like a triangle of knowledge, with the lead characters – Gavin and Stacey, Smithy and Nessa – and then the supporting characters, and then the audience. And really, the way the show works is that at any one point in every single scene, one of those three doesn't know what's going on, and that's pretty present throughout. That's not something we've ever talked about. It's just there. And the triangle moves around all the time. So, for example, the audience know Nessa's pregnant, and the supporting characters know she's pregnant, but Smithy doesn't know she's pregnant. Or it can be both groups of people don't know what's going on. So Jason and Bryn know what happened on the fishing trip. But the audience don't know, and the lead characters don't know.

And nor will they EVER find out. I've recently completely stolen your idea for an answer to the question: 'What happened on the fishing trip?'

Yes, I say, 'I don't know because I wasn't there.'

Gavin and Stacey – notes for eps 4 and 5

Ep 4 – preparing for the wedding

Start in the office - Gavin and Stacey are talking about what happened between Smithy and Nessa at the party.
The crazy thing is, Uncle Bryn actually does believe that they fell over!
I know! So does my mum!
They discuss the arrangements for the Shipmans coming down to Wales for the preparation stuff like choosing the dress, suits and menus.

We meet Dawn and Pete – best friends to Pam and Mick. Dawn is really dirty –
If it's not happening in the bedroom – it's not happening anywhere You gotta keep experimenting babe

The Shipmans drive down to Wales Pam and Smithy in the back. They play car games – at first something simple but then Smithy wants to play "do or die" – a drinking game Gavin can't believe he wants to play this with his parents! But when he explains all the rules – Pam's all for it.
Right Mick – I'm gonna give you three names of people, from history present day – famous or infamous, and you have to say which one of these you'd (a) go on a world trip with but not sleep with but spend every waking hour with, (b)marry and have children with and a cat and (c)have a long hard shag with. Here are your three Saddam Hussein, The Pope and   (Pam chips in) Myra Hindley!

Bryn picks them up from the Severn Bridge just to make sure they find Barry ok Even though Gavin has driven there several times.

The girls go to Pro Nuptia to buy the dress. The boys go to Moss Bros for the suits Gwen wants to pay for the dress She's been saving. Pam tries to change her mind but she insists Nessa says
You're still getting mine tho Pam - yeah?
The girls take ages choosing. The boys get it over and done with in minutes. Except they have trouble with the cravat tie things. Bryn is a bit too hands on with smoothing down the front of Smithy/Gavin's suit. Or he helps them with the cravat. He <u>does</u> know how to do it. He used to wear them?

They all go to the venue for lunch to do a "taster" for the wedding meal?

Gavin and Stacey have to go and meet the vicar to discuss the wedding and the implications of getting married He tells them they have to start going to church and he'd like to see them there tomorrow. It's embarrassing talking about religion.

In the evening Gwen has everyone over to her house for chilli. And because she knows Pam's a vegetarian she does her an omelette! Gwen's house is cramped – they eat their chilli off their laps.

Gavin and Stacey have a catalogue (Argos? M&S?) and are choosing gifts for the wedding list.

Smithy and Nessa have ignored each other all day – need to see them actively ignore each other. But when the wedding gifts are being discussed, Nessa tells them she's already decided on <u>her</u> present to them. She's going to get a tattoo done of their names in Chinese and Welsh on her arm. Smithy is furious –
I'm sorry But I have got to speak up

Pam tells Stacey that Dawn will do the hair and makeup.

Smithy talks to Gavin about the stag do. He wants an eleven day event in Prague. Gavin has to let him down gently and tell him that all he'll be able to manage is a night up the west end. Smithy doesn't want anyone over the age of 35 there. Which discounts Mick and Bryn. Smithy's going to have T shirts made.

Next day - maybe they all go to church – Smithy really gets into it? Bryn is a regular there. He absolutely loves the vicar – has a crush on him – he saved the church as far as Bryn is concerned.

The vicar's sermon – one of those painfully metaphorical ones. He uses the analogy of sandwich fillings – how everyone has a favourite – how everyone makes different choices – just like everyone has a different relationship with God. Asks the congregation what their favourite sandwich filling is. Everyone joins in and has "fun". But Gavin is absolutely gobsmacked Speechless. The vicar gets impatient –
Surely you've got a favourite sandwich filling?
No
Well what was the last sandwich you had? Think??

<u>Ep 5 - Hen and Stag</u>

We start in the office again – on the phone. Stacey begs Gavin to be good tonight on the stag. He says he'll take his phone with him
I thought Smithy said no phones?

Hen and Stag nights – keep them brief. Pam comes on the hen.

See Nessa talking to a very thin friend about the benefits of purging.

Brief stag- get in Smithy's lines –

I try to think of a woman – any woman – who I wouldn't let blow me And I can't Go on – name any woman – go on – Anne widecombe, why not – we'd both stand up to do it Nadia from big brother I still think – yeah. Shut your eyes Great pair of tits – who am I to quibble Jeanette Cranky? I would love to have a go on Jeanette Cranky – not in the outfit and as long as she didn't do the voice

Essex boys come down to Wales next day for rehearsal.

Bryn questions when the stag's gonna be *"been looking forward to it for ages "* They have to have a fake stag for Bryn. Bryn tries to play a trick – like tie Gavin's shoelaces together. It goes badly wrong – Gavin injures himself? Or he "spikes" Gavin's drink with vodka.

Achmed is in the pub – he introduces himself and through their conversation it is revealed that Stacey has been engaged five times before

Gavin has a fit – massive row with Stacey – tells her he thinks their getting married too soon drives off – will he won't he ending? Gavin really freaks out – getting married too soon – *did you sleep with them all – what – you slept with Achmed?*
Last shot – Bryn and Smithy just staring at the floor wondering where Gavin has got to.

<u>Ep 6 will start with Gavin and Stacey's empty office chairs…</u>

"GAVIN & STACEY"

DIR: CHRIS GERNON   DOP: DOUG HALLOWS

ROLL   SLATE   TAKE

PROVISION

DATE: 15 DEC 2006   DAY 35   A

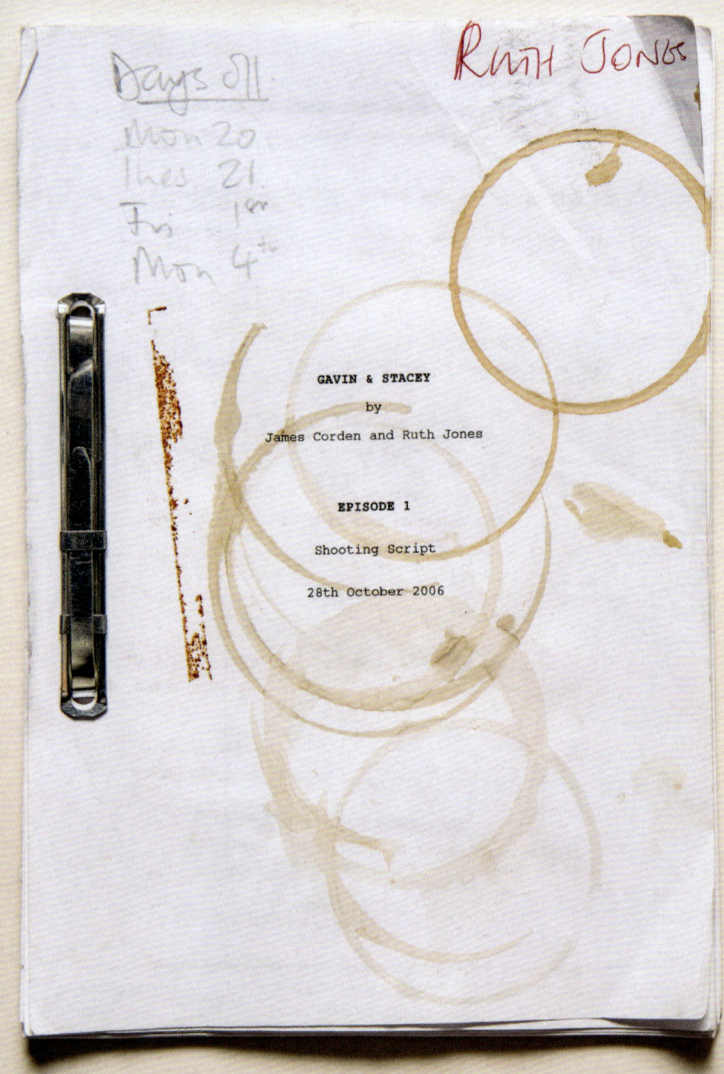

Days off
Mon 20
Thes 21.
Fri   1st
Mon 4th

RUTH JONES

GAVIN & STACEY

by

James Corden and Ruth Jones

EPISODE 1

Shooting Script

28th October 2006

Kate Roberts 'Gavin & Stacey Chinese Symbols'

Blue sky over Barry, where
the Wests live

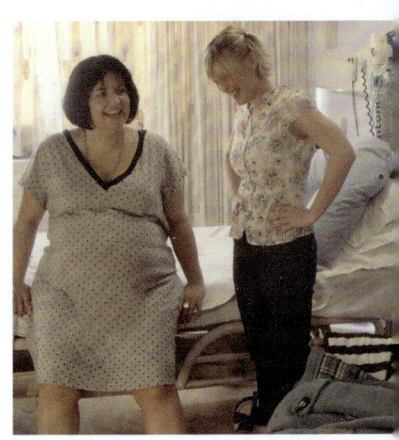

Smithy and Gavin,
best of friends

Nessa at work - as a living
(and pregnant) statue

Series 1, Episode 6 -
Gavin and Stacey's wedding

Pam's 'little prince'
gets married

Uncle Bryn
chats to Dawn
at the wedding

Series 1, Episode 5 -
at Gavin's Stag Night

The **Observer Magazine**

24 February 2008

THE FUNNIEST PAIR IN BRITAIN

Meet Ruth Jones and James Corden

Photograph
Ellis Parrinder

The Observer Magazine, 2008

Friday
21 November

Critics' choice

g a r y

Pick of the day

Gavin & Stacey (BBC1, 9.30pm)

The BBC3 comedy arrives at a new primetime slot in a horse-drawn carriage, awards jangling like medallions. And yet it would appear that the critical acclaim accorded to James Corden and Ruth Jones's sitcom owes as much to a yearning for the comic geniality of yesteryear as it does to the series's individual achievements.

Here, jokes are predicated on gentle domestic misunderstandings and minor grievances are swept merrily aside like biscuit crumbs on a doily. It is an old-fashioned and undemanding world that revels in the minor triumphs of the everyday, and yet, for all its cheer, it rarely manages to elicit more than a smile.

Tonight, in the first episode of this second series, newlyweds Gavin (Mathew Horne) and Stacey (Joanna Page) return from honeymoon to find Smithy (James Corden) in a huff and a seismic revelation in the ladies' loo of their favourite Italian restaurant. Aimless but amiable, it is as substantial as a toasted marshmallow.

SARAH DEMPSTER

Barry folk can't wait for TV comedy's return

'Show may take the mickey a bit ...but we love it!'

BARRY residents will be laughing along when Gavin and Stacey return to our television screens.

While the seafront town might be subject to a bit of gentle ribbing from the BBC hit show it has put Barry firmly on the map.

Shops in Barry are more than happy to soak up the exposure and say Gavin and Stacey is good for business.

Nathan Keelin, 36, who runs Food for Thought delicatessen in High Street, Barry, said he was a big fan of the show.

He said: "Obviously they are taking the mickey about Barry a bit but any publicity is good publicity.

"Since the very first episode customers have been talking about it nonstop. Every town has their Gavin and Stacey. It's nice because I just think, 'yeah, I know that character'.

"I think some of the older people weren't quite sure about it at the start but the youngsters think it's hysterical."

Pat Richardson, 42, owner of The Hair Shop, High Street, said: "The girls here can't stop talking about it.

"I've only ever heard good things about it and I think it's great for Barry. I think people of all ages find it funny. My husband is older than me and he loves it."

One famous fan of the show is

Matthew Aplin

Barry-born weatherman Derek Brockway. He previously told the Echo: "I'm really pleased the series is doing so well and getting the recognition it deserves. It's made even better because it's filmed in Barry. Being a Barry boy, it's great to see the town on the big screen."

Cardiff solicitor Samantha Jones, 30, recently got engaged to her partner John Stray after a similar whirlwind romance to Gavin and Stacey's.

She said: "We always laugh about how we work just like them. I think it's great for Wales as a whole and shows we've all got a good sense of humour."

■ The second series of Gavin and Stacey starts at 9pm tomorrow on BBC3.

■ Next week's TV Live !!

ACTION... The cast of Gavin and Stacey and, above, filming on the streets of Barry.

FUNNY BEYOND THEIR YEARS

We're impressed by the famous faces in supporting roles in Sunday's new sweet romantic comedy on BBC3, Gavin and Stacey. (Yes, that's right: "sweet romantic comedy on BBC3" shock!) Rob Brydon, Alison Steadman, Julia Davis and Matt Lucas make heavyweight comic contributions alongside the young pups in the lead roles, two of whom created the series. But these fresh faces already have impeccable pedigrees. KN

Mathew Horne
Plays: Gavin
Seen before ... as the long-suffering grandson of foul-mouthed Gran in The Catherine Tate Show; as an atheist RE teacher in Teachers; more recently in BBC2 sitcom Roman's Empire.

Joanna Page
Plays: Stacey
Seen before ... you've seen almost all of her before: she was the shy body double who bared all with Martin Freeman in Love Actually. She also featured in Russell T Davies's Mine All Mine.

James Corden
Plays: Smithy, Gavin's best mate
Seen before ... in Fat Friends and The History Boys. Alan Bennett himself encouraged Corden to pick up his comedic pen.

Ruth Jones
Plays: Nessa, Stacey's best mate
Seen before ... in Fat Friends, where she met G&S co-writer Corden; in Nighty Night alongside Julia Davis; Saxondale; best known as Myfanwy, the only gay in the village's only friend, in Little Britain.

Monday 14th May.

Rib-tickling: Matthew Horne as Gavin, with Larry Lamb as Dad and Alison Steadman as Mum in Gavin And Stacey

Chuckle of love

► Can you remember the last time a British sitcom made you laugh out loud? Not in an ironic, postmodern, snigger warning round your armpits kind of way – but a proper belly-laugh ripper? It happened to me halfway through Gavin And Stacey, a love story so sweet yet so twisted it tickled all parts of ribs.

Stacey comes down to breakfast after spending her first night in new boyfriend Gavin's bed. He lives with his mum, Pam, and dad, Mick, and they haven't met her, then in the trots sporting Blues Brothers shades. Looking daggers round the table, Mum is gripped by the fear her sweet prince is a girlfriend beater... 'Well, I've seen it before,' declares Mum. 'Where?' asks Dad incredulously. 'Holby City!'

Give that kind of line to Alison Steadman and you've got comedy gold, but her turn as Mum is just one of Gavin And Stacey's highlights. Writers James Corden and Ruth Jones, familiar from Fat Friends and Little Britain, have created scene-stealer support roles

THE WEEKEND'S TV

Gavin And Stacey
– BBC3 ★★★★☆

Grey's Anatomy
– Five ★★★☆☆

for themselves as Gav and Stace's biffer best mates and Rob Brydon is deliciously creepy as closet case Uncle Bryn. But it's Mathew Horne and Joanna Page as love's young dream who bring Gavin And Stacey alive.

As phonecall flirters struck by love at first sight when they finally meet, this Essex lad/Welsh ladette combo are cute but not cloying, a made-for-each-other pair everyone feels good being around. Mum certainly gave the onion the thumbs up, popping her head round the bedroom door just as Gav and Stace were getting down to it: 'Just to say, your dad's out for the count and I'll put me earplugs in. So, just let yourselves go!' Bless.

► Given that he's cloying, and not half as cute as he thinks he is, it's hard not to clap eyes on Dr McDreamy in Grey's Anatomy without wanting to splat a custard pie in his smug chops. The way he knows one shoulder of his poppy dog eyes and soppy Meredith will be dropping her knickers in the store cupboard in the blink of a stethoscope is just plain creepy. What does she see in him?

But, even though it ended on a Who Will She Choose? cliffhanger, the McDreamy love saga, thankfully, mostly played second fiddle, as season two bowed out with a double bill that demonstrated how much the supposedly supporting characters have fleshed out the bones in Grey's Anatomy's world. Ethics and heartbreak, ambition and loyalty, destiny and disillusion collided as Izzie, George and Cristina got caught up in the fever of love's sweet sickness. Yes, I'm addicted, but no need to go cold turkey – season three is less than a month away.

Keith Watson

When Nessa interviewed Welsh rugby
captain, Ryan Jones, in 2008
to celebrate Wales' Grand Slam
victory at the Millennium Stadium

Autumn 2006, with Ryan Jones
and Gethin Jenkins - filming
The Bridal Fayre at The Vale
Hotel, where the Welsh rugby
team trained and stayed
before a game

This was before the show had ever been seen

Front row (left to right): Mike Phillips, Melanie
Walters, Rob Brydon, Mat Horne, Lee Byrne
Middle row: Larry Lamb, Alison Steadman, Adam Jones,
Joanna Page, Ruth Jones, James Corden
Back row: Jonathan Thomas, Ryan Jones, Adam Jones,
Ian Gough, Gethin Jenkins, Sonny Parker, James Hook

CHAPTER 4

The black bob wig: assembling the cast

RUTH: One of the best early decisions we made was to get Christine Gernon as our director. The director of every single episode.

JAMES: Yes, think how unusual it is for a show this long-running to have the same director.

I met her before you did, didn't I, because I was in a BBC Three series in 2005 called *I'm With Stupid* and Chris directed that.

And while we did look at other directors at the time, we always say, 'Thank god she ended up directing it,' because it's been such a brilliant relationship.

Yeah, and none of the other directors we talked to about *Gavin & Stacey* seemed to light up about it.

While I was filming *I'm With Stupid*, I was talking to Chris about it, and I said, 'Do you want to read the script?' Which was quite naive of me, really, because you don't really do that, you know? You go through a process – agents and all that. But anyway, Chris read the scripts, and she absolutely loved them, and what was lovely was that she was really positive about the show, and we hadn't really had any positive feedback from any other directors. So I said, 'Well, look, do you want to meet James?'

Then she came for a meeting with Baby Cow and you, and we always laugh about the fact that we didn't know what we were supposed to ask a director in an interview. I think you asked something like, 'So how would you approach this, then, stylistically?' – kind of asking a grown-up question. I can't remember what Chris's answer was, but the important thing for us was that we wanted to work with somebody who didn't mind us sticking our oar in. And I think there have been times, understandably, when we've probably crossed the mark, and we've crept a bit into Chris's territory. But once we started filming it was clear she doesn't miss any detail; she's really consummate in the way she directs.

She's very, very happy to collaborate, but also to draw a line in the sand when she needs to. It's a real joy that she's directed every single episode. She just knows the characters inside out.

I think she's probably been put into quite a difficult situation sometimes when you and I have been at odds about something; she's had to have the casting vote. But it works. It works both ways as well, when you and I both say, 'No, this is how we think it should be' – then, you know, she's in the minority. So it's been really helpful to have that triangle of the three of us for the whole history of the show. We've been a team.

When it came to creating the characters, our first thought was Alison Steadman as Pam. We always want every character to be three-dimensional. I think part of that comes from being actors. You want actors to enjoy the notion of a character, so everyone should be layered. We love Alison so much. She's so funny; she's so brilliant. I personally think she is as good as any of those acting dames like Maggie Smith and Judi Dench. I truly believe that. And I think they're amazing. So our thought was, 'If we write a part for her, we know we won't be able to pay her any money, but if we write something that's good and fun enough for her, she will think, "Well, I just want to play this character."'

So we're always thinking about how we want the dialogue to be fun to say. I think we've both been in enough situations where you read a script and you're like, 'I haven't really got much to do here.' You want to give everybody something fun.

I often think, 'Christ, if we hadn't been in _Fat Friends_ with Alison, we wouldn't have had that connection.' But luckily we stayed in touch with her, and you had that connection with her through Mike Leigh, I guess. But if we weren't in contact with her, and we'd just gone to the agent, it would have been dismissed out of hand, I reckon. D'you remember how tense it was when we were waiting for her reaction?

Oh yeah . . . We sent it to her and it felt like there was this really long delay. And we were thinking, 'Oh god, she hates it.'

But in reality it probably wasn't that long. And we found out later that Alison had been filming and just hadn't had a chance to read it. But when she did, she got in touch and said, 'I love it. I know exactly who Pam is.' She said as soon as she read the first scene, about the mother badger crying, she knew she wanted to play Pam. It was such a great feeling – _Alison Steadman_ liked our script!

And then there was Uncle Bryn. And the obvious choice for him was Rob Brydon – who we both knew well.

Yeah, I'd worked with him on _Cruise of the Gods_ . . .

And you'd lost out to him as Best Newcomer at the RTS Awards, don't forget.

Haha, yes, I think you already mentioned that. And you were in school with him, of course.

We both went to Porthcawl Comprehensive (though he's MUCH older than me – well, two years) and we used to do school shows together . . .

I never knew that. ☺

I should just say, I do have a really brotherly–sisterly relationship with Rob. I suppose that comes from our knowing each other for over forty years. We actually played brother and sister in *Human Remains*, the dark comedy he wrote with Julia Davis. What Rob does, which is so sweet – and he's done it more and more in recent times – is that he looks at me as if he's a proud uncle or a brother – in quite a Bryn-ish way, in fact – and then says, 'Ah . . . I'm so *proud* of you!' And he fills up!

He's a sensitive soul, isn't he?

Yeah! When we did the Comic Relief song ['Islands In The Stream' with Sir Tom Jones and Robin Gibb] together in 2009, we went out to Vegas to shoot the

video, and that was just such a brilliant experience. It really was. We had to record the song beforehand, and us in a recording studio was hilarious and lovely. But actually going out to Vegas, being on this set, where we had all these extras dressed as line dancers, was so much fun. We had Tom Jones but only for a certain limited time, so we had to film around his availability. And then the bit where he walks through the crowd, and the crowd parts, and he's coming towards us singing – well, I remember looking at Rob at that moment and we both had tears in our eyes. It was very special.

Rob and I also had another moment like that, when we were both invited to the then Prince Charles and Camilla's Welsh home. Rob was sat opposite me next to Camilla, and I was next to Charles, and there were a couple of times when we just caught each other's eye. I was thinking, 'We went to Porthcawl Comp, you and me! This is mental!'

But before you went for that dinner, weren't we asked to send in a DVD box set of *Gavin & Stacey* to give a context for who you were – and didn't we have to remove the Christmas 2008 episode where Mick and Pam role-play as Charles and Camilla and he wears the big ears?!

Oh god, yes!

Anyway, long before that, when we were first thinking of him to play Bryn, we sent him the script and I wrote him a little note:

---

10 October 2005

Here it is - uncle Bryn is my favourite character - he would be in every episode - broad Barry accent - you'd have to age up – he's mid/late forties. i won't be offended IN THE SLIGHTEST if you're not fussed. you are obviously our first choice. but read it anyway - even if you don't do it - your feedback would be appreciated.
have fun you big star you!

So the thing about the Barry accent is this ... Jo Page will be the first to admit she found it a challenge. And we couldn't really have Stacey with a Swansea accent and the rest of the family with a Barry one. So we decided that the West family came from Swansea and moved to Barry a few years back. Probably only Welsh people would notice that they speak with a different accent from Nessa or Dave Coaches. And Mel Walters is a Swansea girl, and Rob is actually from Port Talbot way, so it all made sense.

When Rob first got the script, he said he knew exactly who this character was – a sort of older, white-haired uncle who was quite fragile – but for us the key to Bryn was that he's actually a lot younger than you might first imagine, and he is in fact very active and enthusiastic, with his home gym, his cycling gear, etc. The way Bryn dresses makes him seem older than his years, but his age is kind of indeterminate, really. I think I slightly panicked when Rob had that initial reaction to the character of Bryn and said how he was going to portray him, because if it had been someone I didn't know, it would have been easy to say, 'Oh no, no, that's not the direction we want to go in,' but when you're working with people who are friends, there is always that sensitivity. The upside to working with friends, of course, is that you've got sort of a shared grammar, and shared experiences and a shared code of reference. But the downside of it is that it can be quite difficult to be upfront. So I was relieved when his reaction to hearing our idea of Bryn was, 'Oh yeah, I see what you mean.'

There was this day in Australia when I was in Sydney doing *The History Boys* and Rob was shooting the sitcom *Supernova* over there, and I knew *Gavin & Stacey* had been green-lit by this point so we agreed to meet up. We had a great day; he took me to a restaurant called Catalina. I tried an oyster for the first time – spat it out in a napkin. I didn't like it at all.

I have to say, I'm amazed Rob likes oysters. He just doesn't seem the type.

What *type* of person eats oysters?

I dunno . . . just not a Rob Brydon type. I think Bryn would give them a go, though – he definitely has an adventurous side.

We took a ferry over to Manly Beach, and we got fish and chips, and we sat on the beach, and I started telling him a bit more about my ex-girlfriend's relative, who the character of Bryn was loosely inspired by. As soon as he heard me talk about the character and how mind-blown Bryn was by a digital camera not having any film in it, he started doing this riff – he was finding the character already.

We definitely cast Rob and Alison first because we knew them and we knew they'd be brilliant.

Then, when we were finding the rest of the actors, we also realized the idea of a script for a new BBC Three comedy produced by Baby Cow with Alison Steadman and Rob Brydon attached would immediately pique their interest; you're immediately going to get actors excited to read that script. It sounds like a savvy producers' trick on our part but it didn't feel like that at the time.

As for the role of Gavin, we'd been thinking of who could play him, and I think I said, 'What about

that guy who's in *The Catherine Tate Show*?' Which
is how Mat Horne came into the frame.

And I mentioned the girl in *Love Actually* who plays
the stand-in for the sex scenes. This was, of course, Jo
Page, and when we brought her together with Mat there
was an instant chemistry between them. I met Jo in the
toilet on the day of her audition. We were in Spotlight
in Leicester Square, and I went to the loo and she was
in there. I said hello to her and she was like, 'Hi there!
Oh my god! Oh my god! I'm just *so* nervous,' in classic Jo
Page style. I remember going straight back into the audition room and saying, 'She is our Stacey, definitely.' But
we did film them together, in a scene where they kiss,
and Mat read with a couple of other girls, so we knew
quite quickly he was going to be Gavin.

Then we had Toby Whale, the casting director, helping to cast the show. He'd cast *The History Boys* and
was so imaginative. He had suggested Larry Lamb
to play Mick, Alison Steadman's husband, so to
speak. And it was just a case of seeing the chemistry
between them as well.

For me, a moment I remember so clearly is when, in
episode three of the first series, Stacey and the Wests
have come up to Essex, and Pam is drunk because she's
found out they're going to get married in Barry and she

calls Gwen a 'leek-munching sheep shagger'. Then Gwen is joining in the row and Bryn comes in and silences them all, saying, 'Will you just look at yourselves! We live in a cynical world. All that matters is that Gavin and Stacey will commit the rest of their lives to each other, and I for one will be proud when they do.' And Mick just goes, 'Me too.' Sometimes Larry does these things that are so subtle. But Mick is the one who calms things down; he's the leveller. He's the voice of reason.

In the rehearsals for series one, Larry came over to me and asked about Mick and the nature of his relationship with Pam. I just said, 'She wears the trousers until he wants them back.' That's their relationship. Pam is Pam, and he'll let her go, but the second it's getting out of control, he'll say, 'Now, now, now, come on.' Their relationship is so key to the show.

I love how incredible they are as a couple. So believable.

Yes, I love how they fancy each other, and all the stuff about role-playing as Charles and Camilla.

The chemistry between them is just gorgeous. You so believe they're a married couple and that was apparent straight away. Same with Gavin and Stacey. Mat and Jo made that whole family dynamic feel so real.

I think perhaps the most difficult part to cast was Gwen [Stacey's mum]. Mel Walters auditioned for that role in the Welsh College of Music and Drama, and there was a trumpeter practising next door. Probably, in reality, Mel is only a few years older than me and there's a small age difference between her and Jo, too, but I think that's right for the characters, and I think in *The Finale* she so comes into her own. Anyway, I think Mel was the last of the main characters to be cast, but she was absolutely perfect.

Then we got Rob Wilfort [as Jason], who came in and initially read to be Gavin – he's such a great actor; he's so nuanced. I was re-watching the scene in *The Finale* where we find out about Gwen and Dave Coaches, and Rob is just superb in it. He's so consummate and committed to what he does. When you have a big scene with lots of characters, it's all about what you're doing when you're not saying anything or doing anything. He does these tiny little things, these little details, and I think he's a massively important part of the whole show.

Yeah, he's brilliant.

As for Julia Davis as Dawn, I think she really loves it. I think she's a genius the way her mind works. The things she comes up with – even in our

WhatsApp group, she comes up with stuff that's so left field – and I think I might be sort of speaking for her a bit here, but I get the feeling that she has just really enjoyed being able to sit back and perform someone else's words, but still put her own unique take on it. And what's really interesting about the way Julia works is that in the read-through she'll be quiet, and you can hardly hear her – like, she's very low energy – and it's as if she just lets the performance grow and grow. Whereas some people come in and they'll have a full-blown performance straight away, Julia just builds and builds and builds, and then when we're filming she might say one word in a certain way that will just throw you.

Like 'black puddin"...

Haha, yeah, when they're all on the landing.

And again, the chemistry between her and Adrian [Scarborough] is phenomenal. The fact that she's taller than him adds so much. And when we did the 2019 special, we really wanted to give them more to do because we loved them as a couple, but because of the nature of the show, we couldn't just transplant them to Wales. If we had done that, there would have been the danger of the show getting too sitcom-y. In

theory, for example, we could have created a scenario where Dawn and Pete are having trouble with their boiler and they're going to have to go to Wales to use Bryn's hot water or something, but that wouldn't have been right for *Gavin & Stacey*. We had to stay true to the show.

But they have that great scene in the 2019 special when Dawn thinks Pete's a drug addict 'like Zammo in *Grange Hill*'. So they still had a showcase for their characters.

> DAWN
> It's Pete . . . . He's a junkie.

> MICK
> You what?

> . . . . .

> DAWN
> Pete was in a lovely mood. Now
> I know why! 'Been off his tits
> all morning, high as a lark!

> . . . . .

> DAWN
> So, I open the glove box in
> search of a charger. I'm
> rustling around in there and
> what do I find?

                    PAM
    A syringe?

                    MICK
    Pills?

                    DAWN
    I find...... this. (Holds up
    cannabis joint). Cannabis!

                    PAM
    Is that it?

                    MICK
    Bloody hell Dawn! Bit of
    weed? I mean, it's hardly
    Breaking Bad.

                    DAWN
    It's a gateway drug Michael,
    it's how it all starts!

                    PAM
    Dawn, it's a bit of spliff.
    Well, me and Mick used to
    smoke it all the time before
    Gavin was born.

When it came to Nessa, I thought a lot about her look. Originally she was going to have what we'd call an 'Ely facelift' – this really scraped-back look, with a really tight ponytail with extreme highlights. I actually went

and had the highlights put into my hair. But what always happens with TV production is they send you to a posh hairdresser's, and they won't do anything that's too unsubtle. So the highlights were really subtle, and I was thinking, 'Hmm, I'm not sure they're really saying anything about this character.'

Then, one evening, I was going to Mark Gatiss's fortieth birthday party, and the theme was the sixties so I'd been to Shepherd's Bush Market and found a little black bob wig, which I've still got. I dressed up with that wig on, and I sent a picture on my old Nokia phone to our director, Chris Gernon, and I said, 'What about this look?' And because the quality of picture you'd get on those old phones was terrible, Chris asked, 'Who's that in the picture?' I said, 'Well, it's me.' And she went, 'Oh my god.' That's when I suggested that could be the look for Vanessa . . . with that hair.

One of the characteristics we decided on for Nessa before we wrote the scripts was that she sang 'Wild Thing' at people's weddings – we had that sort of 'rock' idea for her. And there was just something glorious about her right from the start, right from that outfit and hair. She's so sexually confident, and that seemed to go well with her having this slightly goth-ish, rock look with the heavy eyeliner, wearing lots of leather. And the fact that seventeen years later she still has the same hairstyle is hilarious to me, although I think, ironically, she has more hair now than she did back then, haha.

Sometimes we do see Nessa without the make-up; one of my favourite episodes is when we're in Dave's caravan in series three and she has a pink dressing-gown on and no make-up. I loved that. I loved Dave's caravan. There was also a scene where I had to try really hard not to laugh. 'My tools, my bag, my cloak . . .' and then Rob Brydon coming in with, 'Good god, the atmosphere in this caravan . . .'

As for Smithy, he was originally called Kyle in the treatment, and he and Nessa were going to be the funny fat friends of Gavin and Stacey's, I guess.

He was loosely inspired by somebody I knew. He's not based on him, but inspired by him. It's very, very important we should say that. He was a kitchen fitter, and he was just kind of a regular Essex guy, really . . .

But I think there's something really tender about him, and when we had brilliant Pam Ferris playing his mum in series two and Sheridan Smith playing his sister, you got an idea of his upbringing and that it probably wasn't that secure. We don't really know anything about his dad. He's mentioned at Gavin's stag party, but he obviously wasn't very present in Smithy's life, and so he seeks solace in Pam and Mick, who are essentially his adoptive parents.

He's a lad, but he has got a real soft side. He's a bit of a teddy bear. It's been interesting watching his development. You know, when you think about some of the things we had in the scripts in the early days, we probably couldn't get away with them now. Like when he said, 'I'm not going in there bareback,' about having sex with Nessa. And also his response to seeing Nessa is that of a very regular guy who was then – when we started writing the show – in his twenties. But if you compare the Smithy in that last episode with the Smithy in series one, he's been on quite a journey.

I think it's just life, isn't it, that we all mature and change, and we see him becoming a dad, taking that responsibility. We often laugh about his girlfriend, Lucy, who was seventeen, and we never see or meet, so of course that was a part we never had to cast.

But as for the other characters, they were all now in place.

Our actors were there.

We had our crew.

It was time to shoot the show.

CHAPTER 5

Gone fishing: filming the first series

RUTH: Once we'd gathered the cast, the first day of filming was in London in 2007. It was me as Nessa and Stacey on Dave's coach driving around London, and we did the scene where Smithy gives Nessa her pants back and says, 'So, I'll give you a ring.' And she says, 'Why?' and, 'Get a life, Smithy.' And Gavin and Stacey say goodbye to each other. We filmed the Leicester Square bit where Gavin and Stacey first meet. Do you know what? When we watched that footage of those first scenes the other day for the documentary we've made about the show, I couldn't get over how young our voices sound.

JAMES: Oh yeah, and everything else. It's really strange watching myself back from those days.

We look so childlike.

When I look at myself from eighteen years ago, I couldn't feel more like a different person.

Oh, I am definitely a different person...

As you should be! It was eighteen years ago. And it's all so unusual – that the show and these characters have gone on so long, and us writing and making the show has gone on for that long, and to have it all documented. It's actually why I feel sorry for young people now, because every single thing you do is recorded. Every mistake. Sometimes I want to say, 'You're really going to regret eating that on video . . .'

On the first day of filming, once we actually started making the show, I was a bit sad because it felt like you were Mat Horne's friend now and not mine any more. When the two of you really bonded, I guess I felt a little bereft. Because I think the relationship between you and I has gone through a lot of interesting waves over the years, but we are at our best when it's just us and we're on our own, and we're enjoying each other's company and we're writing. Then as soon as other people are around, the dynamic changes, doesn't it? I don't mean in a bad way. It just changes. And I think, in the first series, I just did not know what was coming. Also, I was living at home, and everybody else on the show was staying in

the hotel, and that really did impact my experience of filming. Because no matter how much it's great to be at home, because you've got your home comforts, you still feel like a bit of an outsider – like, massive FOMO.

But our friendship endured, didn't it? It's one of the things I'm most proud of: you and me. And all we were thinking about with that first series was, 'We have to make this work.' I think we were both aware that you don't get a plethora of opportunities to make your own show for the BBC.

We both had quite exposing moments in the first episode, wearing that thong. Not the same one, mind. But *a* thong.

Here's some real friendship: we were filming the shot when you were laid spread-eagled on your front in a thong . . .

Oh yes!

. . . and Chris Gernon, our director, was like, 'OK, so we're going to remove the dressing gown now.' And you were calling out for me: 'James, James . . . can you just check it all looks . . . OK?' And I did my best to have a look and I said, 'No, it's fine; we're all good!'

In those situations all you're thinking is, 'This has to work; there's another scene where I've just stripped down to my pants on the front lawn.' But you're going, 'This has to work. You have to make this show as funny as can be.' I remember the first read-through of series one so vividly, because I just couldn't believe the laughs it was getting in the room. Stuff that we didn't even know would be that funny. All the call-backs and running jokes and references would get this roar, and I remember looking at you and thinking, 'Fucking hell, people are really laughing at this.' That was mega.

Yeah, and Nessa would get a lot of laughs. I enjoyed playing her so much. And I liked how her catchphrases just developed over time, organically. With 'What's occurrin'?', I can't actually remember where it came from, but someone I was at university with told me I'd got that from him. But I don't remember that at all. He was adamant that he always said 'What's occurring?' when we shared a flat and stuff. So he thinks I stole it from him. But Ian, if you're reading this, I promise you, I didn't! We tried once to put a different version of the phrase in; I think it was in the Christmas special in 2008 we tried out 'What's appertaining?' But it never took off. Which proves my theory that you can't manufacture a catchphrase.

I love it when she says, 'Where to's she now?' in the wedding episode.

That is genuinely a Welsh thing. But it's great when Smithy gets so annoyed about it.

> SMITHY
> Ok, I'm glad you brought
> it up. Because I've got a
> girlfriend who a lot of people
> here know. So I'd appreciate
> it if . . .

> NESSA
> Where to's she now then?

> SMITHY
> What?

> NESSA
> Where to's she now?

> SMITHY
> Right, either speak English
> or learn Welsh, because that
> 'where to's she?' do you mean
> where is she now?

> NESSA
> Yeah

                    SMITHY
          Say that then.

                    NESSA
          Where is she now?

                    SMITHY
          Sixth former's Netball
          tournament in Southend. She
          couldn't get out of it, she's
          wing attack.

I also love the details we drop about Nessa's love life [see appendix]. I think I said at some point, 'Can we have some of her past conquests come into it?' Then I think the first mention of someone Nessa has slept with is when she tells Stacey she's pregnant in series one, episode four, and Nessa says it's not any of the people she's slept with – not Nigel Havers, and not any of Goldie Lookin Chain. And I think perhaps we built on it from that, because the John Prescott thing – although that's in episode three – we wrote in situ on the day of filming. We wanted those moments to be believable, but also a little bit silly.

We did have a discussion about whether to have John Prescott and Noel from Hear'Say make a cameo appearance in that final episode of series three. I quite liked the idea. But I remember Chris the director pointing out how there's something more mysterious about it if we don't actually see these people that Nessa's had a relationship with, which is true. But then we thought we would do it just that once, so people would go, 'Oh god, she really did have a relationship with John Prescott!' Because I've often seen Nessa written about, presuming that she makes up all these stories. And I always think, 'Why do you say she makes them up? Maybe she didn't make them up!'

Do you know, I had a few requests when John Prescott died, asking if I wanted to comment, and I just wanted to say, 'You know it was fictitious, right? Nessa is fictitious, so she doesn't have actual memories of him, because she doesn't exist!' I think it would have been a bit disrespectful, really. Fifty years in politics and then suddenly you get some bloody fictitious comedy character talking about him.

In amongst Nessa's stories, there's also an allusion to 'the big boss from Harrods', but we don't actually say his name. We just call him a 'crackin' little fella'.

Yeah, Nessa says something like, 'And his son was trouble! He kept texting me from his boat and in the end I had to say, 'O! Back off!'

I had to do an interview for the Richard & Judy Book Club last summer on Zoom, and I was sitting there with Richard and Judy on my screen. And I was thinking, 'Oh my god, Nessa's had an affair with you.'

Then, when it comes to recurring jokes and call-backs, there's the fishing trip. The first mention of it is in series one, episode five. I remember us writing that because we knew Stacey would have a brother, and that he'd turn up eventually. I said, 'What if he walks in and everyone goes silent?' And you said, 'Why?' And I said, 'I don't know . . .' But I just thought, 'What if the atmosphere is ice cold for some reason?' So Jason arrives and everyone's like, 'Welcome home! Come in!' And then Bryn walks in, and it just cuts it dead.

It's one of my favourite scenes . . .

Basically, at that moment, Mat as Gavin is the audience going, 'What's going on?' And then it was just a riff, wasn't it? 'You were as good as gold before we went on that fishing trip . . .'

That's an example of how brilliant Rob Wilfort is as Jason, because he's so nuanced . . .

It's just so bizarre how those two words, 'fishing trip', have become such a part of the show.

My taxi driver this morning asked me if we're going to find out what went on during the fishing trip.

Only Bryn and Jason and Dave Coaches know! Robert Wilfort has it right when he explains to all the many people who come up to him and ask about the fishing trip that the whole joke is we never find out what happened on the fishing trip!

On 1 April, someone released a doctored photo of the one we did to announce *The Finale*. In fact, the same one that's on the cover of this book – where we're holding a *Gavin & Stacey* script. And our faces had been replaced by Rob Brydon's and Rob Wilfort's with the title on the script: *The Fishing Trip*. People actually believed we were making a spin-off. But it was an April Fool someone came up with!

It says something that people want to believe it so much. It's a compliment, really.

With Smithy and Gavin, I think your and Mat's relationship is so, so believable as a friendship. I really do. I think with Nessa and Stacey it is different because there's an age difference there, and they are very different people, whereas I just love Gavin and Smithy's relationship and the fact that Smithy is part of Gavin's family in a way. He never really had that family life, so Pam and Mick have become his parents, really. That adds a fraternal level between the two of you as well, doesn't it? And there's a lovely bit in *The Finale*, at Smithy's stag, where Mick talks about what Smithy means to him and Pam, which we'll get to later.

Those social events, like the stag and hen nights, and the get-togethers at Pam and Mick's, are one of my favourite things about *Gavin & Stacey*. I think, because it is essentially about two different groups of people coming together, it's always lovely when you get those two sides of the group meeting up. So we had to try and make those gatherings believable.

That's why we had to end the show after three seasons! We were just starting to run out of organic, believable ways for them to get together. But in terms of the spirit of those get-togethers – which I do think is probably the thing I enjoy most about the show, actually, and I think what lots of people like as well – it's that they all really like each other, and you want to be there with them. You want to be in that pub on Christmas Eve; you want to be at Pam and Mick's when they're dancing to Madness. Those are great times, and really that is down to having such good actors – that's the truth. They're so good. They're just so good as a group. They're all great ensemble performers, but they're also all actors who should be the leads in shows.

We've got a company of leading actors all playing character parts in an ensemble. So when you hand over the script which says, 'Everyone's dancing and having a great time,' I think because of the atmosphere on set, which bleeds into the real-life friendships, you totally get that mood. For example, when Mat and I met on series one, we met eight days before we started filming, and we're meant to have had a thirty-year relationship where we're best friends. So the two of us were like, 'Well, we're going to fucking do that, then.' You just want to ingrain all of it with history and the love, and you need to believe in these relationships.

So there are the get-togethers, and then we have the entrances like 'World In Motion' and 'Step Into Christmas' . . .

Well, that's all you, that is.

I think we were very lucky, because while the show jumps in location, timeline and all those things, we've got some characters that can just arrive at the door, you hear 'ding dong', and it's Smithy doing 'World In Motion'. Which is a great example of that. And obviously there was a lot of England vs Wales stuff in that series, and there was an element of that with that choice of song, but then when you hand it over to this cast, suddenly you get Larry shouting, 'Hear me now!' which wasn't a scripted line.

The idea of Smithy being asked to 'step in' – to 'Step Into Christmas' – was one that I had after I heard the song on the radio one time, because we were always thinking, 'How are they revealing themselves? How are they showing how much they love each other?' 'Step Into Christmas' was a perfect example of that.

And do you remember when Gavin and Smithy had the argument in series one, after Smithy got upset that Gavin had got engaged? We were thinking they needed to have something they shared together, a saying like, 'Make friends, make friends, never never break friends' – that type of thing. And you went, 'Well, why don't we just use that?' And that's an example of another thing about your relationship with Gavin that I love: it's that little-boy thing that you have between you, because you were in nursery school together and all of that. There's that bond.

I also like the bit where I say, re: Gavin and Stacey, 'Will everyone stop calling it a honeymoon? It's just a holiday. Your phone's been off for weeks!' It says so much about how Smithy feels.

That sulkiness! Then Stacey says, 'He did talk about you, Smithy.' And you say, 'But when?!' And she says, 'When we played a game of tennis and we said "If Smithy was here now it would be a really good game . . . "' Which is

really touching. And one of the other elements of the show I'm most proud of is how we get to those more poignant moments. There's that scene in series one, episode six, when Bryn tells Stacey what her dad says in the note he left to her for her wedding day.

Yes, that's a real turning point in the show.

They're on the way to her wedding, and the way he reads her dad's letter is so moving . . .

```
              BRYN (to Stacey)
         Now, there's something I've
         got to give you, but I won't
         give it to you if you don't
         want it..

                   STACEY
         What is it?

                   BRYN
         It's from your father it is.
         Now he wrote it six weeks
         before he died with strict
         instructions to give it to
         you on your wedding day. Bryn
         hands the letter to Stacey but
         Stacey hands it back.

                   STACEY
         I can't
```

BRYN

Do you want me to read it to
you? [Stacey nods]
Do you want me to do it in
your father's voice, with the
lisp and everything? [Stacey
shakes her head]
OK . . . *Dear Stacey, if you're*
reading this, it must be your
wedding day. But if it is
not and Bryn has just left
it lying around, then tell
him he's a waste of space and
can never be trusted to do
anything properly. Ha! *When*
I think back to the day you
were born I was the happiest
man on the planet. I won't
lie to you, Stace, and I'm
not ashamed to say it, but I
cried. Buckets. But I never
imagined in a million years
that I wouldn't be with you
on your wedding day, walking
you down the aisle and giving
you away, I tell you, whoever
'he' is , he's the luckiest
man alive. I'm so sorry I'm
not there for you today,
Stacey, not in body anyway,
but I'll be there in spirit,
and please remember that
whenever you need me, I'll
be listening. Because you'll
never stop being my beautiful

baby girl. Have a wonderful
day, my darling, I love you
always, Dad.

I love it. But you have to earn those moments. You've got to be careful because audiences won't let you get away with it if you're forcing it. We're so cautious of that all the time.

The audience knows when you're manipulating them. We're also pretty careful to find the comedy in those moving moments. There's always something funny about to come along, we hope.

One of the funniest scenes in the first series was the cameo from Matt Lucas. I hero-worshipped Matt. Has anyone ever been funnier? George Dawes! One of the funniest characters. So the idea of getting Matt to come and do a cameo in that first series was really because we loved him. Also, we were trying to do anything to get some eyeballs on the show, and *Little Britain* was huge. I think Matt and David were in the middle of an arena tour at the time, and Matt came and did us a real solid, a real favour, while they were in Cardiff. He came to the hotel where we were filming and did that scene in two hours. But I lost it. He's just so funny. I was laughing for most of the two hours we filmed with him. I mean, what a gift to get to work with him all morning. You know, I've been lucky enough to work with both Matt and David. They are just so brilliant.

When I did *Little Britain*, Matt used to be a terrible giggler, so it wasn't a surprise to see him that day with the giggles, which you did as well . . . It was just really nice that he did it, that he came to do that cameo. He's really funny, and weirdly good at doing really butch parts like Jammy! It was when he cupped your face in his hands . . . you were in agony trying not to laugh!

Scenes like that and the entrances and the songs and the singing are just joy. Joy is the currency of the show . . .

Then there's our beautiful theme tune . . . Do you remember how we chose it?

Well, I really love that Stephen Fretwell album *Magpie*, and for a long time we thought about having a piece of written score as the theme. A few different people like David Arnold wrote pieces; he wrote one which had a Welsh harp on it, and it was beautiful, but it just didn't feel quite right. And I kept saying how I really love that drum sound and the piano chords on the Stephen Fretwell song 'Run'.

I met someone the other day who said when he got married to his husband they walked down the aisle to it because they were such *Gavin & Stacey* fans!

I think the theme tune is one of the most important things when you're making a TV show.

And we're very lucky, because we had *The Office* and *The Royle Family* to inspire us. I think those two shows have been very ingrained in me – more than anything else – and what Ricky and Stephen did in *The Office* was key. Because you can imagine a version of it with a trombone on the soundtrack, right? The show could be exactly the same, but you have Brent waking up in the morning and he gets in the car and drives in, and gets to the office in Slough, and then he goes, you know, 'I'm more of a chilled-out entertainer.' And every frame could be the same, but it doesn't tell you, it doesn't inform you, in the same way that the song 'Handbags And Gladrags' does.

It's the same with *The Royle Family* and 'Half The World Away' by Oasis, when those characters arrive on the sofa.

Both those shows had lovely, simple title sequences, but we truthfully couldn't afford one, and if we had it could have been a crane shot of Barry Island and a big shot of Essex and a sign saying, 'This many miles to London,' or whatever. That's probably what someone would have come up with. But because we literally couldn't afford a title sequence, we went with a black card with white writing, and I wouldn't change it for the world.

So I just kept saying, 'Let's have something that feels a bit like "Run" by Stephen Fretwell.' And then, in the end, it was like, 'What if it's that?'

I think the actual musicality of that song relates really well to the show: the way it starts in such a quiet way, and then it builds. There's just something almost ordinary about it to start with. Then it becomes something else.

What's so odd with our show is there are so many things that were knee-jerk choices or decisions, which actually you realize have a much greater meaning. Like the idea of that song, when you look at the lyrics: 'Run, run like the wind, don't wait for a thing, there is nothing here for you, but if you stay, well then let me say, I'll go out of my way for you.' On some level, it just feels like it's Nessa and Smithy's relationship. It's clear and yet so fuzzy. It's complicated and yet very straightforward. And then just this notion in the song: 'Tell me tomorrow, I'll wait by the window for you. I'll wait by the big house for you. I'll wait by the squeezebox . . .' These two have literally waited for each other to wake up to it, and then the last thing anyone sees of her is on her knees, a foot and a half from a window, asking a question. I don't know . . . There's so many things like that in the creation of this show that feel just right, almost magically.

CHAPTER 6

Semi by the sea: the second series

RUTH: Series two was a challenge in the sense that we never intended to write one.

JAMES: Yeah, we'd always felt that the arc of the story was going to end with Gavin and Stacey's wedding in series one, and that would be that.

But the BBC asked for a second series even before the first one had finished going out. And we couldn't exactly say no . . . so we had to think what would be the logical next steps for our characters. Gavin and Stacey were happily married – albeit with the little cloud hanging over them from when Stacey told Jason at the wedding that even though they were going to live in Essex, they'd be coming home to Barry every weekend. This was news to Gavin and it meant there was some potential tension for another series. And of course, we knew by then that Nessa was pregnant.

Which was essentially a cliffhanger. So it seemed that maybe the story wasn't as complete as we thought it was . . .

That final shot of Nessa at the end of series one always makes me a bit sad. When I watch it back, I always think, 'God, it was really harsh,' when she goes 'Smithy?' and he's like, 'What?' and she can't tell him, and he just dismisses her and walks off. Ending on that moment, having seen the bride and groom being so happy, was quite full on. Just her standing there alone in her brides-maid's dress. It was a bit brutal!

We didn't intend for it to end so poignantly, but the episode length had to be exactly right – like, bang on thirty minutes. And we'd run out of time, which is why there are no credits at the end. It just fades to black with the Baby Cow logo.

I remember I was really unhappy that day and I was very on edge all the time. And in that moment I felt a bit like Nessa was feeling. But y'know, Nessa isn't meant to be vulnerable. She's this powerful, confident woman. So that final shot was a bit out of my – and Nessa's – comfort zone!

We were picking up from that ending going into the second series. We had a direction to go in, which was driven by Nessa having a baby, and Stacey coming to terms with being an Essex girl. Both of these situations had the potential to be funny, but also moving. And after we'd resolved the long-distance relationship of Gavin and Stacey in series one, we realized we had another long-distance relationship with Smithy and Nessa, and there was going to be a baby involved. And how they were going to navigate this unusual co-parenting situation! Thankfully, the BBC gave us seven episodes, rather than the normal six, and at one point I think there was talk of eight episodes. But, looking back, we had a lot to fit into the second series – too much for just six episodes.

The opening of series two was that lovely scene where Pam and Mick are at the airport waiting for the honeymooners to come home. And Pam's made a sign, which she drops as soon as she sees them. And there's that sequence of them walking back to the car park ... Do you remember the guy in the linen suit?

Oh yeah, the supporting artist who was determined to get seen! He walked incredibly quickly and would not let the Shipmans out of his sight! It's so funny watching it when you know what to look out for. He's proper going for it.

I suppose when you compare the opening ep of series two with that of series one, they've got a very different feel. Because, of course, by now we know the characters. But also there's a lot of drama going on. Smithy's sulking at Gavin for not texting him from his honeymoon, and Stacey's coming to terms with the fact she's no longer living in Barry. Gwen's even redecorated her bedroom. We had to think in terms of what the impact would be on both families now that the happy couple have finally got married.

Then there's the scene where everyone's in Capriccio's, the Italian restaurant, which was so joyful. Like a reunion of both our families in the opening episode. Because they had a *reason* to get together. Which was something we always had to be mindful of – why in reality would these two families get together? In series one it was quite straightforward, but series two presented a new challenge.

We managed to get Pete and Dawn into the scene as well, sitting there all embarrassed because they've been caught out having dinner with Seth, who they're contemplating a threesome with. I just love the idea that Seth is there, and he's so quiet, and then he leaves, and that becomes this mantra for the rest of the episode, with Julia as Dawn crying about how 'Seth's gone'. I think there's

something really funny about that episode where you've got the repetition of 'Seth's gone' and you've got Nessa's announcing she's pregnant 'and Smithy's the father'.

Dawn sobs

> PAM
> Dawn! What's the matter,
> Dawny? Dawn!

Dawn squeals

> PAM
> Oh, stop it! DAWN, stop it!
> (Slaps Dawn)

> DAWN
> Seth's gone. (Sobs)

> PAM, STACEY, NESSA, GWEN
> Who's Seth?

> DAWN
> The . . . (mouth's black)
> fella. We met on the internet.
> Our counsellor said we could
> inject some passion into our
> relationship if we introduced
> a third party to the bedroom.

. . . .

                    DAWN
He says . . . he's very
sorry, but our photo is not
representative of the two of
us as a couple, and he feels
he's been misled. He can't go
through with it. I mean, the
shame of it, Pam! Yes,
it was an old photo. But have
I changed that much in 15
years?

                    . . . . . .

                    DAWN
What you lot doing in here
anyway?

                    STACEY
Nessa's pregnant.

                    PAM, DAWN
What?!

                    STACEY
And Smithy's the father.

                    PAM
Oh, my Christ!

And we've got Julia being slapped in the face by
Alison.

It makes me laugh every time, because I know that Julia loves comedy that is really extreme, and I think she really enjoyed getting hysterical in that scene in the toilet with Pam and Stacey. She loves being just on the edge of corpsing. She says that if she's not nearly corpsing, she knows it's not funny, and I think she loves working with Alison so much. It's a great relationship between those two.

And Julia definitely encouraged Alison to slap her quite hard.

There's also the scene between Bryn and Smithy in the restaurant, which I think shows Smithy's character so well – that vulnerability, and his thirst for friendship, because friendship is so important to him. In a way, that's why he's ended up not getting married until he's well into his forties, because his friends are his life. That's where he's found the security he doesn't have at home. I think you see that friendship at Gavin's stag party, or when they're in the pub and Gavin tells him he's got engaged – the deceit that Smithy feels, the disloyalty, the betrayal. It's quite difficult for him to deal with.

```
                  SMITHY
        I'll be your best mate.


                   BRYN
        Will you?
```

SMITHY
Well, I sure as shit ain't got
one any more have I?

BRYN
Come on, Smithy . . . You're a
young man. You've got your
whole life ahead of you. You
don't want to be tied down to
an old fogey like me.

SMITHY
You're not old Bryn. Are you?
How old are you? (Looks at the
crown of his head.)

You also see that vulnerability and how important his friends are when he goes off to the driving range. My real-life sister – also called Ruth, with the nickname Rudi – has a cameo in the episode, serving at the drive-through when they're all looking for Smithy.

Her actual character name is 'Drive-through Worker Number Six'.

And it's where Smithy's sister works, i.e. the character of Rudi played by Sheridan Smith. The scene at the driving range was filmed on the coldest night of the year, and I had to wear three plasters on my nipples because they were sticking out so much, and they still poked through.

There was certainly a lot of drama in those opening two episodes.

Oh yeah . . .

For me, what I loved at the beginning of series two was that Nessa was back in her power. You know, she's driving a fucking truck. I was so proud of myself for doing the trucking scene. I didn't know this at the time, but you can drive a seven-and-a-half-tonne truck with a normal driver's licence. You don't need to train. But I was taken out to practise the truck driving and I was told the thing you have to look out for is, when you go around a corner, you've got to give it more space. So I was driving round Cardiff with this guy, and I remember at one point pulling up to the lights by a bin lorry, and the driver could not believe his eyes when he saw me. Maybe just because I was a woman driving the truck.

Anyway, that's one of the funniest outtakes: when I'm in the truck, in that road, pulling away from Pam and Mick's, so proud of myself; just the way I pull away, feeling really cool. And I didn't even realize until afterwards, when they told me, I'd scraped all along the side of this car and knocked off the wing mirror. It belonged to a neighbour of Doug and Julia (who owned Pam and Mick's house). It was his pride and joy. And I said to the producer: 'Please, can I go and apologize?' But they thought it would be best to leave it to them . . . I often wonder about that car. And its owner. If you're reading this, I really am ever so sorry.

Yes, we had to go and apologize and pay for it. I remember the funniest thing about it was Larry Lamb whispering to me, 'She's hit the fucking car!' You can see it in the outtakes.

In that scene, just before Nessa gets back in the truck, she kisses Mick full on the mouth. I love that idea that she's got no boundaries, because she does it to Gwen as well. She kisses Gwen on the lips on her wedding day. She's just very pansexual!

I like the fact that Nessa once worked for Eddie Stobart! And the CB radio handles she comes up with as well: Robert Mugabe and Dame Judi Dench. We had other options: Courtney Love was one. And Debbie McGee!

One thing I get asked about is the fact that in episode three of the first series, when the Welsh lot are visiting the Essex lot, Nessa is talking to Mick at the bar and he asks her if she drives. Nessa replies, 'I don't, Mick. Which is a shame, because I loves a good ride.' So people have said to me, 'How come Nessa says she doesn't drive, and then in series two we find out she's been a truck driver?'

Well, here's the answer: Nessa says she *doesn't* drive, not that she *can't* drive. Subtle difference. Haha, it makes it sound like we planned all that but we didn't!

So, the ending of episode one when Nessa says, 'I'm pregnant and you're the father,' was quite unusual in that episode two followed on directly from it. It was the only time we haven't started an episode with a phone call between Gavin and Stacey. I mean, technically you could say ep six of series one doesn't start with a phone call because it's Gavin and Stacey's wedding day. But at least we see their desks. And their phones.

Of course, the finale of *Gavin & Stacey* isn't the first time Smithy proposes to Nessa. He actually gets down on one knee at Pam and Mick's in series two, because he feels he *should* propose. And everyone else is like, 'What?!'

And we've also got the whole story with Stacey not wanting to live in Essex and all of that. And there's some really lovely stuff. Like when Stacey's at a loose end, and Pam comes back in her fencing gear, and Stacey describes her breakfast. And Pam tells her, 'What you said just then was really boring.' I know that one of Alison's favourite lines is when Stacey discovers Pam tucking into a packet of ham. 'Promise me thou shalt speak of this to no one!'

'You're eating ham, Pam!'

Thinking back, although we knew where we were going to end series two – i.e. Nessa giving birth, and Stacey and Gavin being reunited after Essex not working out and Stacey moving back to Barry – although we knew that, I feel like we had to find a focus for each episode in a way we'd not had to do before.

Because series one was kind of mapped out: it was the build-up to the wedding. Gavin and Stacey meet, Gavin and Stacey get engaged, Pam has an engagement party in Essex, Gwen hosts the Essex lot for the wedding fayre (and Nessa finds out she's pregnant), we have the stag and hen, and we end with the wedding. Each ep had a natural focus.

But with series two I felt like we had to find a story for each ep – it was more of a challenge. That's why we had things like the phone mast, or Mick's on the telly.

One of my highlights of series two is you doing Nessa as a living statue.

Yeah, I didn't enjoy that! It was revolting, because I had to be sprayed in silver. I remember being irritable that day. I was in a really bad mood because I had to have

the costume, and I had a pregnancy bump as well, and all this silver paint on my skin, which I just couldn't get off (well, I did get it off eventually, but it was horrible). I felt so uncomfortable, and I'm not a physical sort of actress at all, so having to do those movements as the statue, and having to be shown how to do all those movements . . . Oh god, I was glad to get that over with, to be honest.

But you were great! I think you're better at that physical stuff than you give yourself credit for . . .

We did think about having her holding one of the signs that says 'Golf Sale', because we were always looking for Nessa to have funny jobs, but then we went for the living statue instead, which just seemed a bit more Nessa.

And a lot funnier.

There are certain moments throughout series two, every episode, when sometimes it's just a look which I absolutely love. In the scene with Bryn and Gwen in the car listening to the James Blunt song while Bryn sings along, it's when she goes, 'It's the lyrics more than anything, they just don't make sense!' And the way that he just looks at her. It's an absolutely platinum-plated withering look from Uncle Bryn.

Ha! And there's James Blunt singing, 'Look who's alone now . . . Those three wise men they've got a semi by the sea'!

I think one of the most joyful songs we did was 'Islands In The Stream'. We chose it because we had to do a song that would work at the barn dance, and we wanted it to be a duet. So we were thinking, 'Well, what would Bryn and Nessa sing together?' And we wanted it to be relatively up-tempo, but most duets are ballads. In the end, that song sort of showed itself to us pretty quickly. I actually think it's one of the best songs of all time. It's a good example of how music is a big part of the show.

Because Nessa is so self-assured and confident as a character, I had to really go for it when she sings. I had to attack it. I've sung 'Islands In The Stream' many times. Rob had a show just before Christmas last year, and he started chatting to the audience as Bryn, asking for a volunteer to sing Nessa's part. And just as he got someone on stage, I came on from the back, dressed as Nessa, and the audience went mad, and we sang that song again. I feel OK singing it now, but it was quite a challenge at the time when we did it in *Gavin & Stacey*.

I just loved that I got to sing with Rob, but there was a lot in that scene, with the big build-up to the surprise that Bryn had arranged for Gwen, and I think it sort of shows that while on the surface these characters are very benign and civilized to each other, underneath there's this simmering madness that's bursting to get out. Like with Gwen – normally so passive and mild mannered – '*What the HELL is Jean doing here?*'

We never see Jean, of course. Which is delightful.

And that barn dance episode really shows Bryn's inner stress when he's organized something. Just like he was with the stag night, he gets so worked up about organizing these things, but he also loves it. And then, of course, Ness makes that speech, saying, 'There's one person I want to thank,' and Smithy thinks it's going to be him. And then it's not; it's Dave. Then having Jason walk in and the song just stopping – I absolutely love those moments of ridiculous melodrama.

Well, that whole barn dance episode in series two somehow felt on a bigger scale than anything we'd had up to that point.

Yeah, well, series two was a funny mix, really. I remember when we finished filming in the bowling alley, I was really annoyed. Just generally! I think because I had to bowl and get a strike. And in reality I can't bowl to save my life, but Nessa had to be a world-class champion. And I just felt very on show and embarrassed, I suppose.

25 September 2007

Email from Georgina Fallon, Baby Cow production coordinator, to Ruth Jones

Hey Ruth,

Question for you from art department. They are looking into Nessa's bowling ball, and want to know whether you do in fact bowl? Are you as good as Nessa?! If not I think they are going to find another bowling ball too, for a pro, so they just want to know.

Also . . . you're right handed aren't you?

XX

The irony is that we started filming when Nessa takes a shot, and I took aim and bowled and the bowling ball started veering off to the gulley at the side, so I turned round to face camera and came out of character and went, 'Oh, for f***'s sake.' But everyone behind the camera looked aghast, and I think you said, 'You got a strike!' I said, 'Don't be ridiculous!' But when I turned round, I actually had. The bowling ball had curved back round and headed towards the pins and knocked them all down! But because I'd turned round and sworn and come out of character, the shot was unusable! I've still got that bowling ball somewhere, by the way.

Course, series two introduced a load of new characters ... Sheridan as Rudi, Smithy's sister, but also Matt Baynton as Deano. It was Deano who invented the 'kea' – pronounced 'kee' – which is a combination of a tea and a coffee when he can't decide which one to have.

Remember the fight Smithy has with his sister in episode three ... You two were hysterically laughing throughout that whole fight scene. And it rings so many bells, that brother–sister relationship, where it doesn't matter how old you are, you can revert to fighting like that. I like how Rudi is quite aggressive but also has a great affection for her brother.

We have to talk about Doris, as well. You see how much a part of the family she is in series two when they're having fish and chips at Gwen's house, and Stacey thinks Doris is dead! But, of course, she's just dropped off. That scene also shows the bond between Nessa and Smithy over food, and I love those scenes in Gwen's house because they differ so much from the scenes in Pam's house. There's something so cosy and small and simple about the scenes, and I love how Stacey knows the routine that Nessa has with her fish and chips order – you know, having the sausage and then going for a fag.

But, of course, she can't go for a fag now because she's pregnant. So it's a lovely scene where nothing important happens . . .

Yeah, and it was just so lovely working with Margaret John as Doris, just having those moments.

Series two also had that guest appearance from Marc Wootton, who is a great actor, playing the creepy estate agent.

Yeah, he was great. But one of the things I know we always felt a bit odd about in that second series was the scene with Marc when Gavin and Stacey are looking to move in to their own home together and go to look at that really shitty little place. We both arrived on set that day and we knew it was all wrong. As soon as we saw it we thought it was too big, and that's the only time we got upset with the production designer, because we thought it looked like a pantomime set. It had to be a set, because we had specified that there was a shower in the kitchen and all that kind of stuff. So he was only going on that brief. But that was a bit of a wobbly moment for us. I think we were upset with ourselves more than anything, for 'trying' too hard, trying to be funny, y'know?

But then, in the finale of that series, the designer Dave Ferris did a brilliant job recreating the Severn Bridge toll in the car park of HTV Studios, which is no longer there.

Yes, I remember us writing the scene where Ness has gone into labour, and it's coinciding with Stacey telling Gavin that she 'can't do this any more'. So you've got this drama of having to get down there, down the M4, when Gavin and Smithy don't have the right amount of cash for the toll. Of course, now there's no Severn Bridge toll at all, but back then you had to pay in cash; you couldn't even pay by credit card.

And you know, I didn't have the right amount of cash one time when I was driving over the bridge, and they let me off!

Of course they did! We had Helen Griffin, who's no longer with us, sadly – may she rest in peace – playing the really grumpy woman in the tollbooth, and then Ian Hughes played the policeman who stops Gav and Smithy and won't stop talking. I think that's a very Welsh characteristic, to go into all this elaborate detail, while Gavin and Smithy just want to get to the hospital in time to see the baby arrive.

And I think if you're acting a birth scene, you absolutely have to go for it, because otherwise it just looks unbelievable.

Also, as Nessa says, 'To be on all fours is a home from home, for me, love.'

What was funny, though, was I remember thinking, as me, 'I'm not having my bare legs on display', so I kept my tights on. So when Nessa is having the examination, she's still got her tights on, but what I decided was, 'Well, they don't know they're tights; they could be stockings.'

That whole scene was fun, though, and the fact that Nessa was kind of off her face on gas and air, and just wanting sex with Dave Coaches – it was really enjoyable to do. And that's the episode when we find out her middle name is Shanessa, named after the woman from *Big Brother*!

It's a lovely way to end that series, with the baby arriving, and then you've got Gavin and Stacey kissing. And I guess we could have ended it there, because there's no cliffhanger, right?

CHAPTER 7

Next

JAMES: Series one got 500,000 viewers on BBC Three, and we got good reviews, which was probably really important. I try not to read reviews now but I did back then. There were people writing things about it like, 'This is the show I wish everyone was talking about,' and it had a core of really enthusiastic fans. While we were writing series two, we always used to go and get the *Radio Times* because one of their journalists would review that week's episode, and he would write things like 'this show just gets better and better'.

What was funny was that at the time when we were shooting, Mat Horne had also been cast in another BBC Three show called *Roman's Empire* with Chris O'Dowd. It was a Tiger Aspect show and I remember there was a bit of talk that they were going to be filmed at the same time and would come out very close together. And people were like, 'Ah, is that a problem?' And then we got told, 'No, it's OK. They're going to move *Roman's Empire* to BBC Two.' So I thought, 'Oh, does that mean *Gavin & Stacey* is not as good?' It had a bigger budget than our show and I really remember thinking, 'Oh, does this mean we're not any kind of priority?' Then *G&S* got repeated on BBC Two, and it was this sort of underground thing and people were enjoying it.

RUTH: **But then there was a night that absolutely changed the trajectory of the show.**

It was a Saturday night, and BBC Two chose to play the whole of series one back to back from nine p.m., and what was extraordinary was how on the Monday or Tuesday we got these reports that it didn't lose a viewer until episode six, and by that point it's, like, 11.30 p.m., so you're really competing with people being tired. But the fact that it didn't lose a viewer – I think that's pretty unheard of. And then it just started to get more and more attention.

Then there were the BAFTAs in 2008 when we won two, and then we got nominated for, I think, seven Comedy Awards that year, and there were The South Bank Show Awards and all that stuff.

And we just hit that sort of run, truthfully, that I'd watched Rob [Brydon] have, that I'd watched Matt [Lucas] and David [Walliams] have before that. I'd also watched Ricky [Gervais] and Stephen [Merchant] doing it before that, and I'd watched Peter Kay's *Phoenix Nights* do the same – where you hit that thing, where you're flavour of the month – and it was incredibly intoxicating, it really was.

Just to go back to the *Radio Times*, it was being reviewed every week really positively. But then it came to episode five, which is where it got a bit more dramatic, ending on a bit of an 'oh my god' moment where Gavin and Stacey had a crisis because Stacey hadn't told Gav she'd been engaged five times.

Yes, the *Radio Times* said, 'For the first time, this was a misstep. Let's hope they can get back to what they were doing before,' and it affected us so much we couldn't write that day. It absolutely killed us. I'd driven down that morning to Cardiff with the intention of writing and staying at yours that night. It was a Tuesday. We got the *Radio Times* and that review was so devastating. I left about four p.m. to go back to London and I was so broken, and unbelievably I also got stuck in the aftermath of an extraordinary car crash. You know the sort of thing on the motorway where people get out of their cars and wander around trying to work out what happened – it was one of those. It was such an awful day.

But we recovered. After the show moved to BBC One in 2008 with the first Christmas special, and then series three followed it, and by the time the last two episodes aired over Christmas and New Year in 2009, we were getting ten million viewers. It was life-changing.

Back in the day when the show became a big deal, I struggled. When the BAFTAs happened in 2008, for example [James won Best Comedy Performance and the show won the Audience Award], I just found it a bit overwhelming. But you were really good at going, 'Nope, this is what's happening,' and you just took it in your stride. And you were brilliant at that. Geographically we were separated as well: you were in London, and I was in Wales, and after our writing sessions I'd go back down the M4 and I would just hide out in Cardiff.

Yeah, while I went out for a year!

But the irony is – and I don't know if it's just the passage of time or whatever, and you settling down, meeting your wife, Julia, and having the kids – I think you are one of the most grounded people I know. I think this comes from your parents as well, your family, the

solidity of your family background. I'm not saying my family isn't like that, because I think we've got similar backgrounds when it comes to our families, you know – church-going, etc. – but anyway, I think your family helped with this. You have this ability to bring a calmness to situations which I don't think people would expect of you, but you really do. And I think that impacted hugely on me. You'd be really good in the diplomatic service . . .

Ha!

You would, because you're very good when I get hysterical about things, which I sometimes do, and you're just so good at saying, 'What are you worrying about? There's nothing wrong, there's *nothing wrong*.' And I think when I'm getting really frustrated, you just settle things down. You've got such a good heart, James, such a good heart. You bring this level of calm and love, and you go, 'Actually, what matters at the end of the day is our friendship, and let's just get on with life; let's get on with it.' That's really important. And it's had a huge impact on our friendship, because I think there probably are times when we could have had bigger rows, when I've been reactive . . .

Or, if you're in a situation like the last day's filming of *The Finale*, which is a great example of what you're talking about, when you came over to me and you were so upset because one of the tabloids had run this picture of us and we were both wearing wedding rings. And the headline speculated that Smithy and Nessa were getting married, and you were really in a state about it. I just went, 'What are we going to do about it? There's nothing we can do. That's there. We can get really upset about it, but nothing's going to change. One thing we *can* change is that this is the last day's filming of *Gavin & Stacey*, and I abso-lutely refuse to let that infringe on this.' And I think that's just life experience.

But also there have been times over the years when I can remember phoning you when I would get in a state about something. It happened with *Stella*, because the thing with *Stella* sometimes was that my production company was making it. I was playing the lead, I was kind of show-running it and writing the scripts. So I was often quite isolated – not that people were deliberately staying out of my way, but that was just the nature of it, you know. And I can remember one time feeling really under-confident because I had to do this scene which was supposed to be a little bit sexy, and I remember call-ing you, saying, 'I don't want to do this scene. I just feel so horrible and unattractive.' And you were so lovely to me, and gave me such a good confidence boost. I felt really relieved by that.

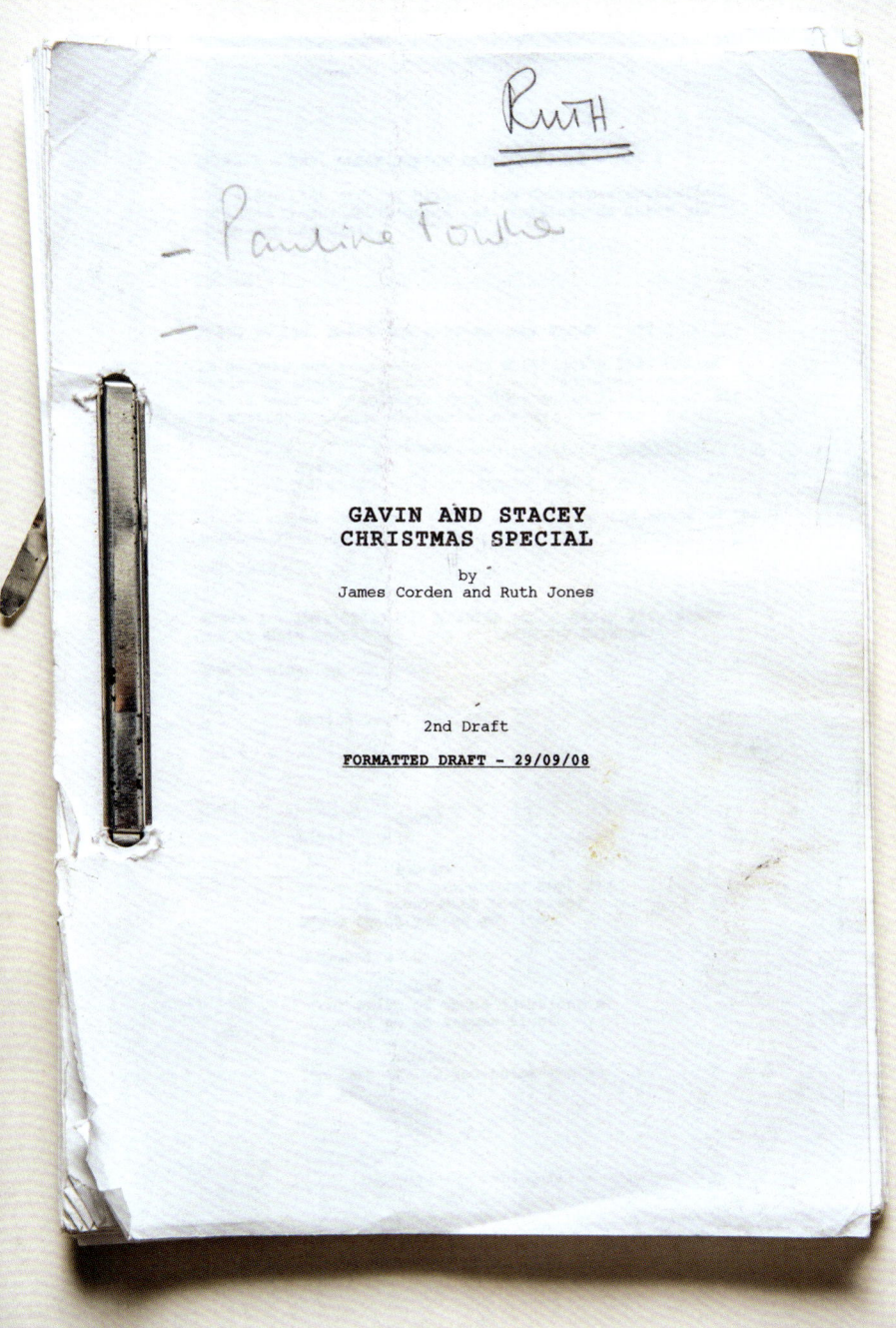

RuTH.

— Pauline Fowler

—

GAVIN AND STACEY
CHRISTMAS SPECIAL

by

James Corden and Ruth Jones

2nd Draft

FORMATTED DRAFT - 29/09/08

'What happened on
The Fishing Trip?'

UNTITLED JACKSON-TRAUB PROJECT

(aka GAVIN & STACY)

Pilot

by

Hayes Jackson & Stacy Traub

Reboot ABC Draft
July 29, 2010

Gavin and Stacey nearly take the US ...

Gavin & Stacey set for US small screen

HIT sitcom Gavin & Stacey has been snapped up by an American television company.

US giant NBC has bought the rights to the British show – famed for putting Barry on the map – and plans to re-stage it for American audiences.

Ruth Jones

Gavin & Stacey tells the story of a whirlwind romance between an Essex boy and Welsh girl and was written by Bridgend-born Ruth Jones in partnership with James Corden.

The hit series has since won honours at the British Comedy Awards.

NBC plans to portray Gavin as from New Jersey and Stacey from South Carolina in the deep South.

The pair will meet in Times Square in New York.

A second series of Gavin & Stacey is due to be screened later this month.

Gavin & Stacey

If only if were just the two of them...

AMERICA

Ruth Jones, Rob Brydon and Tom Jones filming 'Barry Islands in the Stream' for Red Nose Day 2008, in Las Vegas

James Corden and George Michael, Comic Relief 2011 - 'Smithy Saves Red Nose Day' sketch

Smithy fires up the England team for Red Nose Day 2009

With Stuart Murphy, who originally commissioned *Gavin & Stacey*, guest starring as a DJ in the 2019 Christmas Special.

Christmas Special 2019

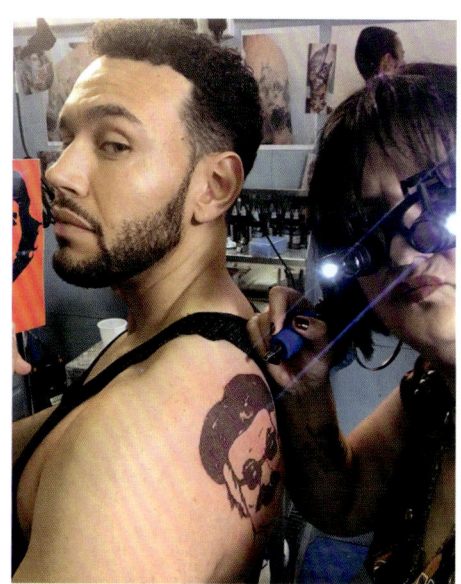

Nessa gives 'Darren' (Kyle Lima) a Che Guevara/Des Lynam tattoo

BAFTAs 2008

Best Male Performance
in a Comedy 2008

BAFTAs 2025

Larry Lamb and our Director,
Christine Gernon

Best Female Performance
in a Comedy 2025

Left to right: Christine Gernon, Larry Lamb, Melanie Walters,
Robert Wilfort, Mat Horne, Joanna Page, James Corden, Alison
Steadman, Ruth Jones, Rob Brydon

14/4/08

thank you

Dear Ruth and
    James

Thank You very much for
Creating Gavin and stacey,
its brilliant. I hope that
You are both Well.
            Love
            Lesley
P.S Mathew Horne is really
Fantastic.

GREETINGS FROM BARRY ISLAND

Wish we were still there...

And I do think you would be the person I would phone if I was in a really extreme situation where I needed help. I would absolutely, 100 per cent, come to you. I mean, don't get me wrong, if I had some minor catastrophe happening in my day, you would be like, 'Can you just tell me when you've got to the point!' But when the chips are down, it's like you are absolutely there for me. When I was in *Sister Act* and I did the first of the dress rehearsals in Ireland, I came out and I'd got the words wrong, and I was crying outside the theatre. I called you, and you were like, 'You'll look back on this day and you're going to wonder why on earth you were upset.' You put everything into perspective for me. It's just fantastic, and I'm very lucky to have you as a friend.

That's the word I think of a lot, actually. When I think about *Gavin & Stacey*, and I think about what the word 'friend' means, and I think about what it's meant to us personally, I don't think either of us think about the show first. Like, my first thought is, I got to make this show with somebody who knows me better than I probably know myself. With a friend who . . . I just don't think I'll ever have a friendship like it again in my life. So, it's so strange to think about *Gavin & Stacey*, and this book is everything in between, and yet the everything in between means more to me today than the show does. The entire thing is just the most extraordinary good fortune, in every way, because I'd have been lost, if truth be told.

Ah, well, that's a little moment we've had there.

I don't know if people would ever realize how much you and I actually say the words 'I love you.'

No, that's true.

And I thought this when I left your house the other day. We'd been writing and I was leaving, and so I leant down to give you a hug to say bye, because it was gonna be a couple of weeks until we saw each other next, and you squeezed my face and you went, 'I absolutely love you.' And I said, 'I love you too.' And then left. And I don't think people would ever know that.

No, they wouldn't.

Particularly not if they saw us in public, where we do often look annoyed with each other.

Oh, like when you annoyed me in a text the other day – or on a phone call, and I just ended in mock anger going, 'I *hate* you.'

And then you hung up!

And I hung up, and then you texted me back, and you just went, 'Well, I love you.'

Thinking back to when the show really took off, I had ended a relationship a couple of years earlier. We'd been in a very long relationship for eight years, I'd moved to London, and then about five months after that, suddenly, the show was huge, and it all felt so exciting.

I also think the experience of being in *The History Boys* was interesting. When that play became such a hit, it had a big effect on me. I can't stress enough how every day the other boys in the cast that I was sharing a room with were coming in with these film scripts, and Dom [Cooper]'s meeting Steven Spielberg and Sam [Barnett]'s going for dinner after the show with Martin Scorsese's casting director, and everyone was just getting this stuff. I remember Russell [Tovey] and Andy [Knott] were both going up for the same really cool indie film project about two boys that go backpacking around the world and they get accused of a murder, and it was the hottest fucking script, and I got a call about it as well. All of our scripts came to the National Theatre, and they had been sent the full script of this movie, and I realized that while they were up for the main roles, my character was, like, a newsagent or something. I was the same age and, if anything, I was more established because I'd done a Mike Leigh movie [*All or Nothing*] and a Shane Meadows movie [*Twenty Four Seven*], but I had this feeling that, fuck, this just isn't going to happen for me.

So then when you write this show, and suddenly within a few years it explodes and you're single for the first time in your life, I don't care what anybody says, it's thrilling. I think we have experienced fame in different ways, you and me. It's something you have actively never wanted, Ruth. Whereas I absolutely embraced it.

Well, I think you're more honest about it, because while I'm much more at ease with it now than I used to be, I did find it difficult at first. But I love it when people love things that I do. I love that people love my characters.

Yeah, I guess no one becomes an actor if they don't want fame on some level, but I was just like, 'Oh, OK, this is it!' But then I also had this feeling that this isn't going to last very long . . . that this will vanish in no time. And so I just decided, 'I'm going to jump into it with both feet.'

It must have been weird for you, too, because you never went away to university, so you never got to do all that student-y misbehaving. I think you missed out on that period when people learn how to misbehave with their mates.

Yes. I started working as an actor when I was seventeen. So when I became famous it was a very intoxicating experience. Suddenly you're invited to these things and you enter these worlds and meet these people, and I had some amazing times and great moments.

And I'm so glad you did. I just went back to Cardiff. It was 2008 when it all kicked off. I set up Tidy Productions with my husband, and I did a weekly radio show on BBC Radio Wales and then we co-wrote this thing called *Ar y Tracs* for S4C, which was a TV film about a team on board a train from Swansea to London – you'd have your cafe buffet car, you'd have the first-class trolley woman, and so on. So we wrote this Christmas film about that. It was quite sweet, actually, and you were in it, playing a gambling addict called Trevor. So I did that, and I just stayed in Wales most of the time and I really did fight against the fame thing.

I used to hate being recognized. I don't know why. Now if people ask for a photo, most of the time I just give it to them. Unless I'm having a really bad day or look particularly crap. I used to be awful; I used to pretend not to be me.

I remember going through Tesco with you once and all these people were asking for a photo with you and you'd be, 'No, no, no!'

Was I? I don't think I was that bad, but was that when you put a sticker on my back saying '45 per cent off'?

Haha. I don't know! Maybe.

I walked round all of Tesco with that sign stuck on my back.
    The only time I get a little bit funny is when people go, 'Oh my god, it's Nessa,' and I'll say, 'No, my name is Ruth.' But generally speaking, now I find it so much easier when people recognize me.

Well, I think you're a lot more comfortable now. I actually think we both are. What you're talking about in both of those things is that your world changing feels uncomfortable. There's two ways you can react to that. You can jump in at the deep end, or you can get out of the pool. There's no middle ground, really. And I think that is just a difference in age and circumstance, you know.

And I'm twelve years older than you. I'm fifty-nine. I was forty when I started this – younger than you are now.

Well, at least you've already paid for your funeral!

True.

After that first Christmas special in 2008, and when the series moved from BBC Three to BBC One, it felt like the show and the characters had taken on a life of their own, and we did have some brilliant times. You and I always used to talk about whether the show would ever be big enough that it would be part of Comic Relief. And then we had an idea for a sketch in which the cast of *Gavin & Stacey* had won tickets to be in the audience at Comic Relief, so they were all coming up to Television Centre to watch it.

Then we had this idea that they all got lost in Television Centre, so Gwen would end up sitting on the set of *The Naked Chef* and show Jamie Oliver how to make an omelette. Pam and Mick would end up in the equivalent of *This Morning* or whatever. Nessa would just keep bumping into ex-lovers, like Dermot O'Leary and JLS and she'd be saying, 'This is depressing for me. I've got too many skeletons in the closet.' And Gavin and Stacey end up having a quick shag in the *Blue Peter* garden, while Bryn ends up on *Top Gear*, talking about his Citroën Picasso . . . And Smithy's bit was that he ended up on the set of *Match of the Day* while they were interviewing the England team, and told them that they're a disgrace, which I always thought was a really funny idea. As it was, everybody was so busy we couldn't find a way to get all the cast together. It would have taken fourteen shooting days, basically, and we didn't have the budget for that.

Then I said to you, 'Can I explore just the Smithy

bit of it? Because I do think the idea of Smithy speaking for every football fan is really good.' You agreed and so we set about trying to do that. But that first Smithy sketch in 2009 was written on the day because we didn't know which players we'd get. They only guaranteed us four players.

Oh, I loved seeing that. It was the way they were giggling. Rio Ferdinand and David Beckham and Peter Crouch – like a bunch of sniggering schoolboys.

And then you and Rob did 'Islands In The Stream' for Comic Relief, which we've already mentioned.

But after that, the Smithy sketch took on such a life of its own. And we thought, 'For Sport Relief, what if he wins Coach of the Year at Sports Personality of the Year?' That felt like a natural progression. Filming that, I was as nervous as I've ever felt. We had a ten-minute window to do it before the actual Sports Personality of the Year show went live, and the sketch was eight minutes long. And then the idea of doing 'Smithy saves Comic Relief' as the last one – that felt right. So I'm very, very proud of them. I really like the idea of Smithy as this no-nonsense motivational coach.

Yeah, so many things came from that sketch, didn't they? Like Carpool Karaoke – that wouldn't have come

about without you and George Michael in the 'Smithy saves Comic Relief' sketch.

Freddie Flintoff had said no to being a team captain on *A League of Their Own*, which was a show on Sky that I was gonna host. Then we did that sketch, and he and I were in a pedalo, and I was saying, 'Go on, you've gotta do it. You'll be great, I promise.'

Aw, he was great, fair play.

He was amazing. But all these things, these sketches, you and Rob having a number one song in the charts – it's just a real indicator of how big the show had become, really.

islands fifth draft

EXT. BARRY ISLAND, SOUTH WALES.

The camera pans across the sea front of Barry, it should
look like the opening of a film with titles that come up
like in old films and it could say: "Nessa and Bryn" in
(BARRY) ISLANDS IN THE STREAM."

INT. BARRY ARCADE.

NESSA is serving ROBIN GIBB with change.

> NESSA
> Alrigh Robin how's it goin
> alrigh?

> ROBIN GIBB
> Alrigh Ness how's it goin alrigh?

> NESSA
> I normally sees Barry down Barry
> so it's nice to see you for a
> change, talking of which, there's
> yours. Now be on your way.

> ROBIN GIBB
> Tidy.

BRYN runs in, he's holding a letter and he is so excited he
looks like a child who's had too much sugar. He is out of
breath but laughing and almost does a little skip and jump
type move when he reaches the counter. NESSA stares at him,
he is now beside himself.

> NESSA
> Alrigh Bryn what's occurin?

> BRYN
> I will tell you what's occurin
> little lady! You and me have only
> been chosen to represent Wales in
> the karaoke world championship.
> We're off to Vegas kid!

> NESSA
> Crackin.

Cut to -

EXT. CALIFORNIAN HIGHWAY, DESERT.

A truck hurtles along. We cut inside -

INT. TRUCK (ON THE CALIFORNIAN HIGHWAY)

NESSA and BRYN are heading for Vegas. BRYN has brought his
sat nav. The road is very straight.

> SAT NAV
> Continue straight on for a
> hundred and eighty miles.

> BRYN
> Thankyou very much.

Silence.

> SAT NAV
> Continue straight on for a
> hundred and seventy nine and a
> half miles.

> BRYN
> Thankyou very much.

> NESSA
> O. Bryn. I'm not bein funny but I
> knows the way to Vegas like the
> back of my hand, I lived there
> for the best part of four and a
> half months remember.

> BRYN
> It must be nice to be here again.

> NESSA
> Not really - this very desert
> holds a lot of bad memories for
> me. I've dug too many holes in my
> time Bryn, too many holes.

BRYN looks somewhat confused. The car starts chugging along
- there is something clearly wrong with it.

> BRYN
> Uh - oh.

> NESSA
> I think we got a problem.

Cut to -

EXT. CALIFORNIAN HIGHWAY.

NESSA has her head under the bonnet of the truck trying to
sort it out. BRYN is trying to hitch a lift.
Unsuccessfully.

> NESSA
> Well we can kiss goodbye to the
> championship. She's blown a
> gasket she has.

> BRYN

Hang on.

BRYN steps out and tries to flag down a huge stretch limo
that is driving past. The car doesn't stop. BRYN is
depressed. NESSA moves away from the engine and into the
middle of the road. She calls at the top of her voice after
the stretch limo at, now some distance away.

                    NESSA
          O!

The car screeches to a halt and reverses. As it pulls up,
its blackened rear window slowly lowers and we see first
BRYN'S elated reaction.

                    BRYN
          Flippin heck.

And then NESSA's deflated reaction.

                    NESSA
          Oh no...

She can't believe who it is either.

It's Tom Jones. Sir Tom Jones!

                    TOM JONES
          What's occurin' pussycat?

Cut to -

EXT.

TOM'S limo drives along at speed. We cut inside -

INT. TOM'S LIMO

BRYN is beside himself and sat between NESSA and TOM in the
back of the car. NESSA is looking out of the window.

Silence.

                    TOM JONES
          I've missed you Ness.

                    NESSA
          O. Tom. I'm not bein funny but I
          got nothin to say to you. I
          appreciates the lift, genuine.
          But don't be harpin on about the
          past. You let me down. Simple as.

                    TOM JONES
          I know and I'm sorry. Bryn help
          me out here will you?

                    BRYN
          Please don't bring me into this
                    Page 3

TJ.

Awkward silence.

Cut to -

EXT. CHAMPIONSHIP VENUE

People are walking in. The limo pulls up. NESSA and BRYN get out and head inside, leaving TOM in the car, calling after NESSA.

> TOM JONES
> Nessa, wait!

NESSA stops and turns to TOM. BRYN rushes on ahead.

> BRYN
> I'll tell them we're here.

And he goes inside.

> TOM JONES
> I want to make it up to you Ness.

> NESSA
> You broke my heart Tom. Simple
> as. But worse than that you took
> my lyrics to sex bomb and you
> palmed them off as your own. Now
> back off.

BRYN comes rushing out.

> BRYN
> O crikey - England just got the
> highest marks in the history of
> the championship. Every judge
> gave them a nine. We don't stand
> a chance.

> NESSA
> We'll let the judges be the judge
> of that.

And she's gone, leaving BRYN standing there awkwardly, desperate to follow but not wanting to offend TOM.

> BRYN
> Right! Well... I ...

> TOM JONES
> I had the best night of my life
> with that woman Bryn. Animal.
> Absolute animal.

BRYN doesn't know where to put himself.

> BRYN
> Thanks for the lift.

And he scuttles off leaving TOM deep in thought, wondering.

INT. CHAMPIONSHIP VENUE

On stage, the MC is introducing the event.

> MC
> Next up, all the way from Wales,
> England, it's Bryn and Nessa.

Polite applause. NESSA and BRYN come to the stage.

> MC (CONT'D)
> Bryn West! You're looking good!

MUSIC begins.

> BRYN
> Thankyou very much!

> MC
> You been on any fishin trips
> lately?

But it's time - thankfully - to start singing.

> BRYN
> "Baby when I met you there was
> peace unknown... etc"

As the song progresses, we see the audience mildly enjoying
it but not totally enraptured. The judges make notes.
[should we see what they write? Eg "average", "not bad"?]
Then suddenly after the second round of choruses who should
appear walking through the crowd from the back but TOM
JONES! who joins in singing in his own unique way. The
crowd love it and go wild for TOM. The panel of judges give
the performance all ten out of ten - holding up the cards
with "10" on it. NESSA finally relents and we see her
forgive TOM - BRYN can't help himself and hugs TOM maybe
saying

> BRYN (CONT'D)
> You saved the day TJ, you saved
> the day!

whereas NESSA gives him one of her hearty handshakes. Happy
days.

Cut to -

INT. TOM'S LIMO

Start on BRYN all smiles, listening to James Blunt's
"Wisemen". Pan across and NESSA is not enjoying it. Pan
across, and neither is TOM.

> NESSA
> Oh Bryn, can we have somethin

islands fifth draft

else on?

               BRYN
But James Blunt's a genius!

               TOM JONES
I like the tune but it's the
lyrics more than anything man,
they just don't make sense.

               NESSA
I agree with Tom.

               TOM JONES
Tidy.

We cut outside the car as -

EXT.

... our heroes drive off into the sunset or whatever, and
we hear BRYN defending JAMES BLUNT -

               BRYN (O.S.)
I know what you mean, but from
what I can work out, there's
these 3 men, blessed with wisdom
who between them own a semi
detatched house by the sea. Not
entirely sure of its where
abouts. And basically they've
been smoking..

Up on screen come the words : "The End."

CHAPTER 8

Diverging paths: series three and the first finale

RUTH: We went back and forth over whether to do a third series. Originally the 2008 Christmas special was going to be the last episode.

JAMES: But that episode asked more questions than it answered.

We had to make sure we weren't selling out the characters and forcing their stories into another series. I think because we'd done a Christmas special and that had ended on a cliffhanger, with Dave proposing to Nessa, we felt we needed to do one more series. We actually announced the third series live on an outside broadcast of my BBC Radio Wales show in Barry Island – do you remember? It was on 21 December 2008 . . . and I think we annoyed the BBC. I think we didn't really understand the protocol. We felt like if we decided to do another series, then we would – not in an arrogant way, just naively thinking it would happen – whereas now look at the hoo-ha surrounding the announcement of *The Finale*, which we couldn't do until we had the budget in place and we had the actors in place. So how naive were we back then to just go, 'Yeah, we'll announce it ourselves'? But it was an incredible event with loads of people in the crowd with 'We love *Gavin & Stacey*' signs. Oh, and, randomly, Robert Plant was on that show as well.

With series three, I think we were confident that we had important storylines for Gavin and Stacey – them trying for a baby and having a hard time with that – and Smithy and Nessa, with the build-up to her marriage to Dave Coaches, after Smithy tells her not to marry him in the Christmas special. Then little ideas for the others started landing in our minds, like them all getting drunk at Mick and Pam's in episode two, which no one had seen before, and it felt natural that that would happen . . .

We also brought in the great Pam Ferris as Smithy's mum, and she's a character who's a bit hopeless. She doesn't want to be nasty. She's not a nasty mother. She's just *hopeless*, and the negativity oozes out of her pores. If you think about when Pam did *The Darling Buds Of*

May, and how vibrant and passionate and positive and life-affirming she was as that character, to be able to then play this character, which is the complete opposite, shows what a fine actress she is.

And introducing his mother was about creating an understanding of why Smithy is like he is, and why Pam and Mick are so important to him. I think it is because of the background that he's come from.

We also brought in Nessa's dad, played by Huw Dafydd, who was lovely, for the christening of Neil the Baby at the start of series three. And so Nessa is now living in the caravan with Dave and Neil the Baby, who she's teaching the difference between Osama and Obama. That scene came from my absolute fear of getting people's names wrong, because I have really massively messed up in the past. Like, I went up to the actor Simon Callow once in a party and I said, 'Oh, can I just say I really, really loved you in the film *Peter's Friends*.' And he said, 'Oh, well, that's nice, darling, but I wasn't in it. That was Stephen Fry!' So I've got a thing about that. And I consciously had to remind myself when talking about President Obama – I would repeat 'Obama, Obama, Obama, Obama', because 'Osama' would creep in. And I sort of always have to do this check beforehand, in my mind, to make sure I am going to say 'Obama' and not 'Osama' and vice versa. So that's where that came from.

One of the best days of filming series three was at the beach.

Yes, having a day on the beach in Barry Island. That was an exciting idea ... I remember Rob brought weights with him that day, so he could pump up his muscles for the moment when he's coming out of the sea like Daniel Craig, and he looked great. I think that was Rob's son's idea, by the way – the James Bond moment.

And Dawn and Pete renewing their vows.

With Gavin and Stacey's storyline, after they find out he's got a low sperm count, we weren't sure if that would work for the whole series throughout all the episodes, but we knew we had Mat and Jo, two brilliant actors, who would make it work.

A scene I absolutely love is in series three, episode five, when Gavin and Stacey are in the car to Essex and they're not saying anything because they've just found out that it's not going to happen yet as far as them having a baby is concerned, and just the way Joanna takes his hand ... Oh, it's so beautiful. And then when she holds him in bed as well and kisses him. There are no words in that scene; it's just Mat and Jo acting their socks off. She just takes his hand and looks at him for a long time, and he's trying to maintain his manly exterior. But you can see all these emotions

on his face. They're both so good in that scene. Those moments are beyond lovely. And there's a bit with Nessa and Gwen on the day of Nessa's wedding to Dave that never happened, when Nessa says, 'A lot of people have been asking if my mother was going to turn up today and I says "yes", because my mother is Gwen.' And she then kisses her on the lips. So you've got that comedy but it's also quite moving. It pays off because Nessa is often quite awful to Gwen. Especially in series three. We sort of made it a running joke that Nessa was terrible to her.

Gwen takes it from everyone, including Bryn . . . He's awful to her quite often.

We had a brilliant Bryn moment in the christening episode in series three when he sings the Labi Siffre song '(Something Inside) So Strong'. When I told him about that idea, I remember how chuffed he was. He loved it.

We knew he'd be brilliant in that scene because he's such a fabulous singer, but what made it even funnier was the backing group, including Doris on drums.

Our producer Ted Dowd tried to coordinate her drumming with his biro – he hid behind a chair or something and used his pen to cue her in, so she could see when to hit the drum – but it didn't work.

Of course, when we saw it in the edit, it was perfect that she's out of time.

There's another great Doris musical scene in series three, when she sings 'There Is A Light That Never Goes Out' by The Smiths. Margaret had to learn that on the guitar. And I remember we were sat at the back of Gwen's garden, and it was a beautiful day, and it was the scene of the barbecue, and she was practising, and there were just two notes she had to play. It turned out Margaret had had a husband called Ben, who was a musician – he played on lots of TV shows like Morecambe and Wise, and with BBC bands and that type of thing. Anyway, he died very young – only in his thirties, I think – and he was younger than Margaret, and I remember she sort of spoke to him under her breath that day to help her get this song right. And then she performed it, and it was great, and I'm not even a Smiths fan. But they played the song at her funeral, and it was really moving.

Then, of course, we had the wedding of Nessa and Dave that didn't happen.

We used the Angry Anderson song 'Suddenly', which we picked because of course it was in *Neighbours* when Scott and Charlene got married. Back in series one we figured Stacey would have loved *Neighbours* and would have expected that song to be played at her wedding. Then we figured it wasn't right for that wedding, but it seemed perfect when we were planning Nessa's wedding.

We really wanted people to think Nessa and Dave were actually going to get married. I really liked how proud she was to walk down the aisle. I love the way she walks – it's so not Nessa. And I think they could have got married and it would have been fine. But as Smithy pointed out, why marry someone you obviously don't love?

Series three was quite a difficult experience, though. Seriously, I think it was quite tough. Because what happens inevitably when something gets bigger, is it *all* gets bigger and you start to get pulled in different directions. And because of the success of the show, the cast are infinitely harder to book now than they were. So there are more pulls on people's time. That was the biggest difference between series one and two, and series three. And there's more pressure. There's more pressure on you to write it, there's more pressure on you to deliver it, and it's all just a bit bigger. Thankfully, the one place we've never, ever struggled is when we shut the doors and we open a laptop, right? All we really need is a room, a laptop, a pen, some Post-it notes and a bar of chocolate.

Well, more than one bar, to be fair.

So we didn't struggle with that. The writing of it was always good. But I do remember one time during that year of me going out, when I don't know where I'd been, what I'd been doing, but I remember coming to your house in a cab.

Yeah, a cab to Cardiff . . .

I was so all over the place and upset – I was heart-broken about something – and hungover. And you literally put me in the front room on the sofa and put a blanket over me. I think I slept all day. I think I slept from, like, ten a.m. till four or five p.m., and then felt so much better.

I gave you some orange squash when you woke up.

You did. So, during that time I would go back to yours, and then just be put in this cocoon.

Then, when it came to the ending of series three of *Gavin & Stacey*, we thought that would be it for sure.

I mean, the ending was great, wasn't it? There was that beautiful aerial shot at the end of what we thought was

the final episode, with the four of us – Gavin, Stacey, Smithy and Nessa – in Barry Island. It's funny to think how things have moved on with technology, because that shot was done on a helicopter. Whereas now you'd just have a drone, and it would have been a lot cheaper. And quieter.

We did originally have Neil the Baby in that shot, which would have been lovely, but the noise of the helicopter was so loud and frightening he was just screaming the whole time. So we couldn't do that. If only we'd had a drone!

When the final day of filming came, I was fucking in bits, man, because I'd been in this not-great on/off relationship, which was finally off, and that happened during the filming of the third series. I remember on the last day feeling, 'Fuck, I've got nothing. Nothing. The show's ending. My relationship's ended. I don't know what I'm going to do. I don't know where I'm going to go.' So I was a wreck that day; I remember not feeling great at all.

No. It didn't have the right atmosphere, either. It felt weird. It was like closing the door on a massive part of my life. And I was really, really down on the last day as well, like you, partly because I didn't drink then, and I wanted to get absolutely smashed. And I wish I had, but all I could do was smoke. So I just smoked loads of cigarettes. It was all a bit hazy around that time. It was a massive, massive part of my life. And it was over.

Well, maybe it feels weird in hindsight because we now realize that was not the last day of *Gavin & Stacey*. But at the time I was thinking that it would be the last day I would ever see you as Nessa. And I was so gutted about that. I was a wreck.

The last-ever scene of series three that we actually filmed was you at the services deciding to go to the wedding and stop Nessa from marrying Dave. And you look at Neil the Baby in his high chair and you go, 'This is all your fault, this,' and Florence + the Machine starts playing. It was so dramatic. But *my* very last scene – and Rob's – was when Smithy meets Bryn and Nessa at a service station to hand over Neil the Baby, because Smithy's going to look after him on the wedding day. We had a photograph done, which was supposed to be Smithy's wedding present to Nessa, of the three of them as a family, and the last line that Nessa says to Smithy is, 'There's only one of you, isn't there?' and it was so sad. And then when they shouted, 'Cut!' . . . was it then that . . .?

. . . I tried to talk to you but I couldn't speak . . . It was very funny, like something out of a sitcom, because there's a line in the show where Nessa says, 'I'd be lost, if truth be told,' and I was hugging you and crying so much. And I was trying to whisper that line to you – 'I'd be lost, if truth be told' – about what was happening in our real lives and ending the show, but you couldn't hear what I was saying because I was crying so much!

You were sobbing. A total mess.

And you went, 'Sorry?' And I said it again – 'I'd be lost, if truth be told' – and you just whispered back, 'James, I'm sorry. I can't hear you.'

And you had to hold your head up and repeat the line, ever so slightly irritated: 'I said, I'd be lost, if truth be told.' You could have even added 'for fuck's sake' at the end.

Honestly, it was like something out of the show.

Yeah, it was quite a *Gavin & Stacey* moment. That was in the summer of 2009 when we finished filming series three, was it?

Yes. They showed the episode on the beach on Christmas Day, and then the last episode was on New Year's Day and it got ten million viewers.

And we truly thought that was that. How wrong we were . . .

CHAPTER 9

The in-between years

RUTH: I think I was away when that final episode aired. I think I was in India.

JAMES: You went to India a lot, I remember. You were never not in India! At that point in your life, you were either in Wales or India. Then India got replaced by Scotland.

That's so true. I'm trying to work out the order of my life! So we shot the first Christmas special in October 2008, then series three in the following June – 2009. Which means I must have done *Ar y Tracs* in October 2009. In case you've forgotten, *Ar y Tracs* was the Welsh-language Christmas film our company Tidy Productions made about the rail crew working between Swansea and London. It was the first thing Tidy ever made. I was Polish in it. I had to play an accordion. Oh my god, so *Gavin & Stacey* series three came out at Christmas 2009 – the same time as *Ar y Tracs*!

Stop talking about *Ar y Tracs*!

It's your favourite thing, James, and you always have to be in everything that I've ever written.

OK, but stop talking about *Ar y Tracs*. And also you were obsessed with India. You started making all these friends there.

Yes, I did become friends with people, like Jagadeesh, the taxi driver. We bought him a tuk-tuk!

Yeah, I'm sure you did.

Anyway … I was in India when that last episode was broadcast. And I'd also started writing *Stella* for Sky. Like, just the very first episode. It would be a year before we actually started filming, but I know that's when I started writing it. And I came back, and we were up for a National Television Award for *Gavin & Stacey*.

Yeah, though we had that argument that night, didn't we?

So, to set the scene, one of the things I think you would probably agree with me on is that we do sometimes wind each other up . . .

Yes.

Exactly. And, well, the National Television Awards were going to be held in January. So I was still in that kind of off-kilter post-Christmas period, and I really didn't want to go out at all, and I'm not a massive fan of red-carpet things anyway. I'm really not. And if I'm feeling overweight and not feeling like dressing up, there's nothing worse than going on a red carpet in a big fancy dress when you're feeling overweight. And I just said to you, 'Oh, I'm not going to go.' And you were like, 'Oh, for god's sake, then it'll just be me going, and then you're just gonna look really cool for not going.' And I went, 'But I just can't face it. I can't face going on that red carpet and people taking pictures of me and asking questions. I just can't face it.' So anyway, all of the cast ended up going except me, and we won the award, which was lovely. And I was at home, watching in my pyjamas, cheering you all on from my sofa . . .

And then we went up to get the award, and I said, 'Ruth Jones can't be here tonight because she can't be arsed.'

No, I think you said, 'Ruth Jones can't be here tonight because she can't leave the house.' And then you added, 'I'm serious, she literally can't leave the house.'*

And then when you said that, my face just dropped. I couldn't believe that you were saying it. I could not believe it. So I texted you, saying: 'I will never speak to you again. Don't ever call me.' I felt so *humiliated*. But when I look back at it now . . . And we were laughing about this yesterday; you said, 'Ruth, the thing is, everybody thought it was really funny, and everybody just thought you were really cool for not going to the NTAs.' And I said, 'Well, that's not how I remember it. I just remember feeling really humiliated.' And you went, 'Can we just agree that, yes, I shouldn't have said it? Can we also agree that you massively overreacted?' And I was like, 'Yeah, I guess I did.'

But I know you said, 'She literally can't leave the house,' because then I had texts from people like my hairdresser asking, 'My god, are you all right?' She thought I had extreme depression.

So, yes, I definitely used to overreact. Nowadays I wouldn't let myself overreact to your wind-ups, but then you don't really wind me up as much as you used to.

Quite soon after that, we had the *Radio Times* Covers Party, and I remember going to it, and I hadn't spoken to

* In fact, what James actually said was: 'Ruth can't be here because she can't be arsed . . . and seriously, it's the most she can do to leave the house at the moment.'

you for maybe two weeks. I hadn't answered your calls or anything, and then I just saw you across the room at the party, and you looked at me, and we walked up to each other, and laughed, had a hug and made friends.

It's all related to the fame thing, I suppose, and how I wasn't very good at dealing with it back then. I just don't think my personality lent itself to that lifestyle. You're really good at that stuff. You just know so much more than me, and you're much more knowledgeable about things that are going on – current things and pop culture – which is why you're so good at the chat show, when you're interviewing people. So I was in a very different place. But also because fame – without wanting to be negative or make a dramatic story that's not been there – did sort of separate us. I think I found it difficult to deal with the world that you were in because I felt it was just separating us. You know what I mean?

Yeah, of course.

I mean, I remember once, in the early days – probably around series two going out – I had to write to the director-general of the BBC; it was Mark Thompson at the time. He'd done a piece in which he said James Corden was the creator of *Gavin & Stacey*, and went on and on about you. And so I wrote to him, saying, 'Excuse me, it was *co*-created.' He was very apologetic, to be fair, and I felt awful that I had to resort to doing that. But I thought, 'Hang on a minute, OK, I let most things like that go.' And I'm not talking about you here; I just thought people's perception was wrong, and it was important to remember what happened with the creation of our little show.

And then there was a definite parting of the ways, in that you were going off and enjoying your lifestyle, and I was going off to my very different lifestyle, but also it related to our age difference and where we were in the world. So I was a stepmother and you were single at the time, and I can remember after series three was finished, you came down to Cardiff when, I think, you had a day off from filming the Paul Potts movie [*One Chance*]. You came down to see me, and we went out for lunch in a Japanese restaurant in Cardiff near my house, and I was walking down the road with you and suddenly there were all these people beeping their horn at you, and shouting out to you. It was so extraordinary.

Well, I also think one massive thing is that you don't look anything like Nessa.

Yeah, that's so true . . .

It made such a difference because you could very easily just disappear. Even if people shout, 'Oi Smithy!' at me when I'm with you in shops or what-ever, they sometimes don't notice you at all, and I remember thinking to myself, 'You don't have a fuck-ing clue . . . That's actually Nessa.' It's a nuts thing, that; it's really crazy.

So when *Gavin & Stacey* finished after three series, after my Welsh film *Ar y Tracs* happened, I then went on to do *Stella*, and that was really a bit scary for me, because I knew that everyone was gonna go, 'Oh, it's Welsh and and it's not as good as *Gavin & Stacey*.' And people did say that, but there were also a lot of people that liked it. Also, because it was on Sky, and not as many people saw it, that was a bit of a dive into the unknown for me. I mean, I'm really proud of *Stella* . . . and I'm so glad I did it.

Well, it was brilliant.

It's funny that Stuart Murphy had gone on to become the controller of Sky One, and he basically set about giving us both our own shows. So I was hosting this sports panel show [*A League of Their Own*], and you were making *Stella*, and there he was again.

I found an email recently in which he said that he wanted to buy *Gavin & Stacey* from the BBC!

Yeah, he tried to do that very publicly.

It's funny as well, because when he got that job at Sky,

he said to me, 'I think you could do, like, a sort of a British *Roseanne* – a half-hour sitcom filmed in front of a studio audience, multi-camera,' and I went, 'All right . . .' And I went away and tried to start writing that, but it just didn't work – it wasn't me at all – so I went back to him and said, 'Would you consider a comedy drama, single camera; like, forty-five minutes?' That's what I ended up doing with *Stella*, because I'm not a sitcom writer in that sense, and I don't think *Gavin & Stacey* is a sitcom in the traditional sense.

I really liked what we did with *Stella*, and people still ask about it now. We did fifty-eight episodes, so it was a big part of my life in that period from 2011. Essentially, *Stella* took over my working life from that point on. I did four chat shows for BBC Wales during the 'down' weeks of *Stella* – god knows how I did that. I'd film for four weeks, so basically two episodes, then while the prep was being done for the next two eps, I'd rehearse and film a chat show in front of an audience – *Ruth Jones' Easter Treat*, or *Summer Holiday*, or *Christmas Cracker*. Ricky Gervais came on that one. He was a challenge, to say the least! But, y'know, looking back, god knows how you managed to do a chat show five days a week in the States. Talk about hard work!

Anyway, I was head down, getting on with *Stella*, which started filming early 2011 . . . *Gavin & Stacey* hadn't completely gone away, though, because there'd begun to be rumblings of an American version.

Oh yeah. The first we ever heard of the possibility was actually back in 2008. D'you remember, we went out there for the BBC America showcase, where they were showing different BBC programmes? And some guys wanted to meet us for breakfast the next day.

Yeah, they were agents, I think, and they told us NBC had commissioned two writers to come up with an American version of *Gavin & Stacey*. We knew nothing about it! And so they sent us this pilot script, and I don't know if it was naivety or what, but I remember reading it and thinking, 'Oh no . . . this doesn't feel right at all.'

And nothing really came of it.

But then, years later – like, I think, 2012, so long after series three had gone out in the UK – we got contacted by Jane Tranter, who was working for BBC Worldwide . . . and there began to be a lot of developments of an American version of the show. First, Fox were interested, and then ABC. The Fox show was called *Us & Them* and it was definitely the best of the scripts. I think David Rosen was the writer – and a few episodes were actually filmed and broadcast. So it did look like it might actually happen . . .

. . . And then it didn't – they decided not to carry on after four episodes. So difficult to get a changed format of a show across the line.

We also had the *Gavin & Stacey* book, *Gavin & Stacey: From Barry to Billericay*, which was ghostwritten by the Dawson brothers with lots of quizzes and stuff. I did write the Nessa diaries in there, though – I remember that. What else was happening in those 'in-between' years?

Well, I did the play *One Man, Two Guvnors* for the National. And the first of my two projects with Meryl Streep! And I also did *The Wrong Mans* with Mathew Baynton for BBC Two. And as well as *Stella* you'd started writing your books, starting with the green one!

***Never Greener*, thank you. By the way, the idea of you sitting down and reading one of my novels is just hilarious.**

But I've read all of them!

Fuck off.

I have! I love that bit where it says, 'But this didn't matter in the end, because the phone was ringing at the end of the corridor and she knew she'd have to answer it . . .'
Chapter Twelve! 'Mark had always been handsome. Ever since I met him as a sixteen-year-old. Lithe, tall, blond, golden locks, broad shoulders,

and as we played tennis that day, I couldn't help but wonder what it would have been like if things were different . . .'

Ha! That's one of my least favourite expressions: 'I couldn't help but think . . .' But I wrote that book in 2017, so you'd already gone to the States by then.

One Man, Two Guvnors started at the National Theatre in 2011 and we went to Broadway in 2012. I did *Into the Woods* in 2013 (with Meryl Streep). *The Wrong Mans* was either side of that. We did one series, and then four episodes. And when we were shooting those four episodes of *The Wrong Mans*, I was approached to do *The Late Late Show*, and I agreed to go to America, then the show launched on CBS in March 2015.

And we did *Stella* from 2012 to 2017. So, yes, we were busy! But I do think we lost touch a bit – not in a bad way, but we were just doing our own things and we were physically far away.

But no matter how long goes by in our relationship, I can always rely on you. When I'm in my darkest moments of feeling awful, you will always come good and say the right thing.

For example, I remember when I'd done this chat show for the BBC in 2011, and I'd read some really horrible

things that people had said about it, you sent me this email:

My darling, darling Ruth, you know I understand
completely how you're feeling right now. It is utterly
horrible. But here's the thing, and it's something I think
about in times like this, and it's to do with message
boards. Remember when David Walliams swam the
channel? It was an amazing, incredible thing to have
done for charity. No one could have had a single bad
word to say about it. Well, the day after the documentary
about it was on, there was a thread on a message board
that was entitled, 'How fat did David Walliams look when
he came out of the sea?' I mean, that's what we're
dealing with. The people who write on these boards do
so for effect, so you must, must, must ignore them. The
truth is, you know, and I know when you've done your
best, we know deep down, and that's all you can go
on. Sometimes it works, sometimes it doesn't, but you
are brilliant. You're brilliant and so talented. When you
start reading things on the internet, it starts to damage
the very thing that makes you great anyway. It shreds
all your confidence. I know it's affected mine. You can't
think about the hundreds. You have to think about the
millions that love you and are grateful for all the endless
joys you've given them, and then at the very bottom of it
all, let's say everything you do for the rest of your career
is shit, I mean, awful, which will never, ever be the case,

but let's pretend that it is: you've still made Gavin & Stacey. It's one of the most love sitcoms of our time, and that's what I hang on to. People can say what they like, and they will, but we did that, you and me; now imagine how annoying it is to those haters who wants to write something, because they all do. They haven't done that. They'll never come close to doing something like that. They hate it.

I love you. You're the best person I know. Truly, James

PS: don't die.

I think you said that because I was going on a long journey to India! And I didn't die.

You're much nicer to me than I am to you. Sometimes.

Then there's this email I sent you in February 2011 when you were writing *The Wrong Mans* with Mathew Baynton, and we must have made some agreement to write again and I said:

Sweetheart, don't try and squeeze in the writing with me. I really don't want you to feel obliged. Just because we made a vague promise to write in January. Give *The Wrong Mans* all the proper space it needs. We can work something out. I just would hate for you to feel obliged. That's all. I'm so thrilled about your commission, though not surprised, Matt [Baynton] must be over the moon

And then you replied:

Darling, all I want to do is write with you. Within the next
few weeks we should have some rough ideas on our
dates so we can get something in a diary.

I've kept all these emails! Like, in 2012 I wrote you this:

Conversation with [my husband] David on the platform
at Cardiff station when the announcement was
made in Welsh: one of the place names was 'harbwr
Portsmouth'. I said to David, 'harbwr Portsmouth. That's
Portsmouth harbour.'

And you replied:

Shall we make another series?

**I think I was trying to avoid answering that because I
didn't want to do it. And so my emails to you were maybe
a bit unfriendly but only because I was avoiding the
subject.**
   This one is from 2015, from you:

Are you okay? Your last email is really playing on my
mind. I feel you're cross with me or something, or
like you don't count me as a friend anymore. I hope
you do.

And I wrote back:

> I'm absolutely fine. I'm in Scotland writing. There are
> power cuts, phone lines down and only intermittent
> internet. Bliss. Hope it's going well over there [in America].

Yes, so at least during the time when you were doing
Stella and I was doing *The Late Late Show* we would
text or email; it's just that we didn't really speak on
the phone.

**Yes, and I did recently find an email from 11 August
2015 from you, James, saying, 'Shall we do a Christmas
special?' And I seem to have ignored it. Again.**

**But I remember coming home in a taxi one time in
March 2016, and Adele's 'Hello' was playing on the
radio, and I imagined Nessa singing it to Smithy. I sent
you the lyrics of Nessa's version called 'Alrigh'?' that I
changed to . . .**

> Alrigh'? it's me it is
>
> I was wonderin' if after all these years you'd like
> to meet
> To go over everythin
>
> Bryn says that we should both consider Neil

The baby. 'member Neil?

Alrigh'? O! CAN YOU HEAR ME? OR WHAT?
I'm in Barry Island dreamin about who we used to be
When we were fatter

And free
I've forgotten how it felt before the world fell at
    your feet

There's such a difference between us
And a million miles

Alrigh'? what's occurrin' now?
I musta called a thousand times
To tell you I'm sorry for everythin' that's occurred
But when I call you're always – with Olly Murs
Alrigh'? from the outside
At least I can say that I've tried
To tell you I'm sorry for just losin touch
But it don't matter. It clearly don't bother you much
    anymore . . .
Tidy.

**I think that was one time when we really properly
reconnected.**

Oh, without doubt.

Then later in 2016, we were emailing each other:

> **Me: Now that you've got a lunatic running the country, come back to Britain and make another series . . .**
>
> **Smithy would definitely have voted Brexit. As would Pam.**
>
> **I love you xxxxx**
>
> You: Pam and Mick would have temporarily separated over Brexit. He stayed with Gavin and Stacey.
> I'd love love love us to do a special I truly would x
>
> **Me: Dates. Gimme dates.**
>
> **I could do from October next year xx**
>
> You: Well let's plan to write it end of next year and shoot it the year after which will be 10 years almost to the day that the show ended.
>
> **Me: Perfect. I'll come out for a week in October initially but let's storyline before that in a kind of relaxed emaily way . . . xxx**

But I had my doubts . . . This is an email from me to you in April 2017:

> . . . I worry we won't be able to write together
> anymore . . . we're just in such different places . . . I
> mean the reality is you are now internationally famous!
> And I love that you are, it's what you were always
> destined to be and you've worked so hard for it and
> deserve every drop of it . . . but you're like friends
> with superstars . . . and I still live in Roath [an area of
> Cardiff] . . . and I worry that we won't click anymore
> because there's a gap between us or that I'll be sort of
> shy or stupidly insecure, which I suppose I always was
> so in a way that's no different . . . but I dunno . . . I'm
> NERVOUS I guess. That it won't be the same . . .
>
> I just had to say it.. what if it doesn't work?
>
> I love you
>
> Rxxx

Then you replied:

> If it doesn't work, it won't be for any of those reasons.
> The truth is, I feel more in need of your friendship now
> than I ever have. I long for the simplicity of our lives then
> and I think it's going to be great fun.

If it doesn't work it will be because the characters can't give us the stories anymore.

It's good to be nervous because nerves just mean we want it to be good.

There's no pressure on this until we decide to push the button and talk to the bbc about it. Right now, we can just enjoy it!

X

And then came my birthday. Which I guess was the big turning point.

Oh, of course.

CHAPTER 10

Wild things in Mexico:
the cliffhanger

JAMES: I'd always thought we should do another one. By the end of series three we had ten million viewers on BBC One. And also it just felt like the show wasn't going away. It was on iPlayer and Gold and Dave, etc., so people would just keep saying, 'Will there ever be any more *Gavin & Stacey*? Will you do another one? Go on, do another one.' But we didn't really seriously sit down and talk about it.

RUTH: Let's be honest, it was Mexico that really clinched it.

It was my fortieth and my wife, Jules, organized a massive surprise birthday weekend in Mexico. She flew in my oldest school friend, Richard Shedd, who I've known since I was five – DCI Richard Shedd who speaks about Mick finding the body in series two, episode four of *Gavin & Stacey* was named after him, by the way. He and his wife came to Mexico from New Zealand. I had friends from all over the world fly in. But it was all a surprise. I just thought we were going away – me, Jules and our kids, plus my friend Ben Winston and his wife, Meri, and their kids. Then we got to Mexico.

Yeah, so Julia messaged me in July that year, and obviously she was arranging your fortieth birthday as a surprise, and she asked, 'Would you consider coming over to Mexico for it?' And it was kind of a bit strange, because that was after another period when we hadn't really been massively in touch, as we previously said.

In fact, I think the last time we'd seen each other prior to Mexico was the previous Christmas, when you and the family came over from LA and you were staying in a hotel in London, and I remember going there to see you, and being very polite in front of you. Because at that stage you'd so gone into the stratosphere, fame-wise. And I think that is difficult for people sometimes, if they're not going along on the journey with you, and they don't quite know how to handle you. I mean, there are friends who I haven't seen for a long time, who might for a while have only seen the public me, and they don't see the private me, so there ends up being a little bit of a disparity. And I think perhaps that happened for me and you, James.

So that Christmas, it was a very polite sort of meet-up in the hotel. And then after that would have been Mexico. I don't think I saw you in between. So there was, like, eight months when we didn't see each other. And I think Mexico was really key, because then we spent time talking about what a new *Gavin & Stacey* episode would be. Because despite moments like that email in 2015 when you said, 'Should we write a special?' I just didn't want to go back there at all. And I think you did.

And I suppose my initial reaction to the trip for your birthday – because I'm so bloody cautious about things like that – was 'Oh god, have I got to go to Mexico?' And then I thought, 'Actually, no, I should go,' and my husband, David, was really up for it, saying it would be a really nice thing to do. So, yeah, we arranged it. We flew to Dallas, and then got another flight to where we were going in Mexico, and we had to hide from you.

We'd been allocated our rooms in the resort where you and the family were staying, and you had a sort of little mini villa, and then everybody else was in their rooms, so we wouldn't necessarily bump into each other, but we had to be really careful not to bump into you. We had to hide away the day before your birthday, and I remember we were opposite John Bishop and his wife. Then, the next day, we'd been told where to gather. We knew that you were going to be inside this

sort of villa thing. And so we all had to gather outside and put sombreros on, and there was a mariachi band playing inside the villa. And then, one by one, people had to go in.

Yes, suddenly this mariachi band strikes up, and all these people come in. John Bishop's there, and all these people I know are marching in wearing sombreros. Then Ben opens the laptop, and Tom Cruise is on it, telling me that my mate Sheddy is here, and then he walks in, and then Jules goes, 'There's one more person here . . .'

And then they told me to come in last.

And you walked in, and when I saw you, I just burst into tears. I was so happy to see you. I was just so unbelievably happy to see you.

It was so emotional. And it's really weird, because I don't think I always appreciate how much you love me. And partly I was thinking, 'Surely he'll be more excited about seeing John Bishop, or someone?' But I walked in and you literally burst into tears. I was kind of shocked that it meant so much to you. But it was really emotional, just seeing you. It was like a proper reunion.

Yes, it was amazing. We had the best weekend. And because we'd always laughed about the fact that you had sung 'Wild Thing' at your own wedding, we went to this restaurant and there was a band, and you got up and sang 'Wild Thing' for us, and did it brilliantly.

Well, we were in this gorgeous outdoor restaurant, and the night before we'd had this lovely dinner on the beach for your birthday, and everybody had made a speech. Then, the next day, when we went to this restaurant, we travelled on two big minibuses, and there was a band playing, and everybody was drinking tequila. And I don't know what possessed me, but at the restaurant I said to the band, 'Can you play "Wild Thing"?' And they said, 'Yeah, it's just a couple of chords, really.' So I thought, 'Yes, come on, sing it.' It was just something that I decided to do on the spot. And I knew that the only way I would get away with it was to absolutely, completely give it my all. And not think about the fact that there were professional singers there. I mean, Harry Styles was there, for god's sake, but I had to just go for it. And I did. I improvised the lyrics and made them specific to you. And I just remember singing and seeing your face – the joy on your face. I can't remember what words I sang. I wish I could remember. But I felt so glad that I'd done it afterwards. It felt like

one of those things where if I don't do it, I'll regret it . . . And I loved it.

It was amazing. And Harry Styles was going to you, 'I can't believe you just did that.'

Yeah, he looked a bit in shock. I don't know if it was in a good way or bad. But he was such fun on the bus on the way home – I remember he had this playlist going and right in the middle he put on the Welsh national anthem. And I was singing my heart out at the back of the bus, 'Gwlad! Gwlad! Pleidiol wyf I'm gwlad!' Such a laugh.

Yeah, it was an amazing time. And at some point during that birthday weekend, I said to you, 'Do you want to think about doing more *Gavin & Stacey*? You know, I think it might be time.'

Yeah, we had that conversation sitting by the pool during the day. It wasn't like a drunken sudden decision or anything. It had been mentioned over the years so many times and while I said I wasn't keen to do it, there were times when I did think about it, because I remember I used to make notes and write down my thoughts about what could happen if we did do a new episode. And we used to text each other ideas and things like that as well. So it just felt, because now we'd finally come together after this period of not really being in touch, maybe that made it feel more concrete. We could actually sit down and go, 'Well, what would happen in this special?'

But I think there was something deeper going on as well, you know. I think we hadn't been in touch that much, and it just felt really lovely, actually, to be there with you that weekend, because it sort of brought us back together. I came away from the Mexico trip in 2018 thinking, 'Right, let's do this.'

CHAPTER 11

Coming back: creating
The Finale

JAMES: We agreed you'd come over to write with me in LA the following month.

RUTH: So, September 2018. And I had an idea I emailed you about: 'How about this for a thread?: Pam and Mick have a murder mystery evening!'
  That never happened.

Haha, but you came out to LA in one of our hiatus weeks from *The Late Late Show* in September 2018, and we wrote together for a week. And then you came back the following February.

And it was funny because we wanted to keep it a total secret, and my friends were asking me why I was going out to LA again, and I would just say, 'Oh, for a holiday, and I'm going to go round the studios and stuff,' and they'd ask, 'Are you going to see James Corden?' And I'd say, 'I might do, yeah . . .'

I think originally we had thought we would tell the entire story in that 2019 special. Because in our hearts, the absolute ending had to be that Smithy and Nessa finally got together. Got married, in fact.

Yeah, we had an idea at one point of doing two specials, but one would be a total secret. So the idea was that after we put the special out on Christmas Day of 2019, we'd have another episode on New Year's Day, which was a total secret. So the show would finish as Nessa goes down on one knee and says, 'Marry me,' and then we'd say, 'Find out what happens New Year's Day, BBC One.' We were even thinking that the BBC could put something else in the listings, like a fake show, so there'd be a massive surprise when our show came on instead. But because of my schedule with *The Late Late Show* back then and only having limited time in the summer, and the behemoth task of trying to deliver two episodes, it was too much to take on.

Did you know that's one of my favourite words, 'behemoth'? It's pronounced 'be-hee-moth', isn't it? But sometimes I like to say 'beh-heh-moth', which I think sounds a bit more biblical . . .

That's so funny, because you get so annoyed about the way that words are pronounced. It's the only thing that winds you up. Apart from me, sometimes.

But I do think that's another way of saying 'beh-heh-moth'.

I don't think anyone says 'beh-heh-moth'. In the same way that no one says 'po-tah-to', which really undercuts the entire song – You say po-tay-to, I say po-tah-to, 'let's call the whole thing off'!

And like 'Billy Jo-ell' instead of just Billy Joel – that's another weird pronunciation.

Which no one ever says!

But anyway, once we decided to do one new Christmas special, I went out to LA to work on it with you. It felt like a big challenge because of the ten-year gap between finishing series three and writing that new special.

Even though we'd kept the characters alive, when it got round to actually writing the 2019 episode, we came very close to quitting.

Yeah, we had a crisis. We went through a few days of thinking, 'This isn't going to work . . .'

Some bits we'd written were really good. But then we read what we'd written, about fifty pages, and as a whole it just wasn't right. It wasn't good. We thought, 'Oh no, actually, it's shit.'

Then we had dinner with our partners, Jules and David, and sat there saying, in all honesty, 'Thank God we never told anyone about us writing it because at least we know now this thing that had always been there, where we were thinking with this show, "Should we? Shouldn't we? Can we? Can't we?" – well, now it's gone, it's done.' And I remember saying to you, 'Look, if this is it and if we're never going to write these characters again, we at least owe it to them to go back in and work out why it isn't working.'

And we realized that what we'd written for the characters of Stacey and Gavin just didn't work. Because the show is called *Gavin & Stacey*, and the truth is, if you don't nail those characters and what they are doing, none of it matters. None of it makes sense. It just doesn't. It becomes a cartoon, is the truth. Without them holding it down, the whole show is a cartoon.

Yes, we were looking at 'Does Gavin have an affair?'

Yeah, we wrote scenes where we'd see him having drinks after work, and he's talking to a girl, etc.

It was just fucking soapy. So then we sat down together and talked about what the challenges are in a marriage when you're fifteen years in, and maybe they're just bored and they're not having much sex and the kids are taking over too much. And you suggested, 'What if she's kept the matches from when they stayed at that hotel in London? What if she's kept something from when they first met, and now she's just trying to keep the spark alight?' And we were like, 'Oh my god, he could play the Paolo Nutini song "Last Request" on his phone that was on the radio the first time they got into bed together.' And we basically wrote that scene set in Barry Island. I remember when we came up with the idea of Gavin playing that Paolo Nutini song, I was like, 'Ah, that's like a time capsule, because we all know that song, but we haven't heard it in such a long time.' But the great thing about music is how you're transported back to a moment in your life, even if that moment is not specific. So I remember us writing that scene and I said to you, 'What if he does this? *Remember this?*' And I played the song on my phone, and the hair stood up on the back of both of our necks, and you said, 'Right, we just have to bottle that now.'

We also had this whole discussion about service stations!

Well, what *Gavin & Stacey* really needs ... and the reason *The Finale* is ninety minutes long is because if it was an hour, it would be *all* plot. You need the air to let the characters breathe. You need the other stuff. You need the oven gloves from series two:

```
          PETE (to Mick)
     Do you mind if I ask you a
     personal question?


               MICK
     Sure


               PETE
     Where did you get them oven
     gloves? I tell you why I am
     asking. Dawn got me a pair
     last Christmas. I loved the
     colour. It was like a charcoal
     grey. But I swear I could
     have only picked up two or
     three baking trays, four at
     tops, and they melted straight
     through.


               MICK
     And you never replaced them?


               PETE
     No.
```

>   SMITHY
> So what are you on now, tea
> towels?

>   PETE
> Yeah.

>   MICK
> That's not good.

>   SMITHY
> You're a fool. See that
> blister? That's tea towels.

>   PETE
> I know.

> MICK (hands Pete the oven gloves)
>   Give these a try . . .

>   PETE (puts on oven gloves)
> Yeah that is nice. (uses oven
> gloves to remove lamb roast
> from the oven, puts it back
> in, then removes it again.)
> Can't feel a thing!

You need Smithy's curry order from series three . . .

> Chicken bhuna
> Lamb bhuna
> Prawn bhuna

```
Mushroom rice
bag of chips
Keema naan
and nine poppadoms
And I'd like a Sag aloo as
well please Mick!
```

Well, you need that stuff. And what we realized is that the 2019 special didn't have enough of that stuff in the script, and we knew it was missing something. And then over dinner, my wife, Jules, was talking about how she loves the M4, because of the various services along the way, and then we were talking about it and she asked the rest of us which services we stop at.

Yeah, and I said we stop at Membury because it's got a Waitrose . . .

And I said I never stop at Membury. I stop at Leigh Delamere, all the time. And Heston's good.

Then me and David were like, 'Heston? Are you serious?'

And we looked at each other, and we were like, 'Oh, they should just do *this*. We should do this discussion about service stations. And then that became a key part of the pub scene. And then Nessa and Smithy woke up together the next morning because they got drunk. And then Sonia arrived, and then we couldn't slow down from then on, really . . . it was like turn-ing on a tap. And we were confident we had enough for an episode. And then we were like, 'Oh well, now we're doing it! Now we're shooting it.'

And so you emailed Charlotte Moore [BBC director of content] the next day to arrange a private call. But you didn't mention what it was about.

No, so we sat in the little office that I had in our house, and called Charlotte from my phone. And I said, 'Hi. I just wanted to talk to you about some-thing . . .'

And she sounded all intrigued . . .

And I said, 'The thing is, I'm sat here with Ruth Jones.'

And there was a gasp, wasn't there? Cos she must have guessed what it might mean . . .

And I said, 'We think we may have a show for you. A *Gavin & Stacey* special . . . if you'd be interested in that.'

And she was like, 'Yes, of course!' And that was it. Except it had to stay completely hush-hush.

So we finished the script, and then we had to do these awful rewrites, which was basically either me waking up at five a.m. in LA and you really staying up late. Or vice versa, with you waking up early and me doing it at midnight. It was awful. Not fun.

But we had some great moments on that episode. Nessa giving the taps as Christmas presents was brilliant, and definitely your idea, James.

Yeah, well, the previous Christmas, Nessa and Dave Coaches gave everyone an individual Celebration chocolate, so we needed something in that vein, but even better. It just came to me, and I said, 'I think she should just give everybody a tap!'

That's *brilliant*. You are so good at coming up with such amazing things. You describe yourself as a Duracell Bunny, and you are like that, and sometimes I feel really awful if you suggest something and I go, 'I know, but that means that you have to do X, Y and Z,' but that's how our writing relationship sort of works. But we both love it when we say something that really makes each other laugh, like I remember with the mature cheddar and Smithy saying 'Midge Ure' ... It was so funny and it's lovely when that happens. I think we both get a great sense of satisfaction when we come up with something like that ...

                    GAVIN
          It's a great song.

                    SMITHY
          A modern Christmas classic.

                    GAVIN
          Geldof at his best.

                    SMITHY
          And Majure. Always gets
          overlooked.

                    GAVIN
          D'you mean Midge Ure?

                    SMITHY
          Yeah - Majure.

                    GAVIN
          It's not one word. It's
          two. It's Midge Ure.

                    SMITHY
          Is it? I thought it was
          Majure.
          Y'know like Majure Cheddar.

**And then there was 'Fairytale Of New York', which I loved
doing with Uncle Bryn.**

It was such a magical moment, Bryn and Nessa singing that, but then there was a bit of controversy over that, which was sort of mad and sad, because we'd used the original Pogues lyrics, and I really don't think it had crossed our mind in any way what those original lyrics are. And it was really hard, actually, cos I feel like – and this is gonna sound wrong, but I do think it's true – I feel like often with the show I think I take the brunt of any negative coverage.

Mm. Yeah, well, you were in a really difficult position, cos you were doing a show every night, you were completely in the spotlight, and the controversy was over the use of a certain word. But I was very adamant that it was being misinterpreted, that the lyrics were not being seen in their original context. For me, the etymology of that word is Scouse Irish slang for 'layabout'. And I felt so pushed into a corner with it. Because it goes without saying that there was no intention to offend – the show is about joy and inclusivity and fun. But suddenly I feel I'm being told I'm being offensive. So I said I didn't want to change it, because then that would be admitting to something we hadn't done.

And then I felt pretty adamant that we change it, because I want the show to live for ever. And we're in a time when, for example, *Little Britain* got taken off iPlayer, and they used to fill arenas. What I felt was so upsetting about the Pogues thing was that there was a way to be kinder about it. In truth, it never crossed our minds. We never even wrote the lyrics out. In the script we just said Nessa and Bryn sing 'Fairytale Of New York'. And that was it.

I remember we did an interview in one of the newspapers and they made out they were going to do this joint interview with both of us. Actually, they just wanted to interview you, and included me as a sort of sidebar, which they didn't tell me about. And then they asked me about comedy and about people's tastes, and whether people were more easily offended now, and they used my reply as if I was talking specifically about 'Fairytale Of New York'. And it was me saying something like, 'Oh, none of the characters mean any harm', and, in fact, I wouldn't have said that. If they'd asked me specifically about it, I would have made it clear that that word, like a lot of words now, has a different meaning.

The thing is, because of social media, there'll always be something that's picked up on, some supposed controversy . . .

I'm really glad that I'm not on social media but, ironically, I probably read more stuff about us than you. [In August 2025 I gave in and joined Instagram . . . mainly because there were a few others out there claiming to be me.]

Oh god, you read a thousand times more things than I do.

Oh, I couldn't bear it if I was on social media and someone messaged me like that. But it was unfortunate for you that you had to bear the brunt of that.

But I absolutely am loyal to you, and I realized what an awkward position you were in. So we changed it.

I still love that scene. And ultimately, it doesn't really affect the show that we changed it. The scene is still a brilliant fun night in the pub on Christmas Eve. It's one of my favourite moments from the episode. That and our cliffhanger ending . . .

```
          NESSA (to Smithy)
     I won't lie you're not
     everyone's cup of tea but when
     all's said and done, you're
     tidy. And if truth be told, I
     loves you. I knows it's weird
     alright. But I do. I loves
     you. With all my heart. So,
     will you marry me?

          SMITHY
     What?
```

```
                    NESSA
       Marry me . . .
```

'With all my heart' . . . That's the moment. You are amazing in that scene. It's honestly one of the best bits of acting I've ever seen. What you did in that moment, with that character . . . Because Nessa is this person who's had this unbelievably chequered life, and out of the four of them – Gavin, Stacey, Smithy and Nessa – we've seen Gavin be quite vulnerable when they were trying for a baby. We've seen Stacey be vulnerable when she wasn't happy living in Essex. We've seen Smithy be vulnerable when he had that fear, that moment of terror when he felt Nessa might marry Dave Coaches in the 2008 Christmas special, when he said, 'Don't marry him. I'm not saying marry me. I'm just saying don't marry him.' So in three of the four main characters, we've seen that vulnerability, and yet Nessa has always had this quite stoic, hardened exterior, really.

Yeah, it's always been like nothing really hurts her. Nothing really fazes her.

When we wrote it, I remember thinking that it was going to be really powerful. And then the joy of watching you do it . . . I honestly think it's when she says, 'With all my heart.' It's so good. It makes me tingle now, thinking about it. It's as good a piece of acting as I've ever seen, close up, in the flesh. And I'm so proud of you for it.

It's very lovely of you to say that. It's very lovely. But you know what? The reason that I feel that it was so convincing, that moment, was because you and I have been on this journey for a long, long time. We've known each other since 2000 when we were hanging out at the Crowne Plaza. And so that scene, which we filmed in the middle of the night – because it was set at Christmas, of course, but we were making it in the summertime, so it had to be dark – and we were there, just the two of us, on that street that had meant so much to us . . . I was there as myself, Ruth, looking at you, my dear friend James, and when I said that I loved you with all my heart . . . I was saying it to you.

Had that 2019 special not included the last ninety seconds, I think it would be *fine*. I do. I think it's good, it's got lovely moments . . . You've got Bryn cooking the dinner, and Gavin and Stacey have rekindled their love, which is a brilliant, lovely moment. And services on the M4 is a fun scene.

But that ninety seconds – that proposal – I think earned everything. And we always knew that it was going to end there. So suddenly you've got a cliffhanger. Then you've got something to talk about. You've got intrigue, you know – what did they say? What didn't they say? And that's it. That's just story-telling, I suppose. It's ending a chapter and thinking, 'I'm going to pick up here,' and actually, you pick up somewhere completely different. You just keep drawing people in. That's all we were trying to do.

After the cliffhanger, for a while I felt – and I don't know if I'm speaking for you now, James, but I think for a time we thought, 'Actually, why not end it there? Why not end it that way?' Because we've always felt that those characters carry on living, that they really exist, which I think is mental, but they carry on living their lives outside of our show. It's just that it's not on TV. So people used to say to me, 'Well, you can't leave it there. How can you leave it there?' And I'd say, 'Why not? Why don't *you* imagine whether Smithy said yes to Nessa's proposal, or whether he said no, and what exactly happened after that?' Because there's nothing wrong in leaving it on that cliff-hanger. So for a while we did think that we could just leave it there. But then we both changed our minds about whether there should be more. I think I was keen to do it.

Yeah, I remember you were keen to do it straight away. You were like, 'Let's do it next summer and put it out next Christmas.'

But, of course, COVID happened then.

And even before that, my reasoning was: I think it puts too much pressure on the writing of it to know that you have a delivery date.

Yes, because the way we'd always done it was to write it because we *wanted* to write it.

And then you're not writing with any pressure. As soon as there's a clock saying, 'This starts shooting on 3 July', or whenever, you are up against it. You can't help but feel it, even in your peripheral vision, and so I remember saying to you, 'I'm up for sitting down and writing it, but let's not have a deadline or anything, because you just don't know how long it's going to take for it to arrive, whatever *it* is.' And in the writing of the 2019 special, there was that very real moment when it was done. It was over. So because of that, the idea of putting any pressure on this new one just felt unnecessary. It was a case of 'when it arrives, it'll arrive', and then about two years after that, just as we were coming out of the pandemic, I said to you, 'I'm not feeling it. I'm not sure.'

And also, do you remember, during COVID I thought we could do something? You know, everybody was doing stuff on Zoom, and I thought we could do something

with all the characters and get everybody in the cast to do it. But you were like, 'No, it's really not going to look good.'

You were really pissed off about that. You were so angry with me about it!

Because I kind of felt we could have given that to people, and they would have loved it.

And my point was, you as Nessa could have done something, but the idea of our whole cast setting up their iPhones and reading something that we wrote seemed . . . a challenge.

Oh yeah, you were obviously right. I actually did do something as Nessa during the pandemic, all about social distancing, because I'd been asked to do it. So I wrote something off my own bat: this little two-minute thing where I said, 'If you sees me every day doing my 5k round Barry, don't even think about breaking that two-metre rule, because I will, quite frankly, tell you to back off! Just because you don't feel ill, don't mean you're not infected. You could be riddled.' But it took me ages to do because I had to get the wig on and do take after take. So you were right! You usually are right.

Thank you!

Yes, yes, you were right, but I just had the feeling that I wanted to give something back to people at a time of crisis. You can't blame me for that!

Thinking about it, what we actually should have done – remembering that I was doing an hour of TV every day from my garage during COVID, on *The Late Late Show*, so I was fully aware of how hard it was getting that stuff together – was a live Zoom reading of a *Gavin & Stacey* script, but even then those things don't always work. Anyway, we didn't do that, and then we spoke during the summer of 2023, and by then I was very sure that the proposal in 2019 was an unsatisfactory ending, if it was the end for ever. Like, I love a cliffhanger. But it has to pay off.

And I think people were annoyed – not in a nasty way – but I remember seeing your sister's reaction when we watched it on Christmas Day 2019, and she just could not believe it. She couldn't believe Nessa was left hanging. And when you watch the *Gogglebox* reaction to it, you do go, 'Oh, actually, that is really frustrating.'

Yeah, it's frustrating. Which is great, and it builds anticipation, but it's too frustrating if you don't pay it off eventually.

So anyway, we started to speak about doing one more episode.

I think we both had various points when we talked about doing it, and for one reason or another, you may have said, 'I think we should do it now.' And I was thinking, 'I don't know', and then I can remember a moment when I said, 'I really think we should do this and write it.' And you were like, 'I just don't feel in the right head space.' Because we talk all the time as friends; a lot of the time we were just talking about life stuff. It's weird, sometimes, working with your best friend! Anyway, to get to the point, I said, 'Look, let's just lock in a time.' And it was that summer – August 2023 – and I said, 'Four p.m. Tuesday: let's do a Face-Time.' And we were both in exactly the same place . . .

We both had the same idea, didn't we?

Yes, which was: let's do a film.

I'd written down a couple of thoughts I'd had before we arranged this meeting, thinking it could be a film, but we hadn't discussed anything beforehand. And then when we got together, you said, 'I hope this could be a film.' And I went, 'Well, this is what I wrote last night.' So that was quite weird.

So then we really played around with that idea of it being a film, and we wrote some of it with that mentality, and then the more we read it, we both felt the same way, that . . .

. . . It's not a cinema film.

And we realized it shouldn't be. Yes, there's a world where you meet these movie people and you talk finances, and everybody says how *The Inbetweeners Movie* was such a success. But we were like, '*The Inbetweeners Movie* is very different, because that could be a film – irrespective of the show – about four boys going to Spain to lose their virginity. It's sort of an *American Pie* rite-of-passage movie.' The idea of our characters blown up that big, and the expectation of what that should be, doesn't work. The fact is, they've always been in the corner of your room, and that's where they should remain.

And I spend quite a lot of time up in the Highlands of Scotland, and I just thought, 'My friends there will have to drive for two hours to get to the nearest cinema in Inverness. They're not going to do that!' Even so, there was something exciting about the idea of a film.

Yes, it feels like an exciting thing to talk about, but actually what you realize is: there is nothing more exciting than the collective experience of different generations of families and friends sitting around watching the TV on Christmas Day. It's such a wonderfully British thing to do. And you know, when we started the show twenty years ago, the idea that it would be one of those shows that had a Christmas special was far beyond anything we ever dreamed of. Just the notion of BBC One, Christmas Day: that means so much to us, I think.

Also, it's important to remember the pressure of it on both of us, because when a show announces it's the last one, it doesn't always deliver.

We do have that feeling that this is the absolute story we wanted to tell. And because we always thought of it as a film, I think we always said, 'This is probably going to be ninety minutes, right?' We had written about two-thirds when we called the BBC. And they were thrilled. They were over the moon.

But again, you know, we wrote it with the same sense of freedom, really, so we didn't tell the BBC what we were doing till we'd done those sixty-five pages. We didn't call them, because then we just had the freedom of going, 'Right now, nobody knows. So we've got as long as we need with no constraints.'

Although we were conscious of the practicality of it. We knew the latest we could finish filming it would be October to get it on that Christmas, 2024, and even that was pushing it.

But we could have held it for another year. So there was still no pressure to deliver it. So all you're actually thinking about is the characters, and who are they and what are they doing.

Do you know, what was quite interesting was that nobody cottoned on to the fact that it wasn't going to be set at Christmas. We decided that from early on . . .

Yes, two Christmases was a lot, and to do a third would be too much. Too much Christmas music.

Yes, that would be sugar-coating it.

And no one gets married at Christmas.

Yes, we managed to keep a lot of information secret. Though I would say, something that really upset me was back in February of 2024, before the show had been announced – a journalist from *Deadline* leaked the news that there was to be another *Gavin & Stacey* special. I've no idea how they found out. But I was in Dublin at

SCENE **80** SLATE **3914** TAKE **1**

Gavin & Stacey
The Finale

DIR: CHRISTINE GERNON DOP: IAN ADRIAN

DATE **7TH Oct '24** ROLL # **A #97**

Last day on the Wests' street

Smithy and Sonia - the weddin
that never was

Nessa loving Sonia's hen

Doing rewrites for
Finale over Zoom -
Cardiff to LA

Smithy's stag - Smithy (James
Corden) with Budgie (Russell
Tovey), Dirtbox (Andrew Knott)
and Fingers (Samuel Anderson)

Bryn's been on the Ravgift

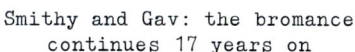

Smithy and Gav: the bromance
continues 17 years on

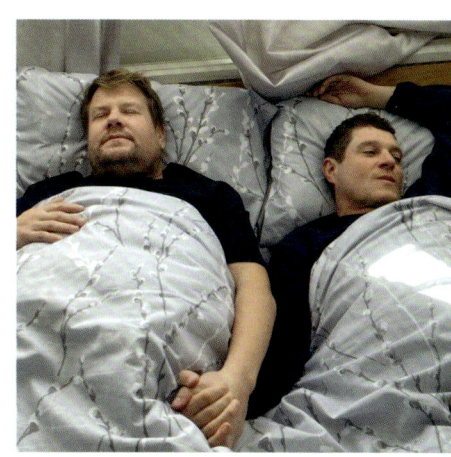

Southampton-bound

Last day at Pam and
Mick's house

Marco Zeraschi,
the Marco of Marco's

The train back to Paddington
after filming

Pam and Nessa

Dave and Gwen, together at last. Who'd have thought?

Last day of filming - James, Ruth, Sophie Hebron (second Assistant Director), with us since 2007

(Ruth had three hours' sleep the night before)

Our brilliant second and fir Assistant Directors, Sophi Hebron and Steve Roberts

wo old Porthcawl Comp kids, Rob and Ruth

A rare cuddle
between Pete and
Dawn (Adrian
Scarborough and
Julia Davis)

Radio 2 Takeover

Deciding on their karaoke song

With Sarah Fraser, our
lovely Producer

James, Mat, Joanna, Ruth
Smithy, Gavin, Stacey, Nessa

The Soiree / the night before
The Stag at Pam and Mick's

The crowds watch Nessa leave

The final shot ever

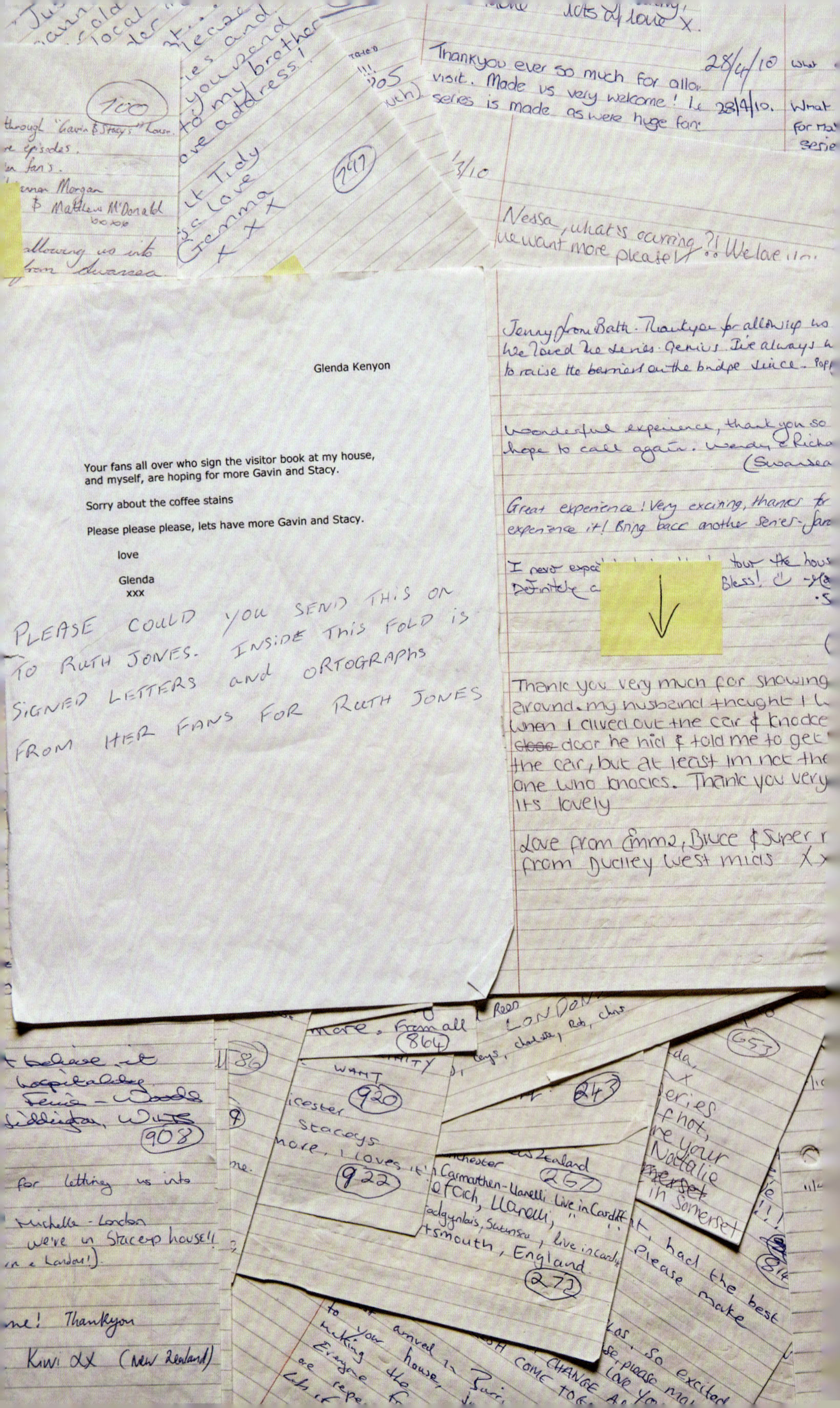

Glenda Kenyon

Your fans all over who sign the visitor book at my house,
and myself, are hoping for more Gavin and Stacy.

Sorry about the coffee stains

Please please please, lets have more Gavin and Stacy.

love

Glenda
xxx

PLEASE COULD YOU SEND THIS ON
TO RUTH JONES. INSIDE THIS FOLD IS
SIGNED LETTERS and ORTOGRAPHS
FROM HER FANS FOR RUTH JONES

(surrounding handwritten note fragments)

through "Gavin & Stacy's" house
re episodes.
fans.
Ciaran Morgan
& Matthew M'Donald xoxo

allowing us into
from Swansea

100

friend
es and
you send
to my brother
ve address!

t Tidy
ts Love
Gemma x
x

747

lots of love x

Thankyou ever so much for allow
visit. Made us very welcome! L 28/4/10. What
series is made as were huge fan.   for ma
                                         serie

28/4/10

Nessa, what's occuring?! We
we want more please!!! Welae in.

Jenny from Bath. Thankyou for allowing us
We loved the series. Genius. I've always h
to raise the barriers on the bridge since. Popp

Wonderful experience, thank you so
hope to call again. Wendy & Richa
                              (Swansea

Great experience! Very exciting, thanks for
experience it! Bring back another series- Jam

I never expec   tour the hous
Definitely a   Bless! C -Ya
                                    S

↓

Thank you very much for showing
around. my husband thought I w
when I arrived out the car & knocke
close door he hid & told me to get
the car, but at least im not the
one who knocks. Thank you very
its lovely

Love from Emma, Bruce & Super r
from Dudley West Mids X >

t believe it
hospitality
Fiona - Woods
Siddington, Wilts
903

for letting us into

Michelle - London
we're in Stacey's house!!
(n a London!)

me! Thankyou

Kiwi dx (New Zealand)

more. From all
864

LONDON

want
920

icester
Stacey's
more. I loves it
9 22

247

653

Manchester New Zealand
Carmarthen - Llanelli, Live in Cardiff
of Cich, Llanelli
adgynlais, Swansea + live in card
tsmouth, England.
272

267

da,
X
eries
, if not,
ne your
Natalie
erset
in Somerset

I had the best
Please make

to   arrived in
kking house,
Everyone   the
are repe

the time doing *Sister Act* and I had to do a lot of publicity for the show. And I went on a national radio show and was presented with all this tabloid coverage saying that there was going to be a final episode. And I had to blatantly LIE – on air. And I hated doing that. But what was worse was that all these friends and relatives were texting me, all excited, saying, 'Is it true? Oh my god, is it true??' and I had to lie to them, too. The thing is, we couldn't announce it until all the cast were booked and the budget, etc. was worked out. I was so upset. What got me was that the news was OUR news to share. Not some journalist from *Deadline*. And he took away that little bit of joy from us. So when we were able to officially announce it, it wasn't as exciting as it could have been, because people were going, 'Yeah, well, I knew that – it was in the press a few months ago.' I actually kept a list of all the friends and family who'd messaged me at the time of the leak, and I apologized to them for lying and explained why it had to be that way.

So then we were into the rewrites. And by then you were doing *Sister Act* in the West End and I was doing *The Constituent*, a play at the Old Vic with Anna Maxwell Martin, and the rewrites were hard. Rewrites are usually the worst bit of the process, but we came up with some really good stuff for this *Finale* episode.

It was a godsend, yes. Smithy's fear of being on his own in the dark, Mick's speech at the stag do ... there was some really, really good stuff. Oh, and Pete and Dawn's argument – we got really hysterical writing that, d'you remember? 'Piss off. Just piss right off.' I don't know why it made us laugh so much. Just the sheer awfulness of them, I guess.

Sometimes we were writing until eleven p.m. We often write in three chunks – like, morning, afternoon, evening – and we just keep going because, as we've explained, so much of it's just us chatting nonsense to each other, and then having to take naps. And this time we talked a lot about 'what should we have for lunch', you know? And then we took walks to get fresh air, so the hours we were writing was probably, like, four hours, even though we might have been together in the room for about twelve. When we were in those shows on stage, first of all we couldn't do Wednesdays, because we both had two shows that day. And then, you know, your show was much more arduous than mine, in many ways ...

No, it wasn't!

You had to do big songs!

You had all the emotional stuff!

Yeah, but mine was only ninety minutes . . . So I got an earlier night than you.

Yes, I guess that's true.

So we were doing probably eleven till four, when normally we would do ten till eight, nine, ten . . . or later.

As long as we were enjoying it, we would just carry on. And we did.

Then we had to break the news of *The Finale* happening to the cast.

Last time, in 2019, we had split it up between us, so you called half the cast and I spoke to the rest. And what we decided to do this time was swap over, so I phoned the ones you'd spoken to last time. It was nice.

Jo Page had the best reaction to the news. I called her and she just said, 'Oh my god. Are you serious? Are you serious? James? Are you serious? Oh my god, so is it all done, then?'

Yes, Jo always has the best reaction.

I also rang Alison [Steadman] and I couldn't get hold of her. She thought it was someone messing around. Because I sent her a WhatsApp saying, 'Hey, Alison, this is James Corden. I played Jamie Rymer in the series *Fat Friends* with you many years ago. Is there a time when we can talk?' And it went grey on Whats-App, and then it went blue, and I remember texting you going, 'She's just not replying.'

And I rang Larry, and I said, 'Larry, are you on your own?' And he said, 'Yeah, it's all right, I've got these Spanish guys with me but they don't know what I'm saying.' With Rob Brydon, I'd had lunch with him a week or so before we decided to contact the cast, and it was one of those weird moments when he just mentioned, 'Oh, you know, people keep on asking me if there's going to be any more *Gavin & Stacey*. And I say the same thing every time.' I was just quiet. And he went, 'Oh my god, is there going to be more?' And I went, 'You can't say anything...'
  Rob was like, 'Wow. I was not expecting that!'

Then, when you've got the cast on board, it becomes such a scheduling nightmare it feels like you're playing Jenga in reverse. You build a script, then someone says they're not available and the Jenga collapses.

But for *The Finale* we didn't get involved with the scheduling, which we had done the last time. People better than us at dealing with it did a brilliant job at making sure the whole cast were available and on set when we needed them.

We also had a WhatsApp group from the last special in 2019, although I'd left at the end of the filming because I'm just a bit weird like that. I just can't bear being in groups. And WhatsApp groups are such hard work. When I did *Sister Act* on stage, I said to everyone, 'Well, I am going to leave tomorrow, and just so you know, I will be leaving the group, but don't take it personally.' So I did leave after the 2019 *Gavin & Stacey* special. And obviously we didn't think we were going to do another one, and you were like, 'Oh god, what's the matter with you? You know, just stay in the group! Because nobody posts on there hardly, anyway!' So then I re-joined for this *Finale*.

And once we got the cast together, I also decided to stay in a hotel with everyone because I really wanted to be part of it, and I had never done that before. Previously, I had been based at home. And it made such a difference. I just thought: this is the last time we're ever going to do this. I want to experience the whole thing. And so me and you were next door to each other in the hotel, and it was just such fun. It was like going on a school trip with your friends.

In series one to three and the 2019 special, the cast stayed at a hotel in central Cardiff, and when you go in you've got the reception, and there's one of those fireplaces on the right-hand side, and then some big armchairs, and then you walk through to the bar, and that's a lot more lively. But Alison Steadman used to sit in her chair and have a gin and tonic, and everybody would sort of join, and it became known as 'Ali's Parlour'. And Ali's Parlour was one of the things that was a little bit of a blot on the landscape in terms of changing hotels. We had to ask everybody on the WhatsApp group: 'How do you feel about this new hotel?' And Rob Brydon replied straight away saying yes, he was up for changing. It was all about stick or twist, and Rob was absolutely twist straight away. So were the others. Except Alison, who said she'd miss Ali's Parlour. And Melanie said she would miss the swimming pool. But we said, 'Well, there is a spa there.' Although really it's just kind of a hot tub. So they were the only two of the cast that were a bit wary about the hotel switch. But I think they were glad in the end. And I told Jo Page separately that they've got an Elemis spa. She went, 'Oh, you had me at Elemis.' So yeah, it was good fun. And I'm so glad I decided to stay there and not at home.

It made such a difference to me. I mean, I would say our friendship today is stronger than it's ever been in the last twenty years since we started writing *Gavin*

& Stacey. And that's remarkable. I don't want to name any names, but everyone else who, twenty years ago, wrote a TV show for the BBC, a comedy show – particularly a comedy show – everybody else has either biblically fallen out, or biblically fallen out and then come back round, just about. There is no other partnership still standing. And that is about more than the success of the show or anything. That's the thing that I think is most extraordinary about all this. Because what it tells you is this working relationship between us, plus fame, plus financial agreements, plus all this stuff, puts an extraordinary amount of pressure on a friendship, and we felt that. We have felt all that, but, within all of it, the friendship has never, ever disappeared. We may have had a couple of sibling-like rows, and I remember one time we had an actual argument on the phone, which never degenerated into shouting or anything, but let's just say you were Tottenham and I was Arsenal, and we were both totally entrenched, right? And you said, 'OK, all right, yeah, OK, yeah, all right. Then, bye!' and put the phone down.

Then you called back immediately and went, 'How are you?!'

The friendship is just so important.

CHAPTER 12

Gathering the gang:
making *The Finale*

RUTH: The filming of the final episode was wonderful, although there were challenges, like keeping all the secrets from getting revealed in the papers, and keeping the return of Sonia as this huge surprise.

JAMES: I remember when the idea of starting the episode that way came to me. I remember it so vividly because I was in America at that point, and this was in the period when we were thinking: 'Will we do it, won't we do it, should we do it, shall we do it?' I had this idea at three o'clock in the morning, and I called you, and I said, 'I wonder if we could trick everybody for the first six or seven minutes of *The Finale* into thinking that they're just going to watch a wedding between Nessa and Smithy?' Because what was really interesting was, after the 2019 special, all people would say to us was, 'What does Smithy say?'

They would never say, 'Who did he choose?' Because I don't even think Sonia was in people's peripheral vision. So I remember calling you on my drive into work before we'd even decided to do another episode and saying, 'I've had an idea if we do one ... I wonder if we could do this.' And then the way that the writing of the show works is: I'll just keep going to you like the excitable Duracell Bunny I am, and suggest something and you'll say, 'Nah.' And then as soon as you go, 'Ooh, yeah,' we both go, 'I know that it's great.' And I remember so vividly having that chat with you, and you going, 'That's really good. I wonder if we can pull it off.'

We've never really forensically plotted the show, but I think in this special we did. We kept asking, 'How do we satisfy this audience? How does every character get their bit?' And so to lull them into this false situation was such a magic trick.

And as I say, the entire 2019 special really comes down to the proposal from Nessa, and you forget that Smithy's told Gavin that he's bought a ring and he's going to propose to Sonia. But five years later, after the cliffhanger, the idea of Sonia being the one he's marrying wasn't even in anyone's mind. So then we thought if we could hide it, and seed it in with all the talk from the characters about there being a wedding, with Stacey talking to Gavin about it, then immediately the audience would go, 'Oh, we're not picking up exactly where we were, but we're going to watch Smithy and Nessa's wedding.' Which is a completely believable and very good special, probably. We'd see them getting ready, the stag do, hen do, bit of jeopardy somewhere. Then you see the marriage, then the reception, then they all sing the Elbow song: 'One day like this a year would see me right' . . . then they get in a car and they leave. That's a very, very good Christmas special, but I don't think it's a great story.

So that notion of taking it all the way, and what we really wanted to do – after seeing in the last special how Nessa and Smithy got drunk and slept together on Christmas Eve – what we were hoping was that the audience would think that they were about to sleep together again.

Then we had that scene very early on of Nessa telling Smithy what she'd said to their son: 'Let your dad cut loose. He's getting married. [A beat] He's getting married.' Then we'd hold. Then we thought that we had to resolve what had happened. So it struck us: what if no one knows? So nobody knows at all that she even proposed that night. He hasn't told anyone, and nor has she, so then you get this thing where – and it sounds a bit convoluted – what you really want is the audience to be going,

'Fuck, I didn't know that he was marrying Sonia!'
And the audience did. Then, oh my god, the audience realizes that the other characters on the show
don't know that Nessa proposed. So you're playing
this poker game with information – the audience is
working out who knows what about who.

And then, after that bit with the salami on bread –
where Nessa and Smithy are talking and she says,
'You doin' that all wrong,' and they share a look –
then they start dancing, and she's pouring wine in
his mouth, and you want the audience to go, 'Oh,
they're going to go to bed together, yeah? Oh, no,
they're not.' Then they have an unsuccessful stag
and hen, and then they meet on the way to a drive-
through, and there's talk about the corn on the cob.
So then the audience are thinking that is where it
happens: 'They're going to sleep together! Call
off that wedding! Nessa and Smithy are gonna get
married in place of those two!' But then you've got
Neil the Baby leaving, and Nessa leaving, heading
off to the ships. These are all just good classic tropes
of rom-coms, really, but it's about making them
surprising.

We tried to keep the Sonia surprise as long as
possible. Because, historically, the show starts with
Gavin and Stacey on the phone. And then often
you go to Pam and Mick's. Sometimes you go to
Bryn and Gwen, but it'll be one of those two, and

then the first eight minutes of every episode, and certainly the specials, is just reintroducing the audience to the eight or so characters that you love, and here they are, and this is what they're doing. And now we're going to get them all together, and that's when the show will really start to cook. So I think that eight minutes or so into *The Finale* was as long as we could go, because you see Pam and Mick, Bryn, Gwen, Stacey, Gavin and Smithy, and then *Sonia*, and then the first person you have to see after that is Nessa. So that was, naturally, as long as we could go, because you can't see Nessa before you see Sonia. And then you really want to see Nessa, quick.

And we have to say how brilliant Laura Aikman was as Sonia.

She's been phenomenal. We had auditions and casting sessions for that role. And Laura was the best combination of all the elements of Sonia. On the one hand she came across as a bit of a monster when she needed to be, but she also had to have something nice and empathetic about her as well. And it's a really, really fine line. I just think it's a testament to her acting that it worked so well.

But during filming, we had the paps on location every day, and my huge fear was that Laura coming back would be leaked. And in fact, one journalist did get in

touch and said Laura had been seen in Cardiff, asking for a comment from us. The BBC just told them they don't comment on filming, and that went away. So Laura didn't stay in our hotel. There was all this subterfuge going on . . .

Yes, I think some people thought we were being a bit melodramatic about keeping Laura a secret, until we started shooting. And then once we started shooting, *everyone* understood. Because it's a ball-ache, isn't it? It's not fun if you're on the crew and you're told you have to call her Susan, and she's staying in different hotel rooms, and she can't travel with other members of the cast – all that stuff. And we had to find out if there was an underground car park where we were shooting.

Steve Roberts, our first assistant director, is just glorious, and he's the guy who has to go and tell locations, 'No, I know we're filming in a John Lewis, and I know they've got a wedding section at the John Lewis, but we can't afford to shut the John Lewis down.' So the John Lewis is open, and we're just using part of it. But also, no John Lewis will let us film after hours, and there's still going to be four people who work for John Lewis there. So even in the scene where Smithy is walking through John Lewis on the phone, he doesn't mention Sonia's name. And if you're filming in places like that, they'll ask to see the script, because they won't want their establishment associated with anything that's incredibly inappropriate or whatever. Also, we weren't using the words 'Gavin & Stacey'; we were calling the whole production 'Toffee Apple' for reasons of secrecy. And so then it was decided we needed to build a John Lewis, at which point we were like, 'What? But we're in a John Lewis and it's shut down, and they've got a wedding section!' The design team were like, 'OK, we can do that!' And so we created our own bit of John Lewis.

But then as soon as we started filming, there were hundreds of members of the public there waiting to see it, and there were paparazzi, and something was being written about the show every day. Apparently, three paparazzi had moved to Cardiff from London, and they were staying in an Airbnb, and their sole job was to find out where we were filming.

One of the hardest things to hide was when Sonia and Smithy – Laura and I – were in the car together, because the photographers could use their long lenses, right? So we actually closed a dual carriage-way, and then only shot in the middle of it. So Laura would get out of the car, I'd drive up to turn around and come down, and then she'd get in. Repeatedly. And that was day one of filming.

So there was a lot of paranoia, but that's because we just felt like it was such a treat to hide the surprise of Sonia, and get that moment of shock from the audience. And it was amazing to witness that response at the press launch; it was all we wanted and all we could have asked for.

Laura filmed her parents watching it on Christmas Day. They had no idea she'd done it. And it was so brilliant to see. The utter shock on their faces! But you know what? As satisfying as that reveal of Sonia is, I think that perhaps the best scene in *The Finale* is when Gwen's affair with Dave Coaches is revealed. It's certainly one of my absolute all-time favourite *Gavin & Stacey* moments.

That's you, Ruth. Because you had always asked, I would say, for every series after series one: 'Should Gwen get a boyfriend?' Because you're always thinking about how to integrate a character better. And I think we may have even tried to write something earlier, but it was just that we'd have had to do so much backstory, with respect to Gwen as a character, for it to pay off. You've got to spend time with a character who I don't actually think has ever been in a scene on her own. So the show is these four main people, and then these are the characters around them, and that's the alchemy, right? And so we thought, 'Wouldn't it be great if Gwen is seeing someone?' And it was your idea. You were like, 'What if it's Dave Coaches?'

And suddenly – because we'd really, really tried to put Steffan, who plays Dave, in the 2019 special, but when we'd looked at it in the cold light of day, it didn't work – we had this dream option. Luckily, two things had happened in 2019. He was very busy shooting two things at that point, and he was due to start rehearsing a play and finish shooting something else. And we weren't convinced that the scene we had for him was right. We just weren't. And Steffan was so chill about it that we thought, 'OK, that's fine.' And it was actually better for the story: he's left town, he's gone. And *now* it's the greatest thing for the story, because actually, what we realized was: Steffan hadn't been on the show for fifteen years!

And sitting at home with my family who'd not yet seen it, or at the press screening at the Ham Yard hotel, the reaction when he walked in was *HUGE*. And then you realize: 'Fucking hell – people really care. They care about all of these characters.' And then you think, 'Oh my god! He, Dave, is the only person that knows about the fishing trip.' And so when those things happen, actually what you do is go, 'Ah, we're not in charge of writing this show. It is laying itself out for us.' There's something nobody could plot. It just bubbled up. And that's how the whole finale feels. It really, really does . . .

I think it's the best scene we've written. And I think everybody is at their peak. The great thing about this show is sometimes you want to use one thing from one take and one from another. But we also have such good actors that you're spoilt for choice. Some of the stuff that Rob Wilfort does is so real – I'm not sure he really gets the credit he deserves. It doesn't even feel written. Also, the best thing about that scene – if you go back and just watch Steffan – is that when the fishing trip is mentioned, his eyes do something amazing.

Yeah, I think the reveal of Gwen and Dave Coaches is my favourite scene. And what I love about it is that it is all about the way that, as a nation, we Welsh are so melodramatic in our reactions. So having Jo Page going, 'Dave. Dave Coaches?!' and Rob Wilfort as Jason, who, as you say, is an amazing performer. I love his response to Dave, when he says, 'We didn't know if it was just . . . sexual'.

'Yeah, all right, Dave.'

And then you get Rob Brydon coming in, going, 'HOW LONG?! HOW LONG?!' in his Lycra, with a camera on his head. It was an absolute joy. And I just got to sit there, literally vaping away, watching this scene. All I had to

say was, 'Oh, Gwen, you doing these omelettes then or what?' And I was just corpsing the entire time, because it was like I was in the audience watching it.

But I think it was so exciting to have Gwen have a relationship. It was just so lovely. As you say, James, I think I'd always been rooting for Gwen to meet someone and there was never really a suitable time for that to happen in any of the series. Also, I guess it's a testament to the show and people's fondness for it. I guess people have been watching it on Gold or iPlayer or whatever, so they know Dave and they get the significance of that scene, because Dave hasn't been in the show for fifteen-odd years. So for him to walk in like that ... It was so low key, but so powerful, the way he walked in, said 'All right?' And then Nessa's reaction, going, 'All right, Dave, how's it going? All right?' And Dave replying, 'All right, Ness, how's it going, all right?' I love that completely unfazed response. It was just fantastic. When you and I were writing it, as always, we'd sort of act it out, and just get so hysterical because of the extremity of it. And then ending with everyone *nearly* finding out about ... the fishing trip.

And Rob Brydon epitomizes that Welsh melodrama thing, when he gets so intense. Of course, we had it in episode three of the first series, when he finds out he's going to London for a party. The extremity of his reaction is what makes it. 'A party? In London? This Saturday????'

Yes, it turns into this huge melodrama when Bryn arrives in his cycling gear. I think at some point we were thinking, 'How would he get there that quickly?' And we've got this constant and valid question, which is: why does Bryn come in the back door of Gwen's when he lives over the road, and he would be very likely to have a key? So for a long time, we'd say, 'Well, he doesn't want to disturb anyone.' He is the type of person that would probably have keys for a lot of houses on the street, but then you don't want someone in a different room having to get up and let him in. So you just can't do it. But then you think, 'Well, why is he around and what's he doing?' So I thought, 'What if he's on a bike ride?' And I just love the idea – because Rob Brydon is actually very fit and Bryn has his home gym, remember, and he's probably very much got into cycling, and probably cycles with a few other guys, and would make an investment in all the gear and the GoPro camera and all that stuff – so, yeah, I just thought: 'What if he comes in full Lycra gear?' And his performance is so dramatic, and actually, that's the show: drama without being dramatic in any way. And people do shout in life, and they do get angry, and they do care, and they do feel often like they've been betrayed if they've been lied to.

It was you who suggested he should come in wearing the cycling gear, and when he says, 'Secrets and Lies, Secrets and Lies,' that also works as a call-back to that episode three when they go to Essex, and there's this big argument going on with Pam saying, 'Oh, give it a rest, you leek-munching sheep shagger,' and then Bryn chimes in with, 'Will you just look at yourselves?' It is a call-back to that moment, but also a lovely little nod to your being in the Mike Leigh film. A lot of people wouldn't get it, but those who do really appreciate it.

I'm just such a huge Mike Leigh fan that the ability to have the phrase 'Secrets and Lies' in that scene was so perfect. At one point I wanted him to say, 'Secrets and lies! We're all in pain! Why can't we share our pain? I've spent my entire life trying to make people happy, and the three people I love the most in the world hate each other's guts, and I'm in the middle! I can't take it any more!' My original idea was that maybe Rob did all of Tim Spall's full speech from *Secrets and Lies*, but I can see it would have been too much!

Apart from that scene, I think it was important that we sort of wrapped things up for all the characters in this finale. So there's a lovely moment between Mick and Pam...

>   MICK
> Who'd have thought you and me
> would be the last two standing
> out of all our friends?

>   PAM
> Well no, there's Sue and Bill,
> remember?

>   MICK
> Oh yeah. How is she now, Sue?

>   PAM
> She's good. She's back
> from Turkey; still in a bit of
> discomfort but she's already
> dropped three dress sizes.

>   MICK
> You're gonna need a new
> nickname!

They just have this little moment together. We directed that scene, didn't we? Cos Chris Gernon was ill that day and we had to step in ... thankfully we had a great first assistant director, Steve Roberts, and a great director of photography, Ian Adrian, so we didn't have to do much! We were so relieved when Chris came back, though.

If we're talking about our favourite scenes in *The Finale*, I have to mention that really great call-back to the corn-on-the-cob scene in series two. Actually, our editor said that was her favourite scene in the whole final episode, and I have to say it's one of mine – when Smithy says, 'I do want a corn on the cob,' and Nessa whispers, 'I know.' It's a magnificent performance from you, Ruth. And then the moment is gone. And so then the audience is thinking, 'Oh, they're really not gonna get together.' That's all part of building the tension of: why aren't these two together? You're thinking: 'Fuck, why aren't they together yet? They should just be ripping each other's clothes off.'

What was quite funny for me about the KFC moment was that it's all about a strong sexual connection between Smithy and Nessa, which you and I don't have in real life, obviously. So while I can do the moments of love between us, the sexual bit was kind of more of a challenge, but we just dived in. And because it wasn't anything too overt, because it was just that moment of you saying, 'I do want a corn on the cob,' and you've got the comedy of it being essentially a conversation about a vegetable – a corn on the cob representing their sexual liaison – I had to make that real when I whispered, 'I know.' Whispering was the best way to do that.

I remember how much we were laughing when we did the original corn-on-the-cob scene. Because the whole

idea of me and you doing anything that's kind of sexual is hilarious. Because they've never kissed, for example. I think we decided that really early on.

Well, we wrote a scene in which they were kissing on that first night they met, coming out of the lift or something and going into the room. We wrote 'Gavin and Stacey are walking together and Smithy and Nessa are like animals snogging each other', and then it came to filming it and we were just like, 'Nope!'

                    SMITHY
          Do you want that corn on
          the cob?

                    NESSA
          Is that a euphemism?

                    SMITHY
          What? No. I'm just saying
          there's one corn on the
          cob left, and you can have
          it ...(long pause)... If you
          want it?

                    NESSA
          Do you want me to have it?

                    SMITHY
          I can see the benefits of
          having it. I'd just be worried

how you or I would feel after
having it.

NESSA

Makes no odds to me as it
goes. If I have it, it'll be
a nice addition to the meal.
If I don't, then I'm pretty
full up already. Question is,
Smithy. Do you want the corn
on the cob?

SMITHY

Don't get me wrong. When I
look at it there, all hot
and dripping in butter,
just inviting me in.
I've got a real hankering
for it.

NESSA

Like a real need?

SMITHY

Mhmm. But id just be worried
that if I ate it tonight, I'd
be expected to eat it more
frequently.

NESSA

I wouldn't worry about that if
I was you. Corn on the cob is
a once in a blue moon treat as

```
far as im concerned, which one
eaten, will soon be forgotten,
and won't be mentioned ever
again. To anyone.


                SMITHY
     Well that's good to know.
Long pause . . .
(Nessa licks corn on the cob and feeds
to Smithy.)


                SMITHY
     Oh god.


                NESSA
     So . . . shall we uh?


                SMITHY
     Yeah.
```

We just couldn't kiss, no. But I think it's really good for their characters as well. So when they get married at the end of *The Finale* we had to explain to the registrar that Smithy and Nessa never kiss.

They'll never kiss, and that's part of the reason why it can't carry on. We don't want to see them as a couple. It would be awful. It would be a terrible show. You don't want to see them doing that.

Them not kissing was a chance to have a bit of comedy during this big moment as well. We always try to keep those bits of comedy in, like when Bryn is reading the letter from Trevor [Stacey's father] to Stacey en route to the wedding, and it's an emotional moment. But Bryn says, 'You want me to do it in your dad's voice, with the lisp and everything?' I love that undercutting of the emotion. I think it's what makes the show so lovely.

One of my favourite moments is when you say the line, 'I ain't got no plans, Smithy, we both knows that.' It's beautiful. I wish there wasn't a cut in there, but you took a drag and flicked the cigarette, and then it cuts back to me. But the reason we cut to Smithy and back to her is Nessa should never take her eyes off him, and she does to flick the cigarette. Ideally, what you want is Nessa saying, 'I ain't got no plans, Smithy,' and it cuts back to her and she's still there. Because then it's really serious.

But it was just a joy watching you all the time.

Oh, babe!

Seriously. What you've managed to do is take this character who, in the same episode, says, 'This is the quietest the slots have been in all the 47 years I've worked here,' and then twenty scenes later, says, 'I'm only 29 I've got my whole life ahead of me.' That is, by anyone's metric, as absurd a sitcom character as you could wish for, and yet you've made her a breathing, walking, three-dimensional human being, and I tell you that there is a bit you do in season two, episode seven, when you have the baby and Smithy kisses you on the forehead. It's *amazing* what you do, because we suddenly see, 'Oh, fuck, she used to love him. Now is he in love with her, and how does she feel about it?' It's magic. Because they've never been tender like that. You're just a fucking world-class actress. You're as good as anybody working.

Oh, that's so kind of you to say. I'm a bit stunned you saying that . . .

I do have to say, I loved playing Nessa more than ever in *The Finale*. I really, really loved it. Because it is a genuine relationship of love between Smithy and Nessa, and because we'd never really seen that, apart from brief moments like the end of the Christmas special in 2008, or in series three when he says, 'Don't marry him.' Or when, as you mentioned, she's had the baby and he comes round and kisses her on the head. But generally speaking, it's always been this front that they've had. So it was a little bit of a challenge to cross into both fields in a way, to still have that kind of weirdness that Nessa has. You have to be able to deliver that.

I loved the challenge of making her be real but still retain her comedy side, saying, 'Oh, love, if I was you, I'd leave it there. You're damaging my mental health.' It was great to be able to keep all of that. Plus I had the 'Hale and Pace' lines. ('I did the knowledge back in the day. Drove a black cab. That's how I fell in with Hale and Pace.') And the Cossack dancing as well. ('I told Gav I was practising my Cossack dancing for a one-off gig on New Year's Eve. Incredibly I still had it in me. I did four or five Slav squats, made my excuses and left.')

I think the only way you can deliver lines like that is to be completely deadpan. You've got to make it as real as possible and absolutely believe in what you're saying. So I had to absolutely believe that I had been doing some Cossack dancing on the doorstep. And also, again – like, I know I said this about the end of the last Christmas special when Nessa proposes – so much of it was my feelings towards you, James, as well, and that was coming into play.

If we're talking other favourite scenes, I love Smithy throwing himself down the stairs!

Yeah, I'm pretty proud of that, because they got a stunt double in and I said to Chris the director, 'What are you talking about? We don't need a stunt double.' Then she said, 'You can't throw yourself down the stairs!' And I just said, 'Of course I can. And we can't cut.' Because it's not impressive enough to have a stunt double. I would argue it's deeply unimpressive if there's a cut in this scene. I don't think it's actually funny. In fact, I think it isn't funny if we see someone tumbling down the stairs, then we cut to everyone watching. Then we cut back to me standing up. I'd go as far as to say that whole way of doing it had to be actively banned! Because how we needed the scene to go was for us to not cut. That's the joy that makes it great. That's why Tom Cruise wants to go to space without special effects. And I'm not comparing the two, but that's his thing. That's why we did that parachute jump together. He was like, 'If I do it with you, people know it's real because you're there.' And it does change your experience when you're watching it, because you're thinking, 'Fuck, they really did jump out of that plane.' So I needed the audience to know me throwing myself down the stairs was real.

Anyway, I didn't get hurt because there was padding, and that was a newly laid carpet, which was pretty chunky with some foam underneath it. And we had a stunt guy who was saying things to say to me like, 'What you've got to do is make sure your shoulder is twisted under your body by the time you go down, otherwise you could hurt yourself.' And I was just like, 'OK, I'm just gonna throw myself downstairs. We'll do it three times, and I reckon one of them will be the one where we don't need to cut, so that stunt guy can stand down. The chubby dude wearing a wig, looking a bit like Smithy, can stand down!' And I really loved doing it. I really, really enjoyed it.

It was hilarious. And I think you are just so consummate as a performer; you absolutely wanted to do it yourself, very like Tom Cruise. And you'd also done all that on stage so you were used to getting bruised and battered. It was a bit like *One Man, Two Guvnors*. So you didn't need the stunt man.

Next favourite scene: Mick's speech at the stag. That was a late addition that came from a rewrite, and that process of rewrites was like adding little bits of paint here and there. The stag sequence was probably the most difficult to write, because we didn't want it to be like *The Hangover* and make it really over the top and hilarious, but on the other hand we didn't want it to be a complete washout. So we were trying to find somewhere in between, and then it was just a case of giving it those textures and layers.

I think in our first draft we probably made the stag too shit! It was all bad, and actually, Chris Gernon the director said, 'Don't we want to see some element of them having a good time?' And we felt that she was absolutely right. So then we rejigged it when we were doing the rewrites, and I don't remember if it was you or me who suggested, 'What if Mick says something that's quite moving within this scene?' And we were both like, 'Yes!'

I think having Mick do that speech, which he did so well because he didn't overplay it, is an example of how there's something nice about discovering things about the characters this late in the day. Because you could say, 'Well, you've never mentioned Mick and Pam wanting another baby before in any of the other episodes,' because we haven't. So if you'd asked us, probably, in series three, when Gavin and Stacey were trying for a baby, if that might have been the time to mention it, that's true, but we didn't. So we took licence, really, in *The Finale*, but it was important for Mick to have that moment. And I have to say, the number of people that have mentioned his speech and when he stands up in the wedding – it felt like he really did get a proper good send-off.

Yes, the biggest rewrite happened in the stag and the hen parties, with the whole quiz at the hen being an addition as well, including Nessa's revelation that Smithy doesn't like to be on his own in the dark. And you're thinking, 'When did he tell her that?' You suddenly start to see these glimpses of things that we've never seen between them.

I think that goes back to when she's protective of him as well in the 2019 special, when Sonia is saying that she bought him a gym membership and all that kind of thing. And you just sort of clock Nessa looking very protective of him, even to the point that – and I don't know if people may have missed it – when he's trying to break his arm by throwing himself down the stairs, she goes, 'I'll do it'. She's offering to do it as a sort of favour.

It was fun to have a stripper in the hen party in *The Finale*, which was also a call-back to Stacey's hen do, and it was nice to reflect on how attitudes have changed. The guy who played the stripper was called Damian, and we actually called him Damian in the script. He was in *Sister Act*, and that was his first TV job.

Whereas the original stripper in the Stacey's hen episode was a real stripper, and he had to say a line, and he was so awful you actually had to dub it, so it's you saying, 'Are you Stacey West? I'm PC Lovelength and you, young lady, are in serious trouble!' I love how Nessa's staring at him and says, 'That. Is. Lush.' And later she has a little bit of the stripper's squirty cream on the side of her mouth; I don't know if anyone ever picked up on that.

But the thing about stag parties is, they are grim once you get to your forties. They are grim now, because really you should just be going to a football match, playing golf and having a nice meal. About fifteen years ago, I went on a pub crawl in Amersham with my friend Richard Shedd, before he went back home to New Zealand; we went to all the pubs that we used to drink in when we were eighteen, and ended up at this club called Winkers in Chalfont St Peter, which is worse than you are imagining. And it was one of those evenings when it was fun for four or five hours, and then people just got so drunk and it became a bit of a 'geezers need excitement and violence every-where' situation, and I just thought, 'I've got to get out of here.' And my friend Andy, who plays Dirt-box, came along to Winkers and he came over to me and said, 'I think the tide might be turning here.' I said we should give it just another half-hour, then I looked up and saw someone get knocked out with a punch. And I just went, 'Yep, let's go.' And we left. We didn't say goodbye. We did a pure Irish goodbye and left. So Smithy's stag was kind of based on that: the idea of trying to cling on to something which cannot be your life any more. You just shouldn't do those things any more.

The line I really like is, 'Latvia didn't work out because of people's finances'. The idea being that in your twenties you've got this disposable income, you've got time, you haven't got kids, you haven't got a mortgage. The pressures just aren't the same. So of course we're going to Latvia. Of course we are!

It's like going to watch your football team away – of *course* we're going to Newcastle. Or of course we're going to Prague. I only decided the day before [West Ham played in the UEFA Europa League Final in] Prague that I was going, because all I was seeing was the horrors. It was the same with England in the Euros. I thought, 'If we go to Berlin for the final and we lose, it's awful, right? If we go and win, it's brilliant, but if we stay home and we lose – thank god we didn't go out there.' So those were the kinds of thoughts in my head when we wrote the stag scenes . . .

But Mick's speech at the stag was also a really nice send-off for him, and we tried to make sure everyone else had a good send-off, too. We did an audit on where we were with the characters' journeys. So with Gavin and Stacey, for example, in the last special they had more of an emotional journey, so in this one we wanted them to have a bit of fun, really.

With Pete and Dawn, it's funny, because we love them – as we love all the characters – and one of the challenges we've had over all the series is that because they very much belong in the Essex world, they've got no real reason for travelling down to Wales. They came down for Gavin and Stacey's wedding in series one. But that was it. So when we did the 2019 special, it was hard for us to justify them coming down to Wales for

Christmas, because why would they come to Gwen's house for Christmas? So it's been nice in this episode, in this final episode, to give them a really good story. Now, I think, because of the nature of their relationship, where they've always argued and have this very tempestuous marriage, it was so great to take it a step further and go, 'Right, in these five years they have actually got divorced,' but the idea that they can't really let go of each other was just lovely. And when we were writing the argument, do you remember, we had such a laugh with that? And then, on the day, coming up with the line of Adrian's saying, 'It feels like I'm in *Baby Reindeer!*'

When you're writing for actors of that calibre, it makes your job 90 per cent easier, because you put it in their hands. And this is true of everybody in the cast. There've been very definite moments throughout the history of the show, back when we were making the first series or whatever, when we might have had scenes where you and I would go, 'Ah, this isn't quite working.' And then you put it in the hands of Alison Steadman or Rob Brydon or Larry or Mel or Adrian or Julia, anyone, and suddenly you go, 'Oh, OK, now it works.' And it's a complete privilege to have a cast like this, who can really make things sing in the most natural way.

As for Bryn, I guess he's always had the fishing trip hanging over him. He had the hangover at Pam and Mick's. He had sweet little moments like wearing the full football kit at the stag, and getting things wrong like with the blow-up doll and all that kind of thing. I suppose he's maybe the one character left with quite a bit of mystery surrounding him. But I think it should be like that.

Then there were two scenes that we wrote but were never able to use in *The Finale* for lack of time. They're set in Bryn's house where Dic Powell is selling him a suitcase for Neil the Baby...

```
EXT. BARRY ISLAND, BRYN'S HOUSE.
Dic Powell is standing there with three
suitcases.

                BRYN
        Choose any one you want.
        This is on me.


             NEIL THE BABY
        Really?


                NESSA
        S'mae Dic be sy'n occurro?


             DIC POWELL
        S'mae Ness.
```

                    NEIL THE BABY
          I dunno, which one d'you
          think Mum?

                    DIC POWELL
          Cês cragen galed, dil-i
          gyd a bag dillad.

                    BRYN
          Dic can you assure me that
          these are all legitimately
          in your possession? None from
          lost property.

Dic looks at them for a moment.

                    DIC POWELL
          Wn i ddim beth sydd yn yr
          un hon.

                    BRYN
          Right, it's between these two.

Cut to

                    --

INT. BRYN'S HOUSE, FRONT ROOM
Neil the baby has all his stuff laid out
in piles - socks, pants, t-shirts etc,
Nessa is sitting there watching and
vaping, Bryn coming in and out with
various boxes.

                    NEIL THE BABY
How do I work out how much
to take? Like how many socks
do I pack?

                    NESSA
You want at least two weeks
worth. Cos let's face it
you're not gonna be home every
weekend

                    NEIL THE BABY
I might be.

                    NESSA
No you won't - you'll have too
much to do. You'll be going up
the West End and what have you.

                    BRYN
The sights and sounds of
the Big Smoke. Like Dick
Whittington and his cat!

                    NESSA
And your Dad'll have a washing
machine don't forget.

Doorbell goes. Bryn goes to
answer it.

               BRYN
    (as he goes)
    Ho, I doubt young Smithy
    knows how to use it mind.

             NESSA
    Good point. Get Sonya to
    show you.

Cut to

              --

Neil the Baby is slowly bringing his
case down the stairs.

             BRYN
    Hang on slugger! Let me
    help you.

Bryn goes to help, and brings the case
down. They stand in the hall. Bryn
smiles at NTB.

          NESSA (O.S.)
          LOOK OUT!!

A second case comes flying down the
stairs. And Nessa follows.

         NEIL THE BABY
    Mum! Look what uncle Bryn
    gave me?

She looks, fans it out, takes a couple
of tenners and puts them in her bra.
A little look of confusion from Bryn.

        NEIL THE BABY (CONT'D)
    But you still got aunty Gwen.
    She'll always be there for you.

             BRYN
    Yes well, that's..

            NESSA
    O. Neil. Don't go there.
    It's a sore point. In all
    manner of ways for Gwen right
    now I imagine, unless she's
    had him tested.

Ding dong. Bryn goes for the door.

          NESSA (CONT'D)
    (to Neil)
    You ready for this.

          NEIL THE BABY
    Yeah.

            NESSA
    Tidy.

CHAPTER 18

Waiting for this moment: finishing *The Finale*

RUTH: I can't believe we haven't mentioned 'Blackbird' yet...

JAMES: Oh god, yes. How lucky were we that Oscar [Hartland], who plays Neil the Baby, could sing and play the guitar. We watched the video of him on *The Voice Kids*, and we all thought: 'He's good. He's really good.' Then we thought, 'Wouldn't it be amazing if no one knows Neil the Baby can sing and play guitar?' So we asked him if he was able to learn this song with enough time. And he did. For me, 'Blackbird' is one of the most beautiful songs, and I believe that you would hear it at a wedding. But then, more than that, you have the idea of watching Nessa – someone leaving their hometown with a broken heart, who you've heard say, 'It's all a bit much for me, and I need a change of scenery' – and you're hearing the words,

'Take these broken wings and learn to fly . . .' And then you're back with Smithy, and you're hearing lines like, 'All your life you were only waiting for this moment to arrive,' and it hasn't been *this* moment he's been waiting for. And I thought a lot about that scene in *Moneyball* where Brad Pitt takes his daughter to buy a guitar, and he says, 'Would you play something for me now?' and his daughter does that, 'I'm just a little bit caught in the middle . . .' and he is so moved. And I've experienced this with my children. You can't believe this person is singing. You can't believe it because they were a baby yesterday. Like, I feel as if my son Max came home from the hospital last week and now he's singing a song with a guitar and that is amazing as a parent. That's hugely emotional, and that was the song. That was it. It was a massive turning point in the spirit of the show.

Even though I obviously wasn't in the wedding sequence, I was there on set, and I had heard Oscar play that the first time. I think I heard it before you, because he brought his guitar into the production office in Cardiff, and there was just me and Chris the director, and Sarah the producer. He came in with his mum, and he told us he'd been practising the song. When we had this idea for him to sing 'Blackbird', we knew he could sing. But it was a bit of a risk, because we didn't know how good he was at the guitar. So he sang it in the room in the produc-

tion office, and it just got me. And of course, he wasn't very polished then. So when he sang it on the day, I was behind the camera with Chris the director, just watching, and when Oscar sang that song I was an absolute mess, because his voice was so pure, and the guitar playing was just so gorgeous. I almost couldn't listen to it; it was too much. So I'm just delighted with that scene; I think it tells a really gorgeous story. I guess there's something so tender about him as this teenager singing that song. I did think there were going to be millions of people watching him, and his mother was so proud as well. It was lovely for him, because he's a brilliant singer, and he's really committed to it, writing songs and playing every day, you know? So, yeah, that was beautiful.

In terms of getting permission to use the song, the BBC have a licensing agreement, which is great for UK transmissions of music, but I think The Beatles sit outside of that, which we didn't know, and it's expensive if you want to use one of their songs. So then we honestly didn't have the money in the budget to pay for it. So I wrote Paul McCartney an email, just telling him that I felt this was a pivotal moment in the show and that I would never request anything if I thought it was going to be in any way derogatory, and I said, 'Look, we have such a history with that Smithy sketch for Comic Relief, and other times we've worked together – is there anything you

could do to help us?' So I don't know exactly how it
worked out, but I think he waived his involvement,
which meant that we could afford it, or something
like that. I don't know the exact details, but basically he replied saying he'd cc'd the person above, and
he wasn't sure if that person got many emails direct
from Paul McCartney . . . so I think that person read
between the lines. And he said in his email that he
was so touched and honoured, and he would love
nothing more than for this to happen, and they'd do
everything in their power to make sure it could, and
then, within twenty hours, it was done, and we had
clearance to use the song.

As for Oscar's performance, it was gorgeous. It's
just beautiful, brilliant. And, bless him, he really
put the work in as well, practising every day, and
he got so nervous on the day. So when we filmed
his footage, there was no one else in the room, and
we did it first thing, so it felt more like a rehearsal.
I remember you and I saying, 'It's eight a.m. and
we're here till seven p.m., let's get it shot now so
that we don't wait till six thirty tonight after a whole
day's filming when the pressure would be intense.'
So he was fresh, and he'd warmed up. I think he did
four takes, and we had three cameras that day, and
he was great. By the time we knew we'd got it, then
he could just play it when everybody else was in
there. And it was just magical. The fact that he was

also one of the original three babies who played Neil the Baby made it perfect, really. Ten years later, he came back in and auditioned for the role in the 2019 special, did his audition brilliantly, and then, at the end of the audition, mentioned to you and Chris the director, 'Oh, you know, I'm one of the original babies that you had.' We're so proud of him.

Then there's the Smithy/Sonia non-wedding as officiated by Anna Maxwell Martin as the celebrant.

I worked with Anna in the play *The Constituent* in the summer of 2024, when we were working on the script for *The Finale*, and it turned out her kids are very big fans of *Gavin & Stacey*. So we'd written this part of the celebrant and, as best you can, you just want to hire the best actors possible. Because what if you get someone who's overwhelmed by it? So I was doing the play with Anna, and she had jokingly said, 'Oh, is there anything for me in *Gavin & Stacey*?' And I just went, 'You know what, there might be!' And she was like, 'Oh, don't be silly.' I said, 'Well, you wouldn't come and do two days as an unnamed character in a BBC budget TV show, would you?' And she said, 'Of course I would.' So we figured it out, and she was just the best. She was just great. She did what great actors do: they take the script and they elevate it, and it's natural and it's good.

I've got a feeling Anna didn't tell anyone she'd done it cos she wanted to see the surprise on the kids' faces on Christmas Day!

Then what appears to be the most moving moment that people have spoken to me about is Mick standing up to agree that Smithy shouldn't marry Sonia, which I was surprised about.

They loved that on *Gogglebox* as well . . . and it was nominated as a BAFTA TV Moment of the Year.

In the filming of the Smithy/Sonia wedding scene, we didn't really tell anybody what to do, other than our cast to stand up at their various points. And when Anna Maxwell Martin says, 'If anyone here knows of any reason, please stand . . .' there are two ladies at the back on Stacey's side who stood up! We didn't tell them to, and one was from Australia. They were just real fans of the show and they were so into it at that moment that they stood up, and then they got really embarrassed. One of them said, 'I just thought she shouldn't be marrying him!' Kind of an amazing moment, really.

After the non-wedding, we had our race against time on Dave Coaches' bus to get to Nessa at the dock. And the stunt! I've never driven through a hedge in a bus, so I imagine it is quite daunting. So with a sequence like that it's all about being true to the show, and then the scene is exciting enough. And then if you put The Maccabees on the soundtrack, it's great. Using that song, 'Pelican', was also a little bit of a gift to Mat Horne because he is the biggest Maccabees fan, and he introduced me to them. He's introduced a lot of people to The Maccabees. I think the original music that our editor put on for that scene was The Libertines, but it just felt too jolly. It didn't have the drive. So we tried out various songs in the edit and on the phone watching the scene with no sound, and then we tried The Maccabees song, and it was just perfect.

When Nessa is finally confronted by Smithy, so many people have commented on the moment when she throws her bag into the boat. I loved that. Because it had to look as if I did actually work on a ship. So I was really glad to have that boiler suit. That was a good call. And, yeah, chucking the bag was a lovely moment, and there was the character of Clayton there, and you can just tell they've obviously got history. She's probably got history with everybody on that boat – Baggy, Noggin, and Crusher, who's still inside. So that was nice. It was also a bit of a Nessa moment, because you might think, 'Well, she didn't really work on the ships', but then you see, 'Oh, actually, she did.' In the same way that you think, 'Well, she didn't really have

a relationship with John Prescott,' and then he turns up at the wedding, god rest his soul.

In terms of writing it, originally it was meant to happen at an airport. Nessa was getting a flight to Carasco where she was going to join a ship.

Yes, but unfortunately we couldn't get permission to film at Cardiff airport.

To be clear, they said they *might* let us film there, but only if we said it was Cardiff airport. And we couldn't do that because it wouldn't have worked in the story. It would have had to be Heathrow. Cos of all the timings. So permission was refused.

So initially we thought, 'Oh no, this is awful. What are we going to do?' Because we had this big farewell, this big reunion scene in the airport, and Cardiff airport was our only option. And they'd said no.

I was really upset to begin with, that they'd said no. I almost took it personally! Like, my home city, for god's sake – the airport is down the road from Barry, planes fly over Barry, couldn't you do this for the show that had its roots there? But y'know, in the end, the person who said no to us actually did us a massive favour.

Yeah, it was Dave Ferris, who designed every single second of *Gavin & Stacey* on screen, who said every day after he'd seen the script, 'I don't think it should be in an airport. I don't think we'll ever be able to make it secure enough. It will still be a working airport. It's going to be very difficult. Should it not be the ships?'

I wasn't aware Dave had said that at the time, but after Cardiff airport turned us down, I said to Chris, 'Surely, with Nessa's work history and the fact she's worked on the ships, it would be lush for her to leave on a boat? Like, in Barry Docks.' And she said, 'Dave Ferris is gonna love you! He's been saying this every day.' We ended up filming in Newport Docks and it was such a great location, it really was. It was a lot of security to get in there. And I have to say, Sarah, our producer, was always on the lookout to make sure there weren't any paps there, because the most important thing we didn't want to get into the press was the image of you down on one knee in front of me. And, thankfully, it didn't. And I'm so glad, because I think that the atmosphere of that location was just so exciting and rich and textured.

Yes, in the end we're very, very pleased it didn't happen in the airport, because when we saw the location, it just would have been a nightmare. And what you realize is *Love Actually* built part of Terminal Five [at Heathrow], right? And they used it twice in

the film. They used it at the very start, with passengers arriving, and then again at the end, and it's
insane that they built part of Terminal Five. But we
couldn't do that. You can't film in Heathrow at all,
and Cardiff airport doesn't have high ceilings and
it feels a bit small in there. And I think doing that
scene outside at the docks works so much better, so it
was a thrilling change.

**Then you and I improvised the big Smithy/Nessa climax,
didn't we? It was about finding the reality of the lines,
so when he says, 'I love you . . . well, not always,' I think
it was just about keeping it real, I suppose, so Nessa not
saying anything, and having it all coming out of him.
That was just so beautiful to film. I loved filming that,
because you're so good at that vulnerability, and we hear
it in your voice. I think the actual writing of the scene
was about capturing a really important moment, and
having her say no, which was a call-back to a line from
an earlier episode when she was dressed as bridesmaid
and said to Bryn, 'You had your chance. You never took
it.' So it was really important, and it was great watching
Gogglebox when they were shouting at Nessa.**

The dialogue for *The Finale* – that took a while,
didn't it? We had to work out: how do these characters speak to each other, when historically they
haven't shown huge amounts of affection for each

other? It's all been left in what *isn't* said, actually, so in 2019 Nessa saying, 'I loves you with all my heart. I know it's weird, all right, but I do' – that's so lovely. So then this time it's about: how does he speak to Nessa? And you get some licence because of the dramatic nature of the journey to get there. Then we just kept going back and forth, and we got that line with him saying, 'I don't know when this thing that was nothing became something. And right now it's everything. But it did. And I know it's been messy and not perfect, but that's because we're messy and not perfect.' That just felt really right. It felt like he needed to say more than just propose, but also we're always trying to get some kind of levity in it, so we came up with Smithy saying, 'I love you. I always have, well not *always*, but most of the time.' It's lovely. And then he says, 'I get it. You don't have to ask me. I'll ask you. I love you – will you marry me?' And that feels like it's just two people who, ultimately, I think, are just very, very afraid of being hurt, which I think is all of us. It's two people who, because of the nature of how this started, can never show themselves to each other fully, and I think we all have that; we all have that with friendships. And the fear of letting your guard down, which is his fear, is so terrifying because they're just not intimate with each other in that way. And they don't want to be. They're two people who set their stalls out, and for a long time we would have been like, 'Are you mad? Are you joking? What?' And then slowly but surely, you know, love is the thing that shows itself to you, and you either accept it and open your arms to it, or you just push it down within you. But it's going to make you do one of those two things, and they've been pushing it down for at least ten years.

What was a really enjoyable bit of an acting moment for me was when Smithy proposes and the camera moves in on my face, and I had to show nothing, and then just a bit of a glimmer. Because Nessa very rarely smiles. So it had to be just in my eyes, and I had to have only a tiny little bit of a smile.

I remember Chris the director, when she was doing the edit, said, 'Well, I hope you'll be all right with the register office scene.' Because she was worried that it was a bit Ruth and James rather than Nessa and Smithy, and I know what she means, and I think probably there is a little bit of that, because I'm really smiling at you and you're really smiling at me, and I know on the day we were getting a bit giggly because we were having to say marriage vows to each other. We did get a bit silly, but I think it worked.

CHAPTER 14

The ending

RUTH: **When it came to filming the very final scene, the montage of the wedding party, there was a scheduling shock. Because throughout the making of the show, our first AD [assistant director], Steve, was always really good at trying his best to make the last scene as near to the end of the filming schedule as possible. The thing is, psychologically, you don't really want to film, you know, two characters in a car, or something anti-climactic like that, as the final scene to the final-ever episode.**

JAMES: But when the first schedule for this shoot came in, the last scene was just Smithy on his phone in the car, and we were like, 'Oh no . . .' And I think because of the way these things work, with it being a six-week shoot, and all the actors booked for just five out of those six weeks as an economical thing, it meant we couldn't have everyone in on the last day. And it was probably the only time we've ever gone, 'No, no, the last day of filming has to be special.'

We both felt it was really important that we filmed the last scene on the last day. And it was so valuable and so important, and it made such a difference, especially because of the nature of the last scene, to have everybody join in with this sense of an ending. I think it was really special. It helped everybody to accept that it was over now. It was good. It was a healthy end.

So I think that final day had been designed not just to achieve the filming that needed to be achieved. I think there was a lot of psychology in helping us to navigate the very, very last day of filming *Gavin & Stacey*. If you look at the script, it literally just says there's a montage after Nessa and Smithy get married, and if you look at the actual schedule for that day, the only dialogue is that last bit with Gavin and Stacey taking the group photo. And so we had a whole day with the whole cast. It was quite a luxury, because normally, you know, you're watching the clock and you're up against it. The rest was all improvised. But it really felt like how Nessa and Smithy's wedding reception would be. We were in a pub, we had food, and we were so blessed that everyone in production made this happen, so that we could have the luxury of a final day when everybody was there and all we had to do was stuff for the montage.

On that last day of filming, there was another problem, though, because the layout of the pub was changed. They had a table where we were going to do the karaoke. There were two tables, in fact, and the way it looked to me felt a bit more like a formal wedding – not *that* formal, because it's still in the Tadross, aka the Dolphin, where we always filmed those pub scenes – but there was a buffet there as well and it immediately felt wrong. It didn't look like how the Dolphin usually looks. So I did what I always do in those situations, and went to find you . . .

Yes, you found me and I was getting changed and you asked if I'd seen the pub layout, which I hadn't, and you said I should just come and have a look at it. Because sometimes you'll show things to me, or I'll show things to you, and we'll go, 'No, it's fine!' But in this case we both had the exact same visceral reaction, which was: 'The characters have to sit where they've always sat in the pub.'

They had to sit where they sat in the 2019 special. Otherwise, I don't even think people would recognize it's the same pub. And then Chris the director was thinking about the depth of the shots, because it is packed into a corner there. But we thought the main thing is the audience has to know they're in Barry, and we have to know they're in the same pub,

the Dolphin, and this corner of the Dolphin specifically. So we ended up with a bit of a shuffle around on
the day, which I think Chris is grateful for now. Then
we filmed the montage of everyone celebrating Nessa
and Smithy in their various ways. And this is where
Chris was amazing: she made all those moments in
the montage feel completely organic. So we didn't
really have set shots planned in advance, because we
just wanted everyone to do their own thing and enjoy
the moment. We did write a rough version of what
was happening, but we weren't wedded to it at all; we
didn't want to impose any of that on the actual scene.
It was just about the camera finding those moments.
And there's no sound on it, so, for example, Alison
at one point wasn't sure about singing a song, until
we said, 'No one's ever going to hear it.' And in the
end, I love what we have in that montage. I think it's
great.

**What was so funny was that everyone put their all into
it. And everyone was a bit anxious about it. I sang Patti
Smith's 'Because The Night', Rob was warming up his
voice, and, yes, Alison was getting really worried that
she was not going to be able to do it. But then we kept
having to remind everyone to relax because we knew
none of it was going to get heard. There were only those
little bits of the speeches that you can just about hear in
there. And it was joyous. And to be able to have that last**

day, the privilege of it, filming in situ, and being able to go, 'These are the last words in Gavin & Stacey, and this is the last time anybody's going to say anything after seventeen years,' and then having the photo taken . . . And Chris the director, being the wonderful woman she is, when she called 'Cut!' on the very last take had arranged for the sound department to play, 'Tell me tomorrow, I'll wait by the window for you . . .' That got us all going, as you can imagine.

I think the whole thing really helped us all to get through it, because if we hadn't had that specific final day, I think it would have been pretty unpleasant, actually. As it was, we were all hugging each other. It was a celebration. It was special.

It was probably the most emotional TV or film set I've ever been on, and it was kind of wonderful. So many of our crew have been with us from the start, and so it was a wonderful way to close it all out.

I also think viewers thought the final moment of the episode would be the scene at the register office with the celebrant saying, 'I now pronounce you man and wife,' and everyone's clapping. I think you absolutely think that's the end of the show. It sort of softens in focus. And then it cuts to the pub, and then we were so aware that we wanted the audience to feel, 'Oh god, we're not going to see them again. This is it!' So that countdown on the iPhone taking the picture, and that Stephen Fretwell song coming in, felt so perfect.

After we wrapped that last shot, I didn't really want to hang around. But there were loads of people outside the pub wanting photos and for us to sign stuff, understandably. I did a few photos, but I really wanted to go, and I think you stayed a lot longer than me. I think we both went back to the hotel. But it was quite weird, that bit of just leaving and packing everything up. I had so much stuff, because I took all my costumes, got all my Nessa stuff, and I took the ceramic hen that was in Gwen's kitchen on the windowsill. I've got that as my keepsake. And I just had loads of bags with presents, and I couldn't take it all in. I did go back to the hotel room, and it was like, 'Oh god, this is so weird.'

And then we had the wrap party, which was amazing. We paid for it rather than using the production money, because we just wanted it to be a really good time, and we didn't want it to be like, 'Here's your token for a glass of wine,' and also we didn't want the BBC to pay for it. It felt really right; it felt like a real thank-you to everybody from us.

It was also the best wrap party I've ever been to. I didn't drink. You didn't drink. And there was so much dancing. We danced and danced and laughed at Jo Page who got quite tipsy on French martinis, which was very funny.

Yeah, the wrap party got to about half one – I think it went on to, like, three or four a.m. but we both decided that we were going to leave – and I went over to thank the DJ, who was so good. I said to him, 'Thanks so much. We're going to head off now.' And just as we were leaving, he started playing Stephen Fretwell's 'Run', and the entire crew just gathered in this huge hug, and I remember looking at Adrian Scarborough, who was crying, and everyone was holding each other and singing. And it was magic, all of it. It was just a magical end to it all. It really, really has been very special.

CHAPTER 15

Christmas and beyond: the reaction

RUTH: The reaction to *The Finale* has absolutely blown my mind. In the build-up to it, we were doing a lot of publicity, from the beginning of December, and it was crazy. The schedule of where we had to be and when was just nuts. And for me, because I am not somebody that dresses up a lot, I knew I'd have to get a stylist and all that. She was great, Stevie B. She was so patient, but I kind of couldn't be arsed. Anyway, all of that was going on, and I remember saying to you at one point, 'God, this is mad, isn't it? But I'm so determined to enjoy every minute of it, because this is never going to happen again. All of this is never going to happen again.' So there were things like going on Graham Norton, and in particular going on the Radio Two Breakfast Show on 23 December, when you and I hosted and we had the cast join us – that was the most profound *Gavin &*

Stacey experience, because it was the last time we were all going to be together, and it felt so lovely and so sad, and it was such good fun.

But it really was the last time, and we knew that this was it before the show went out. And I think all the time building up to that there was always this worry at the back of both our minds – probably more mine than yours – that was, 'Oh my god, what if they find out about Laura? What if it gets into the press about Laura Aikman coming back as Sonia?' Because that would have spoiled the whole thing. But somehow, it didn't get out, and I am so grateful for that.

So anyway, when Christmas came, we did the Radio Two show on the twenty-third, and then we did a thing for Classic FM where we picked our favourite Christmas carols, and that was our last bit of publicity. Then that afternoon we said goodbye – you were going off to buy a puppy, and I was heading back to Wales for Christmas, and we went our separate ways. And I felt a real sense of separation anxiety, saying goodbye to you, though I knew I was going to see you on Christmas Day. But it was really strange, because we'd been together for such a long time, and you went off, and I got driven back to Cardiff, got my car, went down to a family thing in the night, and . . . I started to feel ill.

I just thought, 'Oh, my god. I really feel rough.' I think it was probably everything just coming out, and my immune system reacting to all the build-up. And every-body had been ill. You had been ill the week before. But I tried not to think about it, and then I did the family thing, went back to Cardiff, woke up in the morning and I just felt hideous. But I told myself: 'Keep going, keep going.'

So Christmas Eve came and I did loads of family stuff with the grandchildren, but I was really feeling awful. We were at my auntie's in the night, and I only stayed half an hour. I thought, 'I've got to go to bed. Just go to bed.'

Then on Christmas Day, which is, like, this day that I've been looking forward to for so long because of *The Finale* going out, I just felt like death. I absolutely felt like death. But I drove down to my mum's in Porthcawl. I was doing the turkey. My sister was doing everything else. I put the turkey in the oven and then had to lie down, and I was literally eating my Christmas dinner, telling myself, 'OK, it's OK. It's OK.' Then it was three o'clock, when I had to get in the car and drive to yours, James, and I got there, and there's all your family there, and I just went, 'Don't come near me. I'm really ill,' but they were all really ill as well! They were all taking stuff. So I got there after a three-hour drive, and I really don't know how I got there, but I was so glad that I did, because I had said to you the day before, 'I don't know if I'm gonna make it, because I just feel really rough.' But I think I'd also said to you, actually – before I told you about being ill – I asked, 'Are

you sure you want me to come and watch this with you?
You know, all your family are there, and it's your first
Christmas in your new home.'

And you were so hurt at the prospect of my not
coming, I thought, 'Oh my goodness, I have to!' When
the show came on, we sat in your living room next to
each other and we held hands a lot of the time. What
was so satisfying was just hearing the reaction in
the room.

So sitting there on Christmas Day in your living room
was just phenomenal. It was fantastic, and everything
we could have wished for, really. And of course, when it
finished, I looked at my phone and there were about a
hundred WhatsApp messages and about fifty texts and
emails. And I thought, 'I can't answer these tonight.' I
just sort of left it and went back home.

I went to bed, and didn't get out of bed until 28
December.

I couldn't get out of bed the next day, and I didn't
drink at all over the rest of Christmas. I did just feel very,
very ill for much of it. But in amongst all that, the joy of
watching it – getting to watch it with you, James – it felt
so beautifully wrapped up. It really did. And I had made
a decision that I wasn't going to google anything any
more, because I have had phases of googling my name
or the show, and it doesn't get me anywhere. And I tell
you, that's one of the best things I've ever done; just to

not have that hanging over me was great. So I only know what people think of it from friends and family, really, and letters. People have just said, mainly, how lovely it was to watch something with their family or their friends. I got photos from people of their families watching it together, and it was lovely.

JAMES: I didn't read the reviews, but I got a sense that it had gone down well. I also think you should be very wary of only reading stuff about you that's good, because if you read something that's good and you believe it, then, by definition, you should engage with the stuff that's bad. I haven't actually typed my name into Google in six years, which is the only way you can be healthy, really, because what's the point? You're either the best thing in the world or you're shit, and neither is true. They are both huge lies. So actually, the more you can separate your life and work and go, 'Well, that's the work over there, but this is my life here,' the better it is.

But, yeah, watching it on Christmas Day in our house with my sister, Ruth, sitting in that chair because she didn't want anyone to walk past her . . . And you were here, Ruth, and I was sitting here, and my sister had the chair kind of turned at an angle, and when that moment happens with Sonia suddenly appearing, my sister just had this brilliant look on her face. She looked at me and you, and we were like, 'Yeah!'

I think what we did was make the best episode of the show the last episode ever. And that is nuts to me, but that's the great thing about love stories. If you think of other rom-coms – like, Hugh Grant's character in *Notting Hill* is William Thacker, right, but I don't know who William Thacker is, and I don't know who Julia Roberts's character Anna Scott is either, but by the end of the film I'm longing for them to be together. Similarly, I don't know Harry or Sally's second name, and by the end of that movie, on New Year's Eve, I'm willing them to be together. And that's, in a best-case scenario, a story that lasts for two hours. This is *seventeen years*. It's certainly ten years from the end of the third series and then another five years of 'Will they? Won't they?' So it means so much that all of the things that we thought we could achieve with a story have actually panned out.

That's why I think it's really hard to end *Game of Thrones*, right? How can you satisfy the audience for that whole thing? But actually, what you've got here is something that's just about the characters, then all you've got to do is work out: how do we satisfy them? If you satisfy them, you satisfy the audience. It's like a kid's water toy: you put the water in here, and it's going to end up coming out here. That's it. So with the show, here's Smithy and Nessa, and they're gonna run down here, and they'll come out of it happily ever after, so all we've got to do is put as many things as possible here to make this loop really interesting, and add some sense of jeopardy.

I think that's the joy of writing love stories, isn't it? Let's write more love stories!

There seem to have been lots of 'final moments' to the *Gavin & Stacey* journey, like the last day of filming, or the cast and crew screening, or the Radio Two takeover. But I guess being all together at the BAFTAs in May was the sweetest last gathering.

Aw, it was such an amazing night, wasn't it?! We *were* nominated for the Audience Award, which we didn't win, but actually it didn't matter because we were all there on a school trip, essentially. Eight of us went – me, you, Rob B, Rob W, Mat, Melanie, Jo, Alison and Larry. We turned up in three people carriers and went on the red carpet. And it was so much fun! We sat in the front two rows, and I took my shoes off because I genuinely didn't think I would win Best Female in a Comedy. I had texted you the Friday before and said, 'I'm not going to win on Sunday and it's going to be so embarrassing. I don't know how to react.' And you sent me this lovely text back. You said: 'You just have to smile. And clap. You are the most incredible

actress. Your performance is one of the greatest of all time.' But the best thing was, on the day – and this really calmed me down – you said, 'I'd like you to know I am ridiculously proud of you and to be by your side tonight.'

And when the category was announced I didn't know where to look because the camera was on you, watching your reaction. And you held my hand and I just looked down. And when they announced the winner I wasn't even sure I'd heard my name, but the reason I knew they'd said me was because Jo Page and Rob Brydon were screaming, 'YES!' almost quite aggressively! It was like when Bryn shouted, 'SURPRISE! SURPRISE! SURPRISE!' in the barn dance episode. And I didn't have time to put my shoes on and had to go up on stage bare-foot to accept it. Nessa always comes to my rescue when I'm particularly stressed.

O. I'm not gonna lie – this is immense. I wasn' expectin' to win this no way. I've won a BAFTA before of course I have. In 1976. It was the Barry Arcade Fruity Technician Award. And I was grateful for that, but this? This is crackin . . . Umm . . . I really wasn't expectin to win this and I want to thank the wonderful gorgeous cast, many of whom are here tonight and who've just been so lovely to work with over the years and especially to our director Christine Gernon who directed every single episode . . . to the unsung heroes of our crew and our production team over the years, thank you for making it happen. And a huge thank you to the BBC, such a fantastic institution, which I'm so proud to have worked with so many times. I really would like to thank Stuart Murphy who saw the potential of our little show back in 2005 and to Charlotte Moore the out going director of content at the BBC who has been so supportive over the years – Charlotte you are going to be so missed . . . but . . . the person I would like to thank the most is my dear, dear talented lovely, kind, funny friend – James Corden, with whom I have shared this astonishing journey for the past seventeen years and without whom Nessa Shanessa Jenkins would simply not exist. I love you James, I love writing with you. Long may it continue. Thank you BAFTA!

I was so moved by that. I was, I can't tell you. It was so . . . I was just sat there and I remember looking at you and just thinking, 'Oh my god, this is the greatest last moment you could ever wish to have in the world of *Gavin & Stacey*,' and I just . . . I was so proud of you. It's so richly deserved. I just could not have been more proud of you that night.

Aw. It was an immense night, it was just such good fun. But now, in the aftermath of the show finishing, the

thing I miss most is that lovely time we had when it was just me and you writing. When it was just the two of us. Cos that's the bit we enjoy the most: the writing together, when we don't really have to answer to anybody else. And that's still the case. We don't have to put make-up on, or get dressed up in some costume or answer any difficult questions; we just can get really into the creative world. It was lovely the other day, actually, cos we started working together again on a new project, writing about a new world, this new world that we're creating. It's so lovely when we get that bounce back between us, and we kind of get the engine going. It's really, really enjoyable.

In terms of what I feel like now – and you and I were talking about this the other day, and I said, 'Do you feel sad?' And you said, 'No, I don't feel sad, because we've really genuinely let it go now and it couldn't have gone any better, so now it feels like we're on to pastures new.' And it was so magical, it was such a magical time. And I can really feel so much warmth about all those different events that were leading up to it: the filming days, the writing days, all of it. It's just a massive, massive privilege to be in this position. It really is.

Yeah, and it's nice to have something positive, isn't it? I mean, I get that it's more intriguing to have some argument of some kind, or some disagreement or some sort of tension. I understand that's more dramatic and it's more interesting for the press to write about. But on the other hand, there's something so lovely about people just having had this unified reaction of positivity.

Now we're working on something new. Hopefully we've got some meetings lined up to see where we're going to go with this project, but I think, for us, it's about the writing. And what we've kind of always done is not write to a prescription, as it were. So we know that if we enjoy it, it'll be OK. I mean, who knows? Nothing may come of it. That's always a possibility. But I love it.

I love that you're coming over tomorrow. I do love being in a room with you, and talking about the most ridiculous things. And we'll chat and snack and nap, but then, in between, we might write something decent.

Tidy.

THE END

APPENDIX

Nessa's escapades in full

DAVE
Don't suppose I could tempt
you to a Chinese down mine
later?

NESSA
Oh. Dave, when are you gonna
learn? You can buy me all the
chocolates, all the chow mein
you like but it won't wash
and you knows why. Now, back
off, or I'll tell everyone on
that coach about my trip to
the doctor's. Is that what you
really want?

DAVE

No. Sorry.

NESSA

Look, I think you're a
cracking bloke, Dave, but
let's face it, you're riddled.

DAVE

I know. How is everything, uh,
down there, by the way?

NESSA

Shipshape and shiny now. No
thanks to you.

NESSA

This reminds me of a very
similar situation I was in
with my second husband, Clive.
I was faced with a dilemma,
whether to lie, or not to
lie, and I chose to tell
the truth.

STACEY

And what happened?

NESSA

He died. Firing squad.
Terrible way to go, Stace

and I wouldn't like to see
it happen to you. Smugglers,
we were. And if it weren't
for my relationship with John
Prescott, I'd still be in that
jail right now. So yeah, in
answer to your question, I'd
say no, don't tell him.

                    STACEY
Oh, thanks, Ness. Do you miss
him? Clive?

                    NESSA
I do, yeah. But I don't miss
walking through customs with
a belly full of crack-filled
condoms.

                    NESSA
I used to work down The
Dolphin, as it goes. If you
see Carl, tell him I says
alright.

                    GAVIN
I don't know who Carl is.

                    STACEY
You will.

NESSA

He's got a tattoo that says
"I'm Carl". On his chin.

NESSA

I just can't believe it,
Stace. Of all the people I've
slept with, it's him gets me
pregnant. Not Nigel Havers,
not John Prescott, not any of
Goldie Lookin Chain. No, some
knobhead from Essex.

NESSA

Tidy. I've already spoken
to Noel [Sullivan, from
Hear'Say] He said wherever I
go, whatever I do, he's gonna
be there. Pure and simple.

NESSA

This reminds me very much of
my time with John. Prescott.
I had the lot: a flat in
Westminster, full use of one
of the Jags . . . I didn't

even have to cook – we had a
little Filipino do it for us.
Had a cracking social life.
Many a night we'd have Dave
Blunkett and his bitch round
for dinner. I remember so
clearly thinking, 'This is not
the life for me'. So I turned
to them and said, 'I don't see
the point'. Dave said neither
did he. He could be very dry.
I left that night and I never
looked back. Because I knew
I'd only ever be happy in
Barry.

STACEY
How did John take it?

NESSA
He took it bad. He went mad
he did . . . shouting and
fighting. Next day he punched a
civilian. When I saw it on the
telly I knew that punch was
meant for me.

NESSA
It was March 89 I quit. Then I
went Stobart's.

                    MICK
Eh?

                    NESSA
Eddie Stobart's! I was with
Eddie and the boys 18 month
all told.

                    BRYN
You had a little soft spot for
him, didn't you, Ness?

                    NESS
I did Bryn, I'm not gonna lie
to you. But I wasn't his type.
Apparently. I mean since when
has a great rack and an open
mind not been a grown man's
type? He's a deeply religious
man. Very generous.

                    BRYN
He gave you two trucks
didn't he, Ness?

                    NESSA
He did yes and I regret
selling them now to be honest
with you, but they were a
bugger to park around Barry.

                    NESSA
I'm gonna fire her up and get
on the road, Gwen. There's no
need for us to convoy. Anyway,
I'm stopping off at Heston to
see Ozzie and a few of the
Stobart boys.

                    GWEN
Right, well, should we join
you there?

                    NESSA
No. It's truckers only, I'm
afraid.

                    GWEN
How are you gettin' on
with yours, Ness? Still
battling on?

                    NESSA
I won't lie to you - it's a
tough read. It's putting me
through the ringer a bit.

                    GWEN
What is it actually about, The
Satanic Verses?

NESSA
Don't make me talk about it,
Gwen. I don't want another
fatwa.

STACEY
Ness, is it weird when you
see Smithy? Like, do you just
think "Oh my God! I've had
sex with him"?

NESSA
Stace, if I thought that
every time I saw a man I'd
had sex with, I'd never get
anything done.

NESSA
He's a good bloke, Kev. I've
got a lot of time for him.

JASON
He loved you, didn't he?

STACEY
Yeah, but imagine, if I'd
married him, I'd be Stacey
Spacey!

NESSA

I remember when I was working
in Harrods - I got involved
with the boss. I mean the
big boss. Crackin' little
fella. He used to take me to
the football every Saturday.
Couldn't do enough for me.
But as soon as he got what he
wanted - down there like - he
didn't want to know.

NESSA

I remember my first wedding
day. I woke up in Vegas.
Didn't know where I was.
Looked around: I was in
bed with two of Gladys
Knight's pips.

STACEY (TO GAVIN)

You know when we were away and
I told you I had something to
tell you? And I told you about
Nessa being in the original
line-up of All Saints, but

she had to leave because she
didn't get on with Shaznay?
Well I tried to tell you then.

GAVIN
What? So you made all that up?

NESSA
No that was true. It was a
power struggle.

NESSA
I was personal assistant to
Om Puri!

DAWN
Oh I like him and I don't
normally go for . . . you
know . . .

NESSA
Yeah. He's a great man. Some
say the best in Bollywood.
But he had to fire me. I did
the one thing he asked me
not to do.

PAM
What?

NESSA

I made it sexual, Pam. I was
only there three months.
Between us we directed
over 200 films. Now all I
have to remind me of Om is
this Jamdani Hash and a VHS
copy of *East is East*.

NESSA

I hadn't picked up a trumpet
in 17 years. Jools Holland
and the Big Band were in town
one night . . . they fancied
a jam, and before I know it
I'm there playing the Boogie
Woogie Bugle Boy.

NESSA

I used to drive the sets for
The Who on their world tours.
Great days. Until I found
out some things about Pete
Townshend I didn't like. And
all I'll say, and I'll say it
to his face: where is
the book?

NESSA
So where to are you
heading next?

NESSA'S DAD NEIL
I heard there's a bit of extra
work on Midsomer Murders so
I thought I'd head up there,
show my face and see if I
can get can get a few days
on that.

NESSA
Tidy. Send my love to
John . . .

DAVE
Who's John?

NESSA
Nettles. Bergerac. Dirty boy.
Good job he can't see me like
this or you'd have to put him
on a leash.

GWEN
She [Nessa] lives, Pam,
with a band.

STACEY
They're called The Distance.
Three of them were in

Catatonia, and the little
Welsh one from Hear'Say. Noel.

PAM
Well that's no place to bring
up a child, my love.

NESSA
I know but what can I do?
Richard said I could go there
but Judy won't have it, not
after what happened last
time. What it was, Pam, I was
their nanny back in the day,
and he'd come home after a
morning's work, Judy would be
straight on the whiskey and
me and Rich would make love.
Sometimes for whole Sundays.
And then he'd do his Ali
G . . .

NESSA
I done the knowledge back in
the day, Pam. Drove a black
cab. I mainly worked nights.
That's how I fell in with Hale
and Pace. Picked them up on
Piccadilly, took them home and
moved in for the best part of
a year. Wish I'd shut the door
that night and never left.

The cab got towed, I lost my
licence, and things between
us turned . . . quite dark.
I'll spare you the details but
suffice to say it ended very
badly between me and Gareth
and Norm. That's when I went
back to working on the ships.

[ends]

Acknowledgements

A huge thank you to ...

Lovely Boyd Hilton for helping us with this book and for his immense support over the years.

The fabulous team at Transworld, with special mentions to Kim Young, Bill Scott-Kerr, Susanna Wadeson, Alison Barrow and Charlotte Davey; to Jonny Geller and his team at Curtis Brown, as well as Ruth Young and Stuart Bell.

The *Gavin & Stacey* journey has been an absolute joy and we want to thank everyone who made it possible – our cast, crew and production teams over the years, Baby Cow, Tidy Productions and Fulwell 73; the residents of Barry and South Wales, with particular thanks to Glenda, Doug and Julia, and of course the inimitable Marco Zeraschi and the staff at Marco's cafe. You're all lush.

Finally a big thank-you to everyone who watched and continued watching the show. You absolutely kept the whole thing going.

And that's it for now, alrigh'? We're off.

Crackin'.

Credits

The following permission holders are gratefully acknowledged. Every effort has been made to trace copyright holders and to obtain their permission. The publisher apologizes for any errors or omissions and, if notified of any corrections, will make suitable acknowledgement in future reprints or editions of this book.

Picture section one
p. 1–3 Ruth Jones; p. 4 *top left*: James Corden, *top right*: Ruth Jones; *middle*: Ruth Jones; *bottom left and bottom right*: Mat Horne; p. 5 Mat Horne; p. 6 Ellis Parrinder, *Guardian*, Eyevine; p. 7 *top left*: Sarah Dempster and Gary (illustrator), *Guardian, top right*: *Media Wales, bottom left*: *Radio Times, bottom right*: *Metro Live*; p. 8 *top left*: *Western Mail, top right and bottom*: Ruth Jones.

Picture section two

p. 1 Ruth Jones; p. 2 Robert Wilfort; p. 3 *top*: Ruth Jones, right: *Media Wales, bottom left*: BBC America; p. 4 *top left*: Trevor Leighton/Getty Images, *top right*: Trevor Leighton/Getty Images, *middle*: Toby Merrit/Comic Relief/Getty Images, *bottom*: Simon Ridgeway/Comic Relief/Getty Images; p. 5 *top right*: Ruth Jones, *middle left*: *Radio Times, middle right, bottom left and bottom right*: Ruth Jones; p. 6 *top*: Chris Jackson, *bottom left*: Eamonn McCormack/ Getty Images, *bottom right*: Dave Benett/BAFTAS/ Getty Images; p. 7 *top left*: Oliver Holms/BAFTAS/ Getty Images, *top right*: Rachell Smith/BAFTA, *bottom*: Mike Marsland/Wire Image/Getty Images; p. 8 Ruth Jones.

Picture section three

p. 1 Ruth Jones; p. 2 *top left, top right, middle, bottom left*: James Corden, *bottom right*: Ruth Jones; p. 3 *top left, top right, middle, bottom right:* James Corden, *bottom left:* Ruth Jones; p. 4 Ruth Jones; p. 5 *top left, top right*: Ruth Jones, *middle*: Tom Jackson; *bottom left, bottom right*: Ruth Jones; pp. 6–7 Tom Jackson; p. 8 Ruth Jones.

Quotes

Line from Michael Jackson song 'Ben', written by Don Black/Walter Scharf © MIJAC Music (p. 68)

Line from Stephen Fretwell song 'Run', written by
Stephen Fretwell © Universal Music Publishing
Group (p. 118 and p. 285)

Line from James Blunt song 'Wisemen', written
by James Dearness Hogarth/Sacha Skarbek/James
Blount © Universal Music Publishing Group (p. 134)

Line from 'Islands In The Stream', written by the
Bee Gees, © Sony Music/RCA Records (p. 160)

Format borrowed from Adele's song 'Hello', written
by Adele Laurie Blue Adkins/Gregory Allen Kurstin
© © Emi April Music Inc., Kurstin Music, Melted
Stone Publishing Ltd. (pp. 189–90)

Line from Ella Fitzgerald song 'Let's Call The Whole
Thing Off', written by Ira Gershwin/George Gersh-
win © Ira Gershwin Music, Nokawi Music, Chappell
& Co (p. 205)

Line from Elbow song 'One Day Like This', written by
Richard Jupp, Mark Potter, Craig Potter, Pete Turner
and Guy Garvey © Concord Music Publishing (p. 237)

Line from *Secrets and Lies*, written and directed by
Mike Leigh, © CiBy 2000/Thin Man Films Limited
(p. 247)

Ruth Jones was born in 1966 and hails from Porthcawl in South Wales. She attended Warwick University and the Royal Welsh College of Music and Drama. She is an actress, TV writer, producer and novelist best known for her role as Nessa Jenkins in BBC One's multi-award-winning *Gavin & Stacey*, for which she won a BAFTA in 2025 for best female performance in a comedy. Ruth co-wrote *Gavin & Stacey* with James Corden, and the 2019 and 2024 Christmas specials of this beloved show garnered viewing figures of over 18 million and 21 million respectively.

Ruth also created and co-wrote several series of *Stella* for Sky TV. Other TV work includes *Hattie, Little Dorrit, Tess of the D'Urbervilles, Nighty Night, Little Britain* and *Saxondale*. In 2024 Ruth played Mother Superior in *Sister Act the Musical* at London's Dominion Theatre. Recent acting roles include Elena Ravenscroft in Harlan Coben's *Run Away* for Netflix, and *The Other Bennet Sister* for BBC in which she played Mrs Bennet.

Ruth's four novels – *Never Greener, Us Three, Love Untold* and *By Your Side* – were all *Sunday Times* bestsellers and have sold over a million copies. Ruth was awarded an MBE in 2014 at Windsor Castle, for services to entertainment.

James Corden is a twelve-time Emmy Award-winning host, writer, producer and actor. Born in Hillingdon in 1978, he grew up in Buckinghamshire, where he attended the Jackie Palmer Stage School. Early TV work included *Teachers* and *Fat Friends*, where he met Ruth Jones before the two went on to co-create the BAFTA-winning *Gavin & Stacey*. Playing 'Smithy' was James's breakout role, for which he won a BAFTA for best male performance in a comedy. Other notable TV credits include *Doctor Who*, Jez Butterworth's mini-series *Mammals* and *The Wrong Mans*, which he co-wrote and starred in with Matthew Baynton.

On stage, James starred in *One Man, Two Guvnors* – for which he won the 2012 Tony Award for best leading actor in a play – *The History Boys* and, more recently, *The Constituent*.

In 2015, James made a monumental leap when he took over as the host of the iconic *The Late Late Show* in the United States. During his time as host, he won multiple Emmy Awards and launched globally loved segments such as Carpool Karaoke.

In film, James starred in *The Prom* and received a 2021 Golden Globe nomination for best performance by an actor in a motion picture. His other feature credits include *Into the Woods* and *Ocean's 8*. James also hosts the US interview series *This Life of Mine with James Corden* on SiriusXM.

In 2015, he was awarded an OBE at Buckingham Palace for services to drama.